About the Author

Kat French lives in the Black Country with her husband and sons. She writes romantic comedy full-time, and also writes paranormal comedy under the pseudonym Kitty French.

You can follow Kat @KFrenchBooks.

By the same author:

My Perfect Stranger (previously titled *The Piano Man Project*)
Love Your Neighbour (previously titled *Undertaking Love*)
One Hot Summer
The Bed and Breakfast on the Beach

KAT FRENCH

A Summer Scandal

avon.

This novel is entirely a work of fiction.
The names, characters and incidents portrayed in it are the work of the author's imagination. Any resemblance to actual persons, living or dead, events or localities is entirely coincidental.

AVON

A division of HarperCollins*Publishers*
1 London Bridge Street,
London SE1 9GF

www.harpercollins.co.uk

A Paperback Original 2018

1

Copyright © Kat French 2018

Kat French asserts the moral right to
be identified as the author of this work

A catalogue record for this book is available from the British Library

ISBN-13: 978-0-00-823678-6

Typeset in Meridien by
Palimpsest Book Production Ltd, Falkirk, Stirlingshire

Printed and bound in Great Britain by
Printed and bound by CPI Group (UK) Ltd, Croydon CR0 4YY

All rights reserved. No part of this publication may be reproduced, stored in a retrieval system, or transmitted, in any form or by any means, electronic, mechanical, photocopying, recording or otherwise, without the prior permission of the publishers.

FSC
www.fsc.org
MIX
Paper from
responsible sources
FSC™ C007454

This book is produced from independently certified FSC™ paper to ensure responsible forest management.

For more information visit: www.harpercollins.co.uk/green

For my mum.

My dearest Violet,

I'm not entirely sure if I'm doing the right thing, but in order to honour Monica's memory, I'm going to do it regardless and leave the choices and decisions up to you.

Now – I'm dead, darling. No point beating around that particular bush; I must be, or you wouldn't be reading this letter. I know I should have dealt with this sooner, but I'm afraid I wasn't brave enough – Pandora's box, and all that. Should have talked to your mother perhaps, but the right time never really presented itself. Or maybe I never looked for it. She's too much like me for her own good, my Della; I don't think she'd want this.

Are you ready? Here comes the formal bit.

Violet Monica Spencer, I hereby bequeath to you the property known as number 6 Swallow Beach Lido, and the Birdcage Pier, also at Swallow Beach.

I don't know what you should do with the pier. Renovating it might not be an option; might be better to set fire to the damn thing and let it go out in a blaze of glory. Seriously my love, there may or may not be value in it. Do as you wish. The flat will have value I'm sure, although I expect it'll need a lick of paint after all these years.

Tell your mother I'm sorry. I lied only by omission, but it was still a deception to let her think I'd sold up and cut our ties with Swallow Beach. Truth told, I don't think her memories of the place are happy ones, mine neither, and I didn't want to burden her. So it comes down to you. I have no sentimental attachment, so if you can sell up and make some money, do so without thinking twice. It pleases me to think that some good might come of it, and I'm sure your grandmother would feel similarly.

Bonne chance, child.
Grandpa Henry xxx

CHAPTER ONE

Violet stared at the spikily handwritten letter from her recently deceased beloved Grandpa Henry, unsure what it all meant. She'd heard of Swallow Beach, of course, from a couple of old photographs and the very occasional reminiscence when her mother had had a glass or two of wine, but as far as she knew it was part of her family's history, not present.

She glanced up towards the house, aware her mother was up there in the kitchen right now reading her own letter from Henry, probably explaining all of this to her too. He'd lived in the Victorian villa next door for as long as Violet could remember; her family's connection to Swallow Beach lay in the past, a lifetime ago. Another read through of the letter did little to shed any light, so Violet sighed and let herself out of her workshop at the end of her mum's garden and made her way up to the house in search of answers.

'Mum?'

There was no sign of her mum in the kitchen, nor on further exploration in the living room, dining room or study. Frowning, Violet called out again, running her hand over the familiar curve of the smooth mahogany handrail as she headed upstairs.

'I'm up here.'

Violet tracked her mother's voice to the small, twisting attic stairs.

'In the attic?' she called, even though there was no need because the sound of something being dragged overhead made it clear. 'What are you doing up there?'

Like most people, her parents used their small eaves room for storage. Childhood toys that were too precious for Violet to part with, suitcases that only saw the light of day a couple of times each year, shelves full of dusty school projects and old CDs. And sitting in the middle of it all on the bare board floor, Della, Violet's mum, pulling old photograph albums and yellowed paperwork out of a large, blue-and-white-striped cardboard storage box.

'I'm guessing this has something to do with Grandpa Henry's letter?'

'Silly old goat,' her mum muttered without looking up. 'I can't believe he never told me he hadn't sold the place.'

Violet dropped down on her haunches and touched her mum's shoulder. 'Mum? What are you looking for?'

Her mother looked up at last, her blue eyes red-rimmed from crying.

'What's the matter?' Violet said, startled. Her mum wasn't a crier; she'd only cried once since Grandpa Henry died and she'd loved him beyond words. 'Was it the letters that upset you?'

'I'm not upset,' Della said. 'These—' she jabbed her finger towards her eyes 'are tears of bloody anger. How dare he land this on you?'

Violet tucked her chin-length, blue-tipped hair behind

her ears, trying to read between the lines and work out what was really going on.

'What are you looking for?'

Her mother didn't answer, just pulled an unfamiliar black leather album from the box and blew the dust from the cover. She didn't open it straight away, just held it in her lap and sighed heavily. 'This belonged to Monica. My mother.'

Della so rarely spoke of her mother that Violet was stumped for what to say.

'She loved that bloody pier.'

Again, Violet was lost. What was all this about a pier? Henry's letter was the first she'd ever heard about any pier, yet it seemed to be central to both her inheritance and her mother's current distress.

'I don't understand, Mum,' Violet said. 'What's this all about?'

Della tapped her fingers slowly on the cover of the photograph album. 'This. I thought it was all long gone, but it seems I was wrong.'

Violet slid onto her bum beside her mother and crossed her legs like a child sitting on the carpet for a story at the end of the school day. 'Shall I look?'

Her mum shook her head. 'Not yet.' She didn't look at Violet. 'He shouldn't have let things go on like this. If he'd told me, I could have sorted it out, but now he's gone and saddled you with it.'

From what Violet could see, the album hadn't seen the light of day in many, many years. It had been put to the very bottom of the box; some might say it had been hidden away.

'She was a free spirit. That's what everyone always used to say about my mother.'

Violet sat quietly, waiting for Della to go on.

'An artist. A performer. A dancer.'

This was all news to Violet. Monica Spencer was an enigma; never spoken of fondly, no photographs on the hallway wall amongst the various family shots. So many questions filled her head . . . A dancer? A performer? An artist? Violet herself was an artist, of sorts. Was that where her artistic bent came from? It certainly wasn't from her pragmatic mother or her accountant dad. Even her lovely grandpa had never revealed much about his long-deceased wife; it was as if everyone felt it best to pretend Monica Spencer had never existed at all. Until now.

Violet tried to piece together the scant pieces of the puzzle she had, to at least make up the edges, to form a frame to build the picture from. She knew that her grandfather Henry had never remarried, and her mother Delilah, Della for short, was his only child. Monica, his wife, had died when Della was just a child, and afterwards he'd moved them both here to Shrewsbury to start again somewhere new. Or nearly new; Henry and Monica had grown up and met here, and moved to Swallow Beach just after they'd married. And that was it. All she knew.

'Mum, can I see?'

Violet reached out and touched the album, and Della swallowed hard. 'I haven't opened this in over ten years.'

'Are you sure you want to now?'

'No,' Della said. 'But I don't think I've got any choice. Come on, let's go downstairs. We're both going to need a brandy to get through this.'

'It's not even lunchtime.'

'Trust me. You won't care what time it is.'

As Della got to her feet, a photograph slid from the

album to the floor. Violet bent to retrieve it, and then stood bone still, staring at it.

'Oh my God.' She lifted her eyes to meet her mother's troubled gaze. 'Why did no one tell me?'

Della's ash-blonde bob was shot through with silver, catching the light as she tucked it behind her ears, a resigned look on her pale face. The woman staring up at them had wild black curls and laughing grey eyes. She was crabbing in a rock pool, a slight, blonde child wrapped around her leg.

'It was taken at Swallow Beach,' Della said, gazing at it. 'I was about four, five at most. It's underneath the pier, you can just about make out the ironwork there in the background.'

Violet scoured the image, hungry for more. She couldn't tear her eyes away from her grandmother.

'She's . . .' She shook her head, rocked. 'She's the image of me, Mum.'

It was almost an understatement. Monica Spencer was probably the closest thing to a doppelganger Violet was ever going to get.

Della looked from the picture to her daughter, and then silently took the image and slid it back between the leaves of the album.

'I told you we were going to need a drink.'

Violet frowned as she followed her usually unflappable mum down through the house. Grandpa Henry had mentioned his reluctance to open Pandora's box, but she had a creeping feeling that that was exactly what they were about to do.

Two hours and two large brandies later, Violet had several more pieces of the puzzle to arrange. Poring over the album at the kitchen table with her mum, she'd learned more about her own heritage that afternoon than in the twenty-five years leading up to it. She'd seen all that the album had to offer: her grandparents' black and white wedding picture, them cradling their newborn baby girl, again with their shiny new car in the late sixties. Life events recorded and annotated with dates and names, but the images that touched Violet the most were the unposed ones, the natural, captured snapshots of Monica laughing up into the lens, or ballerina-like balancing along the beach wall, or with her hair tied back by a scarlet chiffon scarf as she painted at an easel.

From the pictures and her mother's memories, Violet learned that her grandparents had honeymooned in Swallow Beach, drawn down south by the bright lights of Brighton and the pretty coastline to explore. Grandpa Henry had been a well-to-do businessman back in his younger days, and he'd been powerless to resist his beautiful, wilful new wife when she'd fallen in love with both the town and its struggling little Victorian pier. Even as they'd watched the For Sale sign being hung onto the closed ornate metal gates, he'd known he was going to buy it for her, that their future as husband and wife lay in Swallow Beach.

It was an idea filled with hope and a plan filled with optimism, and for a while it seemed that they'd been as happy as clams in their beautiful new seafront apartment. Making a success of the pier had become Monica's obsession, and then tragically, when Della was just eight years old, the story twisted when the pier became the scene of Monica's untimely death. The newspaper cutting reported that she'd fallen from the pier at midnight on her fortieth birthday, her body washed up on the dawn tide. Della had needed to leave the kitchen by the back door for a breath of air at that point of recounting the story, flapping her hand at Violet to stay where she was.

Alone in the kitchen, Violet held the picture of her grandmother in her hands and stared into her oh-so-familiar eyes, trying to see more than was there, to understand this woman with who she shared so much. And not just physically. Violet might not paint particularly well, but all of the things she'd ever truly excelled at had been art of some form. She'd dabbled with various mediums over the years, but she always ended up back at her sewing machine under one guise or another. Piecing together intricate quilts, making up clothes from vintage dress patterns – and for the last couple of years she'd been working to build up her own business from the converted old brick-built stable at the end of her parents' long garden.

She laid the photograph down as her mum came back in, sniffing, a balled-up tissue in her hand.

'Sorry, love. Got me there. Unexpected.'

Sitting back at the table, Della placed an envelope down. Violet recognised it as the same pale blue stationery as her own letter from Grandpa Henry. Della shook it until a set of keys fell out onto the waxed pine table.

'These were in my envelope to pass onto you.'

Violet made no move to pick them up, just looked at them, and as she studied them she could almost feel fate trying to give her hand a subtle shove towards them.

'So this pier,' she said. 'Is it open to the public?'

Della laughed softly. 'It used to be.' She shook her head. 'I don't even know if it's still standing, Violet. I haven't been back there in almost forty years. It's probably crumbled into the sea by now.'

Even though Violet had only known of the pier at Swallow Beach for a few hours, the idea of it no longer being there filled her with dismay. She wanted to see it, to walk beneath it and find those rock pools, to hopefully walk the length of it and try to connect with the woman who'd fallen in love with it all those years ago.

'That apartment.' Della shook her head, talking softly to herself more than Violet. 'I can't believe he never sold it.'

'He didn't need the money to come home?'

Della shook her head. 'Dad's business paid well back then. Besides, the house next door belonged to his mum, my gran. We moved in with her when we came back after . . .' She paused, struggling to say it out loud even after so many years. 'And then we stayed here after we lost my gran a few years later.'

There wasn't a picture of the Swallow Beach seafront mansion block in the album, but from the way her mum described it Violet was desperate to go and lay eyes on it for herself. Three storeys, graceful picture bay windows, sweeping staircases. It was an impossibly romantic story, and it sliced straight through Violet's soft heart and ignited her thirst for adventure. Perhaps that was a gift from her grandmother too; adventure certainly wasn't a trait displayed by either of her parents. Her mum didn't go anywhere without making at least three lists first, and her father had a special book in his study drawer for plans. Not to mention the fact that they'd shared the surname Spencer even before they married; it was a standing joke that her mum had chosen her dad mostly because she wouldn't need to change her maiden name on her passport.

Violet pulled the jumble of keys slowly towards her. 'Why have I never heard about any of this before, Mum?'

'Your grandpa didn't like to talk about it,' Della said. The stiff set of her jaw suggested that Henry wasn't the only one who preferred to leave Monica's memory in the past.

'But why?' Violet knew she was pushing too hard, but it just didn't make any sense. Her grandparents had clearly been very in love, and obviously Monica's death must have profoundly affected both Henry and his young daughter, but it was as if they'd tried to wipe her from their memories rather than celebrate her existence.

Della sighed. 'I was eight years old, Vi. My mum left the apartment after dinner and never came home.' A tear ran down her cheek. 'It was a huge scandal at the time, things like that don't happen in Swallow Beach.'

Violet stared at her mum. 'What happened to her?'

Della raised her eyes to the kitchen ceiling, concentrating on the light as if she needed something to fixate on.

'She was found on the beach by an early morning walker, someone out looking for treasure washed up on the dawn tide.' Her face was drawn, remembering. 'They didn't expect to find a body washed up amongst the shells and loose change.'

Violet drew in a sharp breath. 'Do you think she . . .?'

It was a few seconds before Della met her daughter's anxious gaze. 'I don't know, love. All I know is that we left Swallow Beach within days and Dad never spoke her name again.'

Reaching across the table, Violet squeezed her mum's hand. She'd never seen her look so troubled; the morning's revelations had taken a heavy toll. Gathering the letters and keys together, she tucked them back inside the envelope and closed the album.

'Let's not think about it any more right now,' she said,

setting them aside. They were all so desperately sad about Henry's death; this extra layer of murk and mystery suddenly felt like too much to handle right at that moment. 'It's waited all of these years. A few more days won't hurt.'

But even as Violet said it, her fingers lingered on the worn leather edge of the photograph album, desperate to know more about Monica Spencer, the grandmother she was the living image of.

CHAPTER TWO

'Will you marry me?'

Violet stared at Simon, on his knees in the local Indian restaurant that evening. To say his proposal had come as a surprise was an understatement; she couldn't have imagined that anything could top the shock of that morning's revelations. She hadn't even had time to fill Simon in on all of that yet; her letter from her grandpa lay in her handbag at her feet. She'd planned to show him over dinner, but she'd barely had time to order a glass of wine in the Taj Star before Simon pulled a diamond solitaire from his jacket pocket and dropped down on bended knee.

It came as something of a shock; they'd been together for over a year now but marriage was something they'd never even spoken about, and in truth not something that she'd contemplated. She'd just turned twenty-five; too young in her own head for a ring on her finger or a new surname to wrap her head around or a husband to sleep with each night.

It wasn't that Simon wasn't husband material; he was perfectly nice and ticked most, if not all, of the boyfriend boxes. Dependable? Tick. Kind? Tick. Humorous? Almost a tick; it wasn't that Simon didn't have sense of humour, it was more that he was so logical that irreverent humour either went over his head or left him cold. He'd opt for *Panorama* over *The Inbetweeners*, a fact that fun-loving Violet had found out early on; subsequently she'd chosen not to spend many cosy nights in front of the box with him. If they went to the movies it was either his choice or hers; the only movie they'd ever been equally enthusiastic about seeing was *300*, albeit for wildly different reasons. Simon was a history buff, and Vi had a thing for Gerard Butler. They had other things in common, of course, and her parents loved what Simon represented in Vi's life: a safe pair of hands. He was an all-round decent man, unlikely to bring heartache to Vi's door, not the type to eye up the girls at work or run up secret bills playing late-night poker. Violet sometimes thought he was more like her parents than she was.

'Violet?'

Simon's voice wavered a little, probably because he had a dodgy knee and the people at the next table were gagging to know what she was going to say. She smiled, stretched her mouth wide and laughed lightly. Her shoulders lifted around her ears, stressed, because she knew that really there was only one possible word she should say next and she wasn't at all sure she wanted to say it. But she didn't want to say no either, at least not in front of other people. Even the waiters had paused, tikka masalas balanced on their forearms as they watched proceedings.

Because of all of those things, she reached down and plucked the pretty ring from its red velvet box, looking at it as if overcome.

'Simon, I . . .' She paused, as did every single person in

the Taj Star. Simon looked pained; there was no other word for the expression on his face. 'Yes,' she whispered, pushing a smile out for his benefit. 'Yes, Simon. I'll marry you.'

It was only the beginning of the actual sentence in her head. What she really wanted to say was, 'I don't know, Simon. I'll marry you one day, probably, maybe, in about ten years' time – if we're still a couple, which I'm not at all sure we will be because I don't know if you're the love of my life or not.'

She didn't say all of that though; it wasn't as much of a crowd-pleaser really, was it?

Taking Simon's ring from the box, Violet slipped it onto her third finger and tried not to feel as if she wanted to slide it straight off again and hand it back.

Pulling into her parents' driveway, Simon looked across at the illuminated front windows.

'Shall I come inside and we can tell them together?'

Vi looked at her watch, glad they'd lingered for coffee at the restaurant because she could legitimately say it was too late in the evening.

'Let's leave it for tonight,' she said. 'They'll be tired now.'

'But they'll notice your ring,' he frowned.

Violet splayed her hand, and then slipped the ring from her finger. 'There. Nothing to see.'

For a moment, they sat in loaded silence. Had he picked up on the fact that her heart wasn't one hundred percent on board with the idea of getting married? Should she have cried with joy? She was actually feeling quite tearful, but more because she'd had the most overwhelming day of her life than because she was cock-a-hoop at the prospect of marrying Simon.

'I'll come over in the morning then,' he said, watching as she put the ring back inside its box. 'Ten thirty on the nose.'

Violet nodded, pushing the ring into her handbag beside her grandpa's letter. Her plan to share her news with Simon over dinner had fallen by the wayside after his proposal; there was no tangible way to explain her sudden reluctance to tell her new fiancé about Swallow Beach. Leaning in to kiss him quickly with her hand already opening the passenger door to get away, she smiled, small and tight.

'Night,' she said. 'See you tomorrow.'

She glanced over at her grandpa's house next door as she delved in her bag for her keys, forlorn at the dark, empty house. Henry had been a cornerstone of her life forever; a safe corner of the world to escape to. And he was gone now, yet still somehow there offering her a safe haven, a different door to walk through than the one everyone expected her to take. Perhaps he saw Monica in her eyes or somewhere in her smile, knew the wanderlust that made her bones restless in a way no one else could.

'Thank you, Grandpa,' she whispered, then stepped inside without looking back.

She'd been wrong about her parents still being up. They'd left the lights on for her, calling down goodnight when she let herself in and locked the front door.

Still too wired to go to bed, she headed into the kitchen and made herself a coffee, laying her grandpa's letter and Simon's ring on the table in front of her. Left, and right. A more orderly person (her mum, her dad, Simon) might have switched them over – Simon's ring on the left, ready to go on her wedding finger. Violet, however, felt them more appropriately arranged as they were: Simon on the safe and conservative right, her grandpa's letter on the avant-garde, unpredictable left. Looking from one to the other, there was no denying which made her heart beat faster. Opening the ring box, the diamond winked up at her under the kitchen spotlights. Opening the letter, her grandpa's spindly black writing lay stark against the pale blue paper.

Simon or Swallow Beach. Swallow Beach or Simon.

Could she have both? Did she want either? It had been a day of huge revelations and unexpected twists, and now Violet found herself at the end of it with choices to make and decisions to take. Sipping her coffee, she sighed and wished she'd opted for a brandy instead.

Simon's here, love. He's brought champagne!

Violet looked down at her vibrating phone as the message buzzed through from her mum at the house. It was ten thirty exactly. Laying down the box of scarlet feathers she'd just unpacked, she reached for her phone, her heart lead-heavy in her chest.

Ask him to come down, please Mum?

She pressed send, knowing that it wasn't the response Simon would be expecting. He'd probably expected that she'd be there to welcome him on the doorstep, all jiggly with prenuptial excitement and raring to share their news.

Staring at the phone, she half expected her mum to send a second message telling her to get up to the house because Simon had something he wanted to announce. Please don't, Simon. Relief prickled her skin when he emerged from the back door a couple of minutes later and started to pick his way down the long garden path. She watched him, wondering what the right words were to break someone's heart gently. *It's not you, it's me*? She wouldn't insult him with pat lines or stock phrases.

'Violet?'

He opened the door and stuck his head into her workshop. It wasn't a place he ventured often by choice. Violet's workshop was a riot of colour and organised chaos; it didn't sit well with his everything-in-its-place, neat-as-a-new-pin mentality.

'Come in,' she said, sliding down from her stool at the bench to hastily clear a pile of material off the battered velvet armchair she'd up-cycled from a neighbour's garden sale. 'Sit down.'

Simon looked back towards the door, uncertain, as if he didn't understand why they weren't leaving the workshop to go up to the house to break their happy news right away.

'Please, just come in and sit down?'

Frowning, he did as she asked. 'This isn't quite what I had in mind for this morning,' he said, looking uncomfortable as he pulled a peacock-blue reel of cotton from under his backside and laid it on the side table Violet had decoupaged with jungle animals; glossy leopards and jewel-bright parrots.

'I know,' she said, quiet and serious.

His eyes moved to her left hand, to her bare wedding finger.

'There's something I need to show you,' she said, reaching for her grandpa's letter. 'It's this. My mum gave it to me yesterday morning.'

He frowned at the letter as she held it out. 'What is it?'

She didn't answer, just swallowed and nodded for him to take a look. She watched as he sighed, resigned, pulled out the folded letter and began to read. He read it through once, then turned it over to read it from the beginning again.

'You're going to have to fill in the blanks for me here,' he said, laying the letter down beside the cotton reel on the table, looking as nonplussed as she'd felt when she read the letter for the first time. Violet nodded, unsure where to start. She wasn't surprised he was confused; she still felt that way herself twenty-four hours on.

'It seems that my gran, *Monica,* owned a Victorian pier on the south coast. Grandpa never sold it on after she died, and now he's left it to me.'

Simon shook his head, as if he didn't want the information to lodge itself in there permanently.

'Okay.' He drew the word out in a way that said: *You'll have to tell me more, I'm not sure where this is going yet.*

'And there's an apartment with it too.'

He nodded slowly. 'So, you've inherited an old pier and a flat in a place we've never heard of down on the south coast.'

'Yes,' Violet said. 'Mum thought it had all been sold off years ago. It's come as a real shock to her.'

'I can imagine.' He looked at his shoes. 'Is this why we're not up in the house drinking champagne? I brought some, your mum put it in the fridge.'

Violet flinched, wishing her parents hadn't needed to be involved. 'Yes, I guess it is. I was going to tell you about it last night, but you kind of took me by surprise when you . . .' her eyes moved to the small red velvet box on the window ledge 'when you proposed.'

'I have to say, you didn't seem quite as thrilled as I'd expected.'

He couldn't have handed her a clearer cue. Violet felt her heart start to rush, panicky now the moment was here.

'It was a shock,' she said, trying to be diplomatic. 'Marriage is a big step . . .'

'One everyone takes,' he said, reasonable.

'Not everyone,' she frowned. 'But that's not it. I just feel . . . Simon, I'm so sorry, but I don't think I'm ready for marriage yet.'

His brows dropped into a V. 'But you . . . you said yes. You definitely said yes. I was down on one knee, and you said you'd marry me. That's not the kind of thing I could have got wrong, Violet. The waiter shook my hand.'

He didn't pause for breath as the implications of Violet's words sank in.

'I know I did. I said yes, because I didn't want to say no in front of everyone.'

'So you said yes out of pity?'

He looked offended now. 'No! No . . . it wasn't pity, honestly. I'm not saying I never want to get married, Simon, just not yet. I don't feel . . .' She trailed off, because the words in her head were too stark to say out loud. *I don't feel sure you're the man I want to marry.*

'You don't feel what? Like you love me enough?'

His uncharacteristic bluntness surprised her, and her faltering response probably made him wish he hadn't asked.

'I don't know. I'm sorry Simon, but I honestly don't know. All I know is that my heart didn't jump for joy when you asked me, and it should have.'

His brows were so low now they had merged into one dark line across his creased forehead.

'This isn't *Wuthering Heights,* Violet,' he said, almost patronising. 'We're normal people living normal lives.'

She looked down at her lime-green-and-navy-polka-dot polished toes. He couldn't have said anything less inspiring if he'd tried.

'I'm going to Swallow Beach.'

Simon breathed in and out, slow and steady. 'Of course. You'll need to go to make arrangements to sell it.'

Violet shook her head. 'No, that's not what I'm going to do.' Her forthright words surprised herself; up until that point she hadn't been sure what she wanted. But hearing Simon pretty much tell her what to do crystallised it for her. 'I'm going to go and stay there for a while.'

'What?' His eyebrows shot up. 'When? For how long?'

She paused. 'I don't know. Soon. Next week, maybe.'

He looked at the wooden rafters, thinking. 'I'm due seven days' annual leave. I'll take you. We can have a holiday. Shame to use my leave so early in the year, mind.'

There was a look of something dangerously close to piety on his face, as if he was bestowing a favour.

'No, I wasn't talking about a holiday,' Violet said, soft but firm. 'I'm going to go and live there for a while.'

Simon made the mistake of scoffing. 'You're being slightly ridiculous now, Violet. How do you expect to do that on your own?'

Irritation sharpened her tongue. 'Don't you think that's rude, Simon? To suggest that I'm incapable?'

'I wasn't . . .' He looked flustered. 'Is it so wrong to want to get married and settle down? I thought we were on the same page here, Violet. Singing from the same hymn sheet. Your mum and dad are going to be so disappointed.'

'They don't even know,' Violet said.

He shrugged, looking awkward.

'You didn't say anything, did you?'

'Not exactly,' he said. 'But what on earth else would I have bought champagne for? I did say she should dust off the best glasses.'

'God.' Violet pushed her fringe out of her eyes. She

didn't want to disappoint her parents; she was already worrying about telling them she wanted to go to Swallow Beach. Now she had to tell them that not only was she going to up sticks, but she was turning down Simon's proposal too. They were going to think she was off her rocker.

'You're confused,' Simon said, getting up out of the chair and coming to stand in front of her, his hands on her shoulders. 'My timing was off, Violet. If I'd known about your letter I'd have held off to give you a chance to sort it out. One thing at a time, and all that.'

She looked up into his conventionally handsome face, knowing that he didn't mean to make her feel incapable. He freely admitted that he enjoyed taking care of her, that he liked to think that she needed him as her solid rock. And God knows that's what he was; there wasn't a more reliable pair of hands in the land. That was the problem, really; Violet had spent her life being sheltered, she wanted to step out on her own. She hadn't realised how much until Simon proposed; it was as if she was going to move from one gilded cage to another.

Shaking her head, she drew in a deep breath.

'I'm not confused. I'm going to move to Swallow Beach for the summer.'

He stared at her. 'And then you'll come home and marry me?'

'I don't think I will, Simon.'

If she thought she'd been direct enough, she was wrong.

'I know what this is.' He gave her shoulders a reassuring squeeze. 'Fear. It's okay to feel a bit scared of change, Violet. I'm like that too.'

'I'm not scared,' she said, more determined now. 'I don't know how to say this any more clearly without hurting you, Simon. I'm moving to Swallow Beach, and I don't want to go there as your fiancée. I need to feel free.'

Violet couldn't have known it, but she'd never been more like her grandmother than in that very moment.

'I'll wait for you,' he said, a look of indulgence on his face. 'You'll come back, and I'll be here waiting for you.'

'Simon, please don't,' she said. 'I don't want you to put your life on hold. I'm so sorry, but all of this has really made me think, and I've realised that I'm not being fair to you. I think I'm stringing you along. I don't think we have what it takes for forever.'

He set his jaw. 'I'll be here waiting when you come home.' His eyes flickered with dismay. 'Please Violet. Don't tell me not to.'

She picked up the ring box. 'You should take this. I can't even promise that I'll come back.'

He sighed and shook his head. 'It's a good job I know you better than you know yourself,' he said, at last. 'You'll come back. I know it. You go, and I'll be your safety net.' He kissed the tip of her nose. 'I'm going to leave that champagne on ice in your parents' fridge, and leave that ring in your hands. By autumn, it'll be on your finger.'

Short of having a bloody-minded argument, there was nothing Violet could do; he had her backed into a corner, and because Violet wasn't given to arguments, she didn't push. She'd told him the truth; she was going to Swallow Beach and she didn't feel as if she wanted to marry him, now or in the future. The fact that he wasn't prepared to accept it wasn't her fault. He thought she needed a safety net. She knew the opposite to be true. She wanted to step out and walk the tightrope without a safety net, ready to be a roaring success or go down spectacularly.

*

'No way, Violet. Absolutely no way.'

Della stared at her daughter, and Violet stared right back. She'd fully expected to meet opposition from her parents, and they hadn't disappointed her. Her father was resolute that it was a terrible idea, and her mother was hopping mad. In fact, she'd go as far as to say her mother was more furious than she'd ever seen her.

'Mum, I really don't want to fall out,' Vi said. 'But please try to understand, I really need to do this.'

'No. No, you don't really need to do this. You need to marry the perfectly decent man who proposed to you last night, and forget any fanciful ideas of moving to Swallow Beach. Simon has a house two miles from here. You can live there. I'm sure he'll let you go wild with redecorating, and you can still come home for Sunday lunch.'

Vi sat down at the kitchen table, the scene of so many family dinners, discussions and the occasional argument. Violet's adventurous, rebellious streak had often placed her at odds with her placid parents, and every now and then they'd clashed over late nights, unsuitable-length dresses and even more unsuitable boyfriends.

They'd thanked their lucky stars when she'd brought Simon home, even if her dress sense hadn't exactly calmed down. She'd settled into her own style over the years, an eclectic mix of wartime vintage and sixties boho, all carried off with a slash of red lipstick and a collection of hair accessories to rival Claire's Accessories.

She was her own best advert; she adjusted all of her vintage buys to fit her curves perfectly, and made many of the hair accessories herself from feathers and jewels left over from her latest commission. Her business was starting to gather a reputation; she was making a name for herself in the costume world as someone whose eye for detail and carefully honed skills created wonderfully intricate showgirl outfits and feather headdresses. Boned silk corsets, sequinned hot-pants, feather and rhinestone bras. She was carving her own niche, and one day she hoped – no, she *planned* – to supply costumes to the legendary Moulin Rouge. It was the Holy Grail; one day she'd walk under that famous, glittering red windmill and see her costumes up there on that famous old Parisian stage.

Right now though, she had more immediate concerns. She needed her parents to accept that she was going to spend the summer in Swallow Beach; her every instinct told her that it was the right thing to do. She could work from there as easily as from here; there was bound to be space in her grandparents' apartment for her to set up a temporary sewing room. Was it fanciful? Maybe. Was it sudden? Yes. But she was going to do it nonetheless, and she'd really like to do it with her parents' blessing.

'I don't want to redecorate Simon's house, Mum.' His house was a minimal temple of neutral shades; the last thing he'd want would be Violet's jewelled hues and eye for colour un-minimalising his home.

'Fine. Buy a new home. That's exciting, Violet! Buy a house, a big Victorian one you can do up. You'd love that, right?'

Vi shrugged. Who wouldn't?

'In fact, move in next door! It's perfect. We won't sell Grandpa's house, you can move in there with Simon instead. Go wild with the decorating.'

Violet's father looked at his wife, clearly alarmed. The proceeds from Henry's house was their retirement plan; he loved his daughter and of course he'd love it if she wanted to stay so close, but his spreadsheet would be buggered, as would his grand plan to take Della on a walking tour of the Scottish Highlands. He'd have to keep working, there was nothing else for it.

'Mum, it's a lovely thought and I can't tell you how much I appreciate it, but no. Next door would remind me too much of Grandpa Henry. Besides, Simon loves his house, he wouldn't want to leave it.'

Out of the corner of her eye, Violet saw her dad sag with relief and shot him a small smile. She knew how much he was relying on the sale of next door; she wouldn't dream of taking up her mum's offer. Della knew too, really; she was just clutching at any straw going because the idea of Violet going to Swallow Beach filled her with trepidation. Bad things happened to people at Swallow Beach. That bloody pier! Why had her father hung onto the past? God knew their memories of the place weren't good ones.

'Look Mum,' Violet said, keeping her voice light. 'Why don't you come with me for a few days, have a look what state everything is in? It might not even be possible to stay if it's as bad as you think.'

Della had implied that both the pier and the apartment were sure to have gone to rack and ruin, and if that was the case then Violet was going to need to revise her plans. She watched as her mother's expression changed from obstinate to fearful, alarmed when Della sank into the nearest chair with her head in her hands.

'I can't go back there,' she whispered. 'I'm so sorry Violet. I just can't. Please don't ask it of me.'

Why had her grandpa hung onto the place? He mustn't have felt the same feelings of fear and hatred as her mum, or surely he'd have sold it on, severed his connections. Della had been only a child when they'd left, her perception of the events would have been very different to

Henry's, of course. And to Monica's. Violet felt torn, conflicted; the last thing she wanted to do was upset her lovely mum, but the pull towards Swallow Beach was, out of nowhere, overwhelmingly powerful.

'I need to do this, Mum.' She knelt beside Della and laid her head against her mother's knee. 'I promise I'll be careful, and you're probably right that it's a fool's mission, but I still need to go and see it for myself. I'm twenty-five, Mum, and I know you think I've lost my mind not to accept Simon's proposal, but I can't help how my heart feels. Or doesn't feel.'

'He's deferred it,' her father chipped in. 'He's going to wait for you until you come back. A lot on at work anyway, he said.'

Violet wasn't sure if her dad's comments were meant to be supportive to her or helpful to her mum. The latter, presumably, because the idea of someone deferring their proposal due to the pressures of stock-taking season was about as unromantic as it got. Rhett Butler, it wasn't. She'd watched *Gone with the Wind* countless times, mostly for the fabulous boned and feathered costumes, but also for the sweeping, epic – if somewhat unconventional – romance. It might not be a typical love story, but Violet kind of liked it all the more for that because she wasn't a typical kind of girl. She had spiky edges and a taste for adventure; Swallow Beach was calling, and she had no choice but to answer.

CHAPTER THREE

Violet swung a left, her stomach flipping over at the first mention of Swallow Beach on a road sign. Over the last few days she'd loaded the basics of her life into the back of her Morris Minor Traveller, the only car she'd wanted despite everyone advising her to get something newer and more reliable. She'd merrily ignored them all and her trusty woody van had fast become one of her most prized possessions, and right now it held a good chunk of her life in the back of its hatch. There had been little room for sentiment whilst packing up; the essential contents for her makeshift workroom filled the lion's share of the space.

Realising that there was little to gain from standing in Violet's way, Della had valiantly set aside her own feelings to assist her daughter, all the time dropping the words 'temporary' and 'coming home again soon' into the conversation to make sure they lodged well and truly in Violet's subconscious. Her dad had been typically low-key, although he'd insisted on giving her two hundred pounds in fresh ten-pound notes drawn from the bank that morning, just in case of emergency.

She'd hugged them tightly, then watched them stand arm in arm on the pavement as she drove away with a lump lodged in her throat. Simon wasn't there; he'd sent her a *bon voyage* card in the mail, vowing to keep the home fires burning until she returned ready to plan their wedding. Violet couldn't help but feel like an Amish teenager. She'd seen a programme a few weeks back on how they were allowed one wild summer before they settled down to the traditional ways; Rumspringa, they called it. Was this her own personal Rumspringa? Were her family indulging her in the hope and expectation that she'd get it out of her system and return to the fold?

All such thoughts flew out of the window as she passed a road sign welcoming her to Swallow Beach, twinned with a French town she couldn't pronounce the name of. Well, that had to be a good omen, right? Anywhere that was pretty enough to be twinned with a French town had to have something going for it, surely. She couldn't see anything yet; the skinny country lane was the kind where you pray nothing comes in the other direction, the high hedges batting her wing mirrors on either side. And then a few twists later, the lane widened and crested a hill, and for a few seconds Violet paused the car and just sat and looked at the scene spread out before her, entranced.

From her lofty hilltop position, she could clearly see the curved sweep of the bay down below. Her eyes scanned the beach, her heart in her mouth, terrified of disappointment, but sure enough, still standing there on the far right, was the old Victorian pier. Her breath whooshed from her chest, pure sweet relief. She'd told herself over and over that there was every likelihood that it had crumbled into the sea, but there it was, looking almost exactly as it had in the photos in her mum's battered album.

Sliding the car into first gear, Violet followed her nose slowly down the hill into the bay, her heart still banging around in her chest in a way that had nothing to do with the Traveller's springy suspension. The town, if that's what it was, felt like most out-of-season English seaside towns: closed up and waiting. April showers were the order of the day; it had dried up for now, but grey skies ruled and a damp, low hanging sea-mist clung to the air. Hardly the most welcoming weather, but Violet brimmed full of nervous optimism nonetheless. She was here. Now what was she supposed to do?

When she reached the seafront, she nosed the Traveller into one of the empty car park spaces facing the deserted beach, clearly placed there for people to pull in and watch the sunset. If the sun ever came out, that is. Not that it mattered all that much to Vi as she turned off the engine and let her eyes drink in her first good look at Swallow Beach Pier. At *her* pier. Ornate black ironwork reaching out into the sea. It wasn't overly long; and considering its age and the fact that no one would have looked after it in years, it looked to be in pretty decent shape. The scrolls and arches were almost delicate, and balanced over the waves at the far end stood the prettiest of glass pavilions.

'Oh,' Violet whispered, steaming up her windscreen. 'Will you look at that.'

Climbing from the car, she fastened the oversized wooden buttons on her kingfisher-blue felt coat against the brisk breeze, wound her hand-knitted cherry-red scarf around her neck, and locked the Traveller even though there wasn't another soul around. She didn't have a plan; she just felt the need to get closer to the pier.

Following the cobbled pavement along, she slowed as she neared the land-bound end of the pier, coming to a halt in front of two tall, wonderfully ornate gates closing the pier off from the rest of the town. A heavy metal chain bound the gates together, wound several times between the bars and scrolls. A huge old padlock held the chain in place, ensuring that no one set foot onto the wooden boards that lay beyond the gates.

Almost tentatively, Vi stepped closer and reached out her hands, closing her eyes as her fingers made first contact with the cold metal. Sighing deeply, she curled her fingers around the iron and leaned her head forwards to rest against it, imagining her grandmother standing in the exact same spot all those years ago. How had she felt the first time she'd been in Swallow Beach? She'd been on honeymoon, probably full of optimism and excitement. A strangely comforting wash of emotions swept across Vi's skin, making her open her eyes and fill her lungs to the brim with bracing, salty sea air. If she'd been asked to give the emotion a name, it would have been hope.

'Monica?'

Violet twirled around, startled by the voice behind her. She found herself looking up into the bluest eyes she'd ever seen, cornflower bright and wide as they stared at her face. The tall, distinguished man was probably eighty or more, and he looked nothing short of incredulous as he narrowed his gaze and peered closer, then shook his head as if to clear it.

'Sorry. Thought you were someone else then for a mo.'

'You called me Monica,' Violet said. 'Monica was my grandmother.'

Again, the stranger stared, then nodded slowly and sighed. 'Of course she was. Blow me, if you're not the living image of her.'

'You knew my grandmother?'

The man laughed then, those blue eyes glittering and wishful. 'Oh, I knew Monica,' he said. 'And Henry, of course. Is he still . . .?'

Vi shook her head and bit the inside of her lip, holding in the sharp stab of longing for her grandpa. 'No. He died a few weeks back.'

Lowering his gaze, the man removed his fedora. 'Sad news, *mon chéri*.'

A thought occurred to Violet. 'I wonder if you could help me?' she said, digging in her coat pocket for her phone to check the address of her grandparents' apartment. Or her new home, as she needed to start to think of it, temporarily at least. 'I need to find the Lido building?'

The stranger didn't say anything for a second, then he held his hand out. 'I'm Bartholomew Harwood,' he said. 'Everyone calls me Barty these days, you should too.'

Ingrained politeness had Vi reaching out to shake his hand. 'Violet,' she said.

'Violet.' He repeated her name, as if deciding whether or not he approved. 'How perfectly glorious. Lilys are two a penny these days. Violets are rarer by far.'

Glorious and rare? Well, no one had ever said that about her before. Vi decided she rather liked Barty Harwood. He had a rakish, old-school charm and the hint of a wry smile hovering around his mouth, and going on his bright floral shirt, he didn't seem to care much for convention. Tall and well dressed, he looked like a man who had many anecdotes and would be happy to share some of them over a few glasses of good whisky.

'How about I show you the Lido?' Barty said. 'It's not far at all.'

Violet glanced back along the seafront towards the Traveller. 'Is it walking distance? We could go in my car.'

Barty followed her gaze. 'As you wish,' he said, holding his arm out to indicate she should lead the way.

'Have you always lived in Swallow Beach?' She made conversation as she fished her keys from her pocket as they approached her car.

Barty ran his hand appreciatively over the polished wood on the Traveller. 'It's admirable that you don't feel obliged to follow the trends, Violet.'

Violet slid into the driver's seat and reached across to open his door, aware that he'd dodged answering her question. She didn't push it; if he'd been here long enough to know her grandparents, he'd obviously spent a large part of his life here.

He rubbed his hands together briskly as she started the engine and reversed, then nosed her way along the seafront towards the pier.

'Which way?'

Barty inclined his head across the strip of grass that served as a central reservation, towards a building fronting the main road. Following his nod, Violet scanned the scene and found herself gazing at a tall pale-brick villa, double-fronted and far more grand and ornate than she'd anticipated. Stone steps led up to the wide, central front door, flanked on either side by graceful white pillars. Curved bay windows ran up the full height of each floor of the building, and up on the very top gutters, large, white letters proudly spelt out 'The Lido'.

'You weren't kidding when you said it wasn't far,' she murmured, taken aback. She'd imagined that the apartment would be somewhere tucked away at the back of Swallow Beach, not in the grandest building on the seafront. How frankly fabulous.

'Where's best to park?'

Barty directed her down a side street. 'There's a car park around the back for residents.'

Residents. Was she really to be a resident in such a gorgeous place, albeit only for a summer? Following Barty's direction, Vi turned in behind the building and found a well-cared-for, almost empty car park. Even the back of the building was lovely, a rose garden already in early bloom beside the back door.

'Does it matter where I park?' she asked, keen not to wind anyone up on day one by parking in their space.

Barty wrinkled his nose. 'Most people are at work, I expect; park wherever takes your fancy. Have to fight them off with a stick in the summer, mind.' His hand was already opening the door, and he turned away to unfold his tall frame from the low passenger seat.

Sucking down a deep breath for courage, Violet swung her door wide and followed suit.

Following Barty through the back door, Violet found herself inside the ground-floor lobby, light and bright thanks to the many stained windows surrounding the front door and the freshly painted white woodwork on the gracefully sweeping staircase and two apartment doors, one either side of the tiled vestibule. Gold numbers on the doors declared them 1 and 2.

'This is mine,' Barty said, nodding towards number 1. 'And that one belongs to Keris, my granddaughter.'

Vi's jaw dropped. 'You live here?'

He threw his hands out. 'So it would seem. Cup of mint tea?'

Vi narrowed her eyes. 'That's my favourite.'

Barty looked at her steadily, half smiling. 'Who knew?'

You did, Violet felt like saying. 'I better not,' she said, instead. Glancing towards the staircase, her nerves kicked back in. 'I better head on up.' She stalled, jiggling the keys, excited and terrified at the same time. 'Has anyone been up there recently, do you know?'

Barty shook his head. 'Not that I've noticed.' He touched his fingers against his fedora. 'I'll let you get on. You know where I am if you need me. Tap the door for mint tea.'

And with that he turned and opened his own door. Looking back at her as he stepped inside, he paused. 'Do you want me to come up with you?'

Tempted as she was to say yes, Vi shook her head. This was something she needed to do alone.

'Thanks, I think I'm okay.'

He looked at her for a couple of silent seconds, then nodded and closed his door. Violet stood still for a few moments, fighting the urge to knock on his door and tell him she'd changed her mind, she'd love a cup of mint tea and someone to hold her hand and come with her. All she knew about the apartment on the top floor was that her grandfather had paid a cleaning company to go in once a month, but that aside, no one with any actual connection to her family had set foot near the place in decades. It was empty. Waiting. For her? Suppressing the chill that ran down her spine, Violet put her best foot forward and set off up the wide, shallow stairs.

Number 6. The swirled gold number on the left-hand door of the upper-floor landing confirmed it. Violet hesitated at the top of the marble staircase, her eyes flickering towards number 5. Who was her new neighbour? She hoped they wouldn't mind sharing the top floor; they must be pretty used to having it to themselves after all these years.

God, but she was nervous. She'd been so caught up with the romantic notion of moving to Swallow Beach that she hadn't paused to think about the reality of standing here poised to enter the apartment for the first time. She hadn't counted on feeling so alone, or scared, even. She hadn't imagined that she'd be ever so slightly spooked, or feel inexplicably certain that her life was going to change as soon as she opened the door. Shooting a look back towards the staircase, she toyed with the idea of asking Barty to accompany her after all. She almost stepped towards it, then at the last second she pulled herself together, swung purposefully towards her door, and raised the key towards the lock.

'Er, not so fast, cat burglar. Who the hell are you?'

Violet jumped out of her skin, startled by the sudden male voice behind her. His timing couldn't have been more spectacularly off; her heart was already in her mouth – he'd pretty much guaranteed her a heart attack. Swinging around, she tried to look more together than she felt. For a slow moment, she stared down the guy standing across the landing, mostly because she couldn't breathe properly.

'I know,' he grinned, leaning against his doorway and folding his arms. 'It's a lot to take in.' He gestured down at himself. 'I can wait.'

Violet looked away out of the picture window towards the sea, ignoring his smart-arse remark. In truth, he *was* quite a lot to take in. Tall and tanned, so far so good, but also wearing overalls unbuttoned down his bare chest to waist level. He radiated a laid-back kind of charisma that Hollywood directors no doubt wished they could bottle, all dark curls and eyes that said more than his mouth.

'I'm Violet,' she said, aware she sounded clipped and

prim as she raised her chin and looked at him again. 'And I'm not a cat burglar. I live here.'

It was his turn to look surprised. 'No one lives up here but me.'

'Well, now I do.'

'In there?' he frowned towards her door.

'Yes.'

'Since when?'

'Since now. Since this minute.'

He nodded slowly. 'Have you been inside yet?'

Violet bit her lip. 'Not yet.'

'I didn't realise the old place had been sold,' he said, frowning.

'It hasn't. It belonged to my grandparents.'

'Oh, right.' His eyebrows flicked upwards, from confusion to surprise. 'Well, welcome to the neighbourhood.'

When he made no move to go back inside, Violet nodded out of politeness and turned her back on him, raising the key to her lock again. This time, she didn't hesitate. It slid in easily enough; the caretaking company were obviously doing a good job. And because there was nothing else for it, and because she could feel her new neighbour's eyes burning the back of her neck, Violet pushed the door open and stepped back in time.

CHAPTER FOUR

It didn't smell of anything, really. She'd braced herself for it to somehow smell like her grandpa's house, maybe, or of her grandmother's perfume, which she knew was ridiculous. Or, more likely, of stale year-upon-year emptiness. But, no doubt thanks to the diligent upkeep of the cleaning company, it simply smelt vacant, as if waiting to catch the scent of someone new.

Closing the door, Violet stood in the small hallway to get her bearings, lowering her bag slowly to the floor and breathing deeply. She was here. This was it. Little as it was, the square hallway told Violet two things straight away. One, her grandmother had an eye for colour and interior design, and two, she was going to adore number 6 Swallow Beach Lido. It was pure seventies retro glamour right down to the shell-pink Bakelite telephone table, topped of course with a curly-wired ivory telephone, its sharp-angled handset resting lengthwise over the dial. Violet lifted the receiver and placed it against her ear, then replaced it, feeling foolish as she caught her reflection in the mirror over the table. As if there would have been any dialling tone.

Four doors led off the hallway, each of them closed. Turning the handle of the nearest door, Violet pushed it wide and stepped through it, finding herself in the bathroom.

'Oh my God,' she whispered, her eyes darting all around the room. It had all of the usual things – bathtub, loo, sink – but none of them were the usual kind. The huge, turquoise kidney-shaped bathtub had been inset into a surround with steps up, and the whole bathing corner had been lined with mirrors, like a child's music box. It wasn't a wallflower's bathtub, that much was for sure. The loo and sink were squared off and equally bright turquoise, and the forest-green-and-turquoise-swirled wall tiles added to the impact. The taps were gilt, water-spouting goldfish, the light fitting a golden chandelier. It was a Hollywood starlet's bathroom, and Violet found herself almost laughing with unexpected delight.

'Go Gran,' she whispered, turning a tap, glad to see the water flow from the goldfish's open mouth. She hadn't thought to check if the utilities were still connected; it seemed that she was in luck.

Opening the wall cupboard above the sink, Violet found herself looking at a collection of vintage glass-bottled bubble baths and paper-wrapped soaps, all still perfect thanks to being tucked away safe from the daylight. A pang of sadness washed over her at the sight of a glass holding three toothbrushes, two adult, one smaller. Her mum's. Closing the cabinet quietly, she backed out of the room.

Right, so which door next? Vi looked at each of them and chose the one on her right, pushing it open slowly to reveal a single bedroom. She didn't go inside, just stood in the doorway of her mum's childhood bedroom and let the sweet sadness settle over her. The low, white single bed covered with a lemon and white patchwork eiderdown, the chunky white and lemon furniture, the wheeled book-box filled with well-thumbed picture books. Della had been seven or eight when she'd left this room for the last time, and as far as Vi could see, it hadn't been touched since. She didn't venture further inside the room. She would eventually, but of all the rooms in the house she knew that this one was likely to be the most difficult for her personally, because it represented her mum. Clicking the door closed, she moved on to the next, the master bedroom where, once again, glamour reigned.

Violet drew in a sharp breath; it was unique, and wild, and quite stunning. One wall had been hand-painted, a marine-blue ocean adorned with mermaids, some coy, others joyfully bare-breasted with their arms flung over their heads as they basked on rocks. As she neared the wall for a closer look, glints of iridescent gold glittered in their scaly tails, and their eyes seemed to watch with interest, as surprised by her presence as she was by theirs.

'Who did all of this?' she whispered into the quiet room. 'Was it you, Gran?'

The mermaids served as the theme for the rest of the bedroom. The large, low bed's high scalloped headboard had been padded in shimmering oyster silk, and an elegant clamshell chair sat in the curve of the floor-to-ceiling bay window.

Sinking down onto its ink-blue velvet seat, Violet took a few minutes to just let herself be. A tailor's dummy stood beside the chair in the bay, dressed in a floor-length sheath that seemed to be made entirely from sequins and lace and light. Necklaces and pearls had been looped around the dummy's neck, a glamorous makeshift jewellery box.

Every last thing in the room had been chosen with a nod towards maritime decadence; polished curved wooden furniture reminiscent of a luxury ocean liner, the fabulous, huge Tiffany glass bowl suspended from the ceiling an intricate mosaic of rainbow shades. Seventies glam wasn't everyone's style, but it sure was Violet's. So much so that she felt as if she'd been winded; her own leanings towards colour and craft were so clearly inherited from the woman who'd hand-decorated this place with such unique style.

She was starting to understand that she hadn't inherited just her gran's physical looks. All of her life she'd felt very different to her practical, list-loving parents, and now she understood why. Monica's blood ran hot in her veins. Violet hadn't expected to feel an instant connection here, but by God she did. She saw now why her mum had wanted to keep her from this place: she'd known. Della knew precisely who her daughter was most like in the world, and probably feared what that knowledge might do to Violet.

Leaving the bedroom reluctantly, Violet headed for the last unopened door. She opened it slowly, wanting to savour this final new space. It was worth the reverence; the lounge-diner wouldn't have looked out of place on the faded cover of a seventies copy of *House Beautiful*. A low, burnt-orange, oversized velvet sofa sat central in the lounge, accented by curved pale-blond wooden furniture, and the orange and grey oversized flower print wallpaper would have been perfect in an Orla Kiely showroom.

The kitchenette ran across the back of the space, a glossy swathe of orange. A breakfast bar acted as a room divider, complete with stools upholstered in orange and grey stripes. Accents of muted gold warmed and glamourised the space, not least the decadent wheeled glass and brass drinks trolley, still loaded with half-full bottles of colourful spirits and cocktail paraphernalia.

Vi gazed up at the chandelier dripping with clear and orange glass droplets and fell in love. She fell in love with the Lido apartment, and with Swallow Beach, and with her grandmother. Sinking down onto the sofa and wrapping her arms around her midriff, she couldn't decide if she felt like laughing or crying. Because in the most unexpected of ways, she felt as if she'd come home.

'Hey cat burglar. You still in there?'

Violet jumped as her new neighbour rapped on her front door. Unfolding herself from the sofa, she went to open it.

'Hello again,' he grinned. 'I was a little rude earlier. I brought wine to say sorry and welcome to the top floor.'

He held out a bottle of red, and then produced a bunch of white roses from behind his back like a magician.

She narrowed her eyes as she accepted them. 'Did you cut those from the bushes outside?'

'I did,' he said, lifting one shoulder, clearly unabashed at being caught out. 'But I also grew them, so I'm not all that sorry.'

'You grew them?'

He scrunched his nose, as if debating how honest to be. 'Well, I water them sometimes. Strictly speaking, Barty is the green-fingered one of the block.'

Violet liked the idea that the tenants of the Lido worked as a community.

He glanced over her shoulder into the apartment. 'How's everything going?'

She accepted the wine, unsure how to answer the question. 'Okay. Sort of.'

'Need a hand with anything?'

'No, I'm good I think,' she said. 'Except . . . I don't suppose there's a lift in the building, is there? A trade one, or something?' The Traveller was fully loaded, and her sewing machine in particular was going to be a bit of a monster to lug up all of those stairs.

His mouth kicked up at the edges. ''Fraid not. You do, however, have a handsome neighbour with guns of steel who'd carry your stuff in exchange for a glass of wine?'

'A neighbour who hasn't even told me his name,' Vi countered, amused despite herself. He was cocksure, but the mischievous glint in his brown eyes told her that he didn't take himself seriously. Back home in Violet's world everyone took themselves seriously, so he was something of a breath of fresh air.

'I didn't?' he said.

She shook her head.

'Cal.'

Different. 'Short for . . . California?' she said, knowing full well it wouldn't be.

He laughed loud. 'Trust me, my mother is nowhere near that adventurous. Calvin,' he said. 'Calvin Dearheart.'

Jesus, he's straight out of a Jilly Cooper novel, Violet thought, nodding wordlessly. At least he'd buttoned his overalls up before knocking on her door.

'Right, so now you know who I am, and I know who you are, that makes us friends. Now take the flowers, let me help you with your stuff, and then let's get gloriously drunk and tell each other our darkest secrets.'

Well, that was unexpected. Violet swallowed hard, unsure how to reply, because Calvin Dearheart was fast becoming one of the most startling men she had ever met.

*

'Jesus, Violet, what's in here, a dead body?'

Cal appeared on the upper landing with the last and heaviest of her belongings cradled in his arms, her precious sewing machine.

'Careful,' she cautioned, wondering where in the apartment to set up her workroom. She'd upgraded to the eye-wateringly expensive machine last summer off the back of a couple of big theatre costume contracts, and right now Cal was staring at her questioningly, slightly out of breath.

'Where to?'

Up to that point, he'd deposited her bags and boxes on the top landing and she'd ferried them inside as he fetched the next load, but it made no sense for him to put the machine down because she'd have to pick it up again.

'This way,' she said, hesitant. Inviting him inside the apartment felt almost disrespectful to her grandmother, as if Monica's artistic secrets were going to be spilled. And then reality bit; Vi reminded herself that this was *her* home now, not Monica's, and she needed to work out how to live in it, new neighbour included.

Turning her back, she led Cal into the lounge and asked him to put the machine down on the pale wooden dining table. It was an interesting piece: a thin slice of polished walnut on a white plastic pedestal with matching slender-legged walnut chairs. He carefully did as she'd asked, then straightened and looked slowly around the room, wide-eyed.

'Christ,' he murmured, rotating almost three hundred and sixty degrees on the spot. 'I never realised this place hadn't been touched. It's amazing.'

Pride slid down Violet's spine, making her stand straighter. She'd expected him to have a reaction to the place, because who wouldn't, but she wasn't sure which way it would go. She found it mattered that he appreciated her grandmother's taste, because it was so in line with her own.

'It's really something, isn't it,' she said quietly. 'I didn't even know it existed until a couple of weeks back.'

He nodded slowly, taking it all in. 'I think we need that drink now.'

Violet looked at her watch. It was well after three, and she was starving.

'I better go food shopping first,' she said. 'Can you point me in the right direction?'

'I could,' he said. 'Or I could take you to the local instead? They do a mean lasagne, Roberto makes it himself.'

Lasagne was one of Vi's all-time top ten dinners. It was too good an offer to pass up, especially when it was cooked by someone who sounded like they might actually be Italian.

'Go on then. You're on.'

Cal wasn't kidding. Perhaps it helped that Violet was hungry, but Roberto's lasagne was to die for, as was his ice-cold sauvignon and his infectious belly laugh. The Swallow, as the pub was appropriately called, sat a little further along the seafront than the Lido, a hop and a skip away for an evening pint.

'Have you always lived in Swallow Beach?' Vi asked, poking a patchwork of holes in her lasagne with the tip of her knife to cool it down.

Cal nodded. 'Give or take a few years. My family have been here for more generations than anyone can count back.'

'Wow,' she said. 'You must like it then.'

'It's as good as anywhere,' he said, non-committal. 'Pretty special when the sun comes out.'

'Does it attract much of a holiday crowd?'

Again, he looked as if he was hedging his bets. 'Some. Not as much as the more well-known tourist spots further along the coast, but we do okay. We're a bit more shabby than chic, if you know what I mean.'

Swallow Beach sat on the south coast, a forgotten little sister to Brighton's famous pebble beach and the often-photographed Camber Sands. Violet rather liked the fact that it was off the tourist track; she'd been there less than twenty-four hours and already she was starting to feel territorial.

'So what's the grand plan then, Violet?' he said, refilling both their wine glasses. 'Are you here for a week, a month or forever?'

There he went again, coming out with something direct and unexpected.

'The summer. To begin with, at least.'

He nodded. 'And then back to the bright city lights?'

Thoughts of her distinctly orderly suburban life back home at her parents' filtered in.

'It's not exactly that,' she said, not wishing to say anything ungrateful. She knew she was lucky to be able to live cheaply at her parents'; it had allowed her the creative freedom to start the business rather than be forced to take a job she didn't want to cover rent and bills.

Cal laid his cutlery down, his plate almost empty. 'And is there a Mr Violet on the scene?'

Was he fishing? Or was this just another of his direct questions? He watched her steadily, his dark eyes interested. Violet found herself a little dry-mouthed; he was undeniably attractive and easy company. His question wasn't a simple one to answer either, thanks to Simon's insistence on waiting for her.

'No, but kind of yes, a little bit,' she said. 'It's complicated.'

He laughed softly. 'Is that your Facebook status?'

She rolled her eyes. 'I know, it sounds flaky. It's just . . .'

'Complicated?'

Vi smiled, shrugged. 'Yes.'

'Okay.'

He didn't push, and thankfully Roberto chose that moment to hustle over and take away their empty plates.

'Dessert tonight, passion fruit pannacotta,' he said, tipping a wink at Cal.

'Irresistible,' Cal smiled. 'Two please.'

Violet wasn't sure if she ought to feel irritated that he'd ordered for her, but on reflection she found not, especially given that she was a pudding kind of girl.

'Passion fruit,' Cal said, as Roberto disappeared with their plates.

There really wasn't an answer to that, especially after three glasses of wine. 'Indeed.'

'I think we've reached the point in the evening where we trade secrets,' he said, leaning back in his chair.

Violet took him in; the way his faded T-shirt and washed-out jeans followed the definitions of his body, suggesting someone who took care of themselves. He didn't look like a gym worshipper though, more like someone who took themselves seriously. Until you looked into his face, that was; Cal didn't seem able to stop his dark eyes from dancing or keep the ever-ready laugh from his lips. He was easy on the eye, and easy company to be in. Dangerous, in other words. The one thing Violet hadn't come to Swallow Beach for was romance, especially not with her neighbour. If she thought her love life was complicated now, that would be a sure-fire way to make it as tangled as a fisherman's trawl net. And perhaps she was hugely jumping the gun anyway; Cal Dearheart seemed the kind of guy who flirted as naturally as he breathed, it probably didn't mean anything.

'You can go first,' she said, buying herself a little time.

He raised his eyebrows and tapped his fingers on the edge of the table, thinking. 'Right. So, I've climbed a mountain,' he said. 'Three mountains, in fact.'

'Oh,' she said. That confirmed that he was indeed someone who took his body seriously. The idea of walking up a mountain filled her with unfathomable dread. Why would anyone do that for fun?

'Your turn.'

There was a painting on the wall behind Cal's head, a landscape oil of Swallow Beach.

'I own the pier.'

He stopped tapping and stared at her. 'Say again?'

Violet sighed, repeating herself quietly. 'I own Swallow Beach Pier.'

Cal scraped his seat in under the table and leaned forward, his elbows on the table. 'You own our pier?'

Nodding, Vi smarting slightly at the incredulous way he said it; 'our' as if the pier belonged to the town, and 'you' as if she wasn't part of it. Well, she wasn't really, not yet, but her grandparents had been and she felt oddly like she was representing them in the community. His words also gave her pause for another reason; she hadn't for a second stopped to imagine that she might meet resistance to her presence from the locals.

Oh God! Were they all going to hate her?

'My grandparents, Henry and Monica Spencer, honeymooned here. Gran fell in love with the place, and the pier was up for sale so my grandpa bought it for her. They moved here to the Lido lock, stock and barrel on the strength of it.'

'That's some story,' he said, nodding slowly.

She still couldn't tell if he was being off. 'I think it's romantic.'

'Oh, it is, it is,' he said slowly, as if choosing his words with care. 'But you might want to tread a little cautiously, that's all. The pier's become a bit of a bone of contention in recent years. Some of the locals feel that a compulsory order is appropriate to get it out of private hands.'

Violet blinked, feeling her cheeks start to heat up. 'A compulsory order? What does that even mean?'

Cal emptied the rest of the wine into their glasses. 'You know, a forced sale. There was even talk of it being dismantled, although that seems to have gone quiet.'

'No!' The word left Violet sharp and laced with fear; they couldn't take her grandma's pier down. 'Why would they do that?'

'Hey, don't panic,' he said, sliding her glass towards her. 'It's not going to happen. Especially not now you're here.'

'But . . .' She trailed off and swallowed a mouthful of wine. She'd had her rose-tinted glasses firmly jammed on up to now, seeing only romance and fairytale where the pier was concerned. Where *her* pier was concerned. 'Is everyone going to hate me?'

A smile tugged at the edges of Cal's mouth. 'How could they hate a girl with blue hair and candy-stripe nails?'

Violet looked down at her hands. Her mum despaired of her penchant for painting her nails in weird and wonderful designs, and she dearly wished her daughter would stop dip-dyeing the ends of her dark hair all shades of the rainbow. Teal, orange, fire-engine red; she'd tried them all. Right now Violet was in her peacock-blue period. She didn't do it to stand out. She just liked colour, and patterns, and didn't see any reason to be bland.

'Want to go out and look at it now?'

She looked up again and found Cal watching her. 'Yes,' she said quietly. 'I'd love that.'

Darkness had already fallen when they stepped out of the pub, and the nip in the air had Violet buttoning her coat as they crossed the deserted seafront road.

'Is it always this quiet?'

Cal shook his head. 'It's Sunday, and it's cold. Anyone sensible is doing something warm.'

Was that flirty? Did he mean sitting around the table with their family eating a Sunday roast, or did he mean in bed with a lover? It was hard to tell; Calvin Dearheart seemed to have a permanent glint in his eye. Vi didn't pull away when he linked his arm through hers and steered her along the sea wall towards the looming pier gates.

'Have you ever been beyond them?' she asked.

He slanted his eyes towards her. 'Not as an adult.'

She watched him, waiting for more, until he laughed and looked away.

'What kind of kid would grow up in a seaside town and not explore the deserted pier?'

Ah. She nodded, wrapping her arms around herself as they reached the gates. It looked different at night; more ominous and ramshackle, like something from a Stephen King book. It wasn't hard to imagine Cal as a boy, scrambling over the gates with his mates when they thought no one was looking.

'What's it like in there?'

Her eyes moved beyond the gates towards the barely visible glass pavilion perched out over the sea.

He followed her gaze. 'I can barely remember. More sound than it looks, I think. Must be to have survived all these years; a lot of the old piers have fallen into the sea by now unless they've been looked after.'

They stood side by side in the quiet evening, their breath misting in front of them. Violet could taste the sea-salt on her lips, and looking down the length of the wooden pier towards the pavilion, she could easily imagine the sound of footsteps running the length of it, or dancing along it, as she fancied when she thought of Monica.

'I've got the key to this,' she said, touching her fingers against the cold padlock.

'I don't think you should use it tonight,' Cal said. 'Wait until you know if it's safe.'

She didn't answer, just curled her fingers around the gate, much as she had that morning. The truth was she knew it was safe. Her legacy from her grandpa hadn't been neglected; he'd paid for a structural survey every three years. The pier had been given a clean bill of health just the summer before.

It was hard to fathom Henry's thinking; on the one hand he'd left Swallow Beach and never returned, and on the other hand he'd ensured that both the pier and the Lido apartment were maintained. It was almost as if he'd mothballed them for something. For Monica? Not for her mum, surely – Della's reticence about all things Swallow Beach was more than clear. The simple truth seemed to be that he'd kept them because they were part of the woman he loved, and now he'd passed them on to Violet because he'd felt, rightly or wrongly, that she'd know what to do with them.

'Will you come with me tomorrow?' she said. 'At dawn?'

'Are you serious?'

She nodded. 'I'd like to open it up and take a look without anyone knowing I'm here, and that seems like the best time to do it.'

'Will you come without me if I say no?'

'Yes.'

He shook his head and pushed his dark hair back from his face when the wind whipped it forwards.

'How did I know you were going to say that?' Placing his hand on the base of her back, he steered her away from the gates and back towards the Lido. 'Come on, let's get inside, it's too cold out here. I'll come back with you in the morning.'

'Morning catwoman,' Cal said when he met her on the landing early the following morning as agreed. It was a completely nonsensical nickname derived from *cat burglar*, but Violet didn't pull him up on it because, for one, it was harmless, and for two, it was kind of cool. Catwoman wore skintight leather and exuded sex appeal; no one had ever called her anything remotely sexy before. The closest Simon had come to giving her a nickname had been the couple of occasions he'd referred to her as *darling*, which didn't really count. Unless Cal meant *catwoman* in the sense of a spinster who turned to keeping cats out of desperation, which was something else entirely. Caffeine; her brain needed more caffeine before she could distinguish between compliment or insult.

'How did you sleep?'

'Not the best,' she said. 'First night in a strange bed and all that.'

It was a massive understatement. She'd barely slept at all, too churned up by the events of the previous day. Less than twenty-four hours previously she'd been in the relative safety of her parents' familiar kitchen, and now she was here in a strange town, in an even stranger apartment.

It wasn't just that, either. Every time she'd fallen into

fitful bursts of sleep, surrounded by mermaids, she'd found herself thinking about her new neighbour with his easy smile and laughing dark eyes. God only knew why; the one thing she definitely didn't need was any distractions of the romantic kind. And now here he was again, with his low-slung jeans and disreputable air, and she couldn't help noticing how his old leather biker jacket fitted him like a glove or the way his dark hair tumbled forward over his brow. He looked like trouble and laughed like a man who didn't care what people thought. Vi couldn't decide if she found that attractive or scary – a bit of both, probably.

'Got your keys?'

She nodded and patted her pocket. Last night she'd shown Cal the paperwork from her grandpa's engineers confirming the stability of the pier, and it had been enough to convince him they were safe to venture out there that morning as long as the weather was on their side. The huge landing window facing out towards the sea confirmed it; it was one of those rose-bright mornings, dewy, still and clear.

'All set,' she said. She didn't wait for Cal to lead the way. This was her destiny and she was going towards it herself, best foot forward.

Cal watched his interesting new neighbour strike off down the stairs, her blue-tipped hair swinging beneath her chunky red bobble hat. She wasn't very tall, yet she had a presence, an undeniable spark that crackled from her English-rose skin and shone from her unusual grey-green eyes. They were the exact same shade as the sea out in the bay; maybe she was a mermaid washed ashore to tempt him. If she was, it had worked. He was beguiled by the soft curve of her hips as she dashed down the stairs, taking care to step lightly due to the early hour.

'Come on,' she called up, a loud whisper that had his feet moving to catch her up. He'd cancelled a date last night to keep Violet company, and today he was going against his better judgement about the pier. But then it was no good being the black sheep of Swallow Beach if you didn't do stuff that marked you out as rebellious, was it? The thought of how much Violet's presence was going to rile his mother was enough to put a skip in his step as he followed her down towards the street.

She was waiting for him at the bottom of the Lido steps, rubbing her hands together in red-and-blue-striped fingerless gloves.

'Nervous?' he said, unnecessarily because it was written all over her face.

'No,' she said, and then laughed and rolled her eyes. 'Yes.'

'Standard,' he said. 'Come on. Let's do it.'

In truth, he was undeniably fascinated to go onto the pier without climbing the gates like he used to as a kid, and he'd never been inside the pavilion. Aside from the engineers, no one had been inside it for the last forty years.

It took them all of three minutes to reach the gates, and he watched as Violet stood jiggling on the spot, keys in hand. Come on, he thought. Be brave, mermaid girl. He smiled when she turned her uncertain eyes towards him. Had they really only met yesterday? She felt familiar, as if she'd been here far longer.

'Do it,' he whispered. He didn't offer to do it for her; it was one of those things she needed to do for herself. She nodded, turning away, and then stepped forward and slid the key into the clunky black padlock with shaky fingers.

*

Violet found the key fitted easily inside the lock. She'd worried it might be rusted or too stiff, but clearly her grandpa's upkeep of all things Swallow Beach extended to ensuring that the hefty lock keeping the public at bay was fit for purpose. The gates themselves had rusted and creaked though, screeching like angry seagulls as Violet twisted the padlock off and unwound the chains that bound them together.

'Sshh,' she whispered, worried that the noise would attract unwanted attention.

'It's fine,' Cal murmured. 'No one will hear it.'

She pushed the gates open just wide enough to allow them to step through.

'Are you worried it's going to crumble into the sea with us at the wrong end?' she said, turning to look at Cal again.

'Are you looking for a reason not to do it?' he countered, half smiling.

Was she? Kind of. Not because she was scared of it crumbling; she trusted her Grandpa Henry better than that. Her reticence was much less tangible than that, almost a muscle memory of being here before, a whisper of yesterday, a ghost from the past.

She was being fanciful; aware that her gran's blood ran in her veins, that she looked so very much like her, that her spirit seemed to have lain dormant in her daughter and skipped down a generation. In actual fact, Violet was ever so slightly afraid. What had happened to Monica for her life to come to such a sudden, tragic end in Swallow Beach? It was unreasonable to fear the same fate, the sensible part of Vi's brain knew that, but all the same her gran had arrived in Swallow Beach a bride and died far too young as a result. The thought sent a portentous chill down her spine. Maybe her mum was right to fear this place. Perhaps she shouldn't have come here at all.

'Violet?' Cal's hand warmed her shoulder. 'Shall we?'

Buoyed by his presence, she swallowed her fear. It was now or never.

'Yes. Yes, we shall.'

CHAPTER FIVE

The change from pavement to wooden boards underfoot felt like passing from reality to fairytale. She was really here, really doing this, really walking along her grandmother's beloved pier. After just one day here, Vi already felt immeasurably closer to Monica, never more so than as she set foot on Swallow Beach Pier for the first time.

'Okay?'

Cal's reassuring voice was quiet at her shoulder as he closed the gates so as not to attract attention. He didn't touch her; perhaps he sensed she needed to do this under her own steam. She nodded, her gaze lifting towards the glass pavilion at the other end. She'd feared that it might feel rickety, rather like walking the plank, but it was dry and solid beneath the soles of her sheepskin boots. A light sea breeze lifted the blue ends of her hair, and she breathed in slowly, purposefully, filling her lungs with the fresh, salty air as she moved forwards. She was aware of Cal following a few steps behind her, grateful for both his presence and his silence.

'I'm here, Gran,' she whispered. 'I've come.'

Solid as the pier was, Violet caught glimpses of the sand below through the gaps between the boards, and then of seawater as they moved further away from dry land. A slight sense of disorientation made her pause for a second, aware that they were putting their trust in the structure to hold them safely above the waves. Glancing back towards Cal, she found he'd paused too, and his little nod and thumbs up was enough to make her turn back and carry on again.

Half way now. She knew as much because a pale blue stripe had been painted across the boards and inscribed with the faded words 'Half way to paradise'. Vi hunkered down to look at it, tracing her fingertips over the swirled golden letters, glad they'd stood the test of time.

Was it her grandmother's hand? She suspected so. The letters had been accented in gold leaf, and something in the style reminded Violet of the Lido apartment. Looking at it, Vi couldn't help but wonder if her grandmother had paused to look at it the very last time she'd walked the pier. Apprehension twisted her mouth, and then Cal's hand on her shoulder made her look up, shielding her eyes from the low, peach-pink sunrise with her hand.

'It's tradition not to step on the line,' he said. 'Everyone in town knows that.'

Standing, Vi blew on her cold fingers, digesting this new bit of detail about the town's relationship with the pier, even those too young to have ever been on it.

'Right,' she said, stepping carefully over the board. Maybe the rule was a practical one, there simply to protect the paint, or perhaps it was more deeply rooted in superstition. Good luck, bad luck. Was it random, or did fate play a part? Had Violet always been destined to come here?

Giving herself a mental shake, she marched along the pier, her head held high, not stopping again until she reached the end where the boards flared out to accommodate the pavilion. She wasn't just Monica's artistic, impulsive granddaughter. She was Della's daughter, and Della had instilled a forthright practicality in her only child that served her well in that moment.

'Keys,' she whispered, feeling in her coat pocket.

'Do you want me to come in with you?' Cal asked.

Violet slid the key into the lock and found it as well-maintained as the previous one. Despite the fact that the pavilion was glass, it was difficult to see inside due to the dust accumulated over many years standing empty.

'Yes, come in,' she said, unthreading the chain from the door handles and laying it on the floor. As she bent she caught sight of the waves beneath them, a reminder that they were cut adrift from the mainland. Straightening, she rolled her shoulders and pulled the door open, giving it a bit of a shake when it offered resistance.

'Smells a bit.' She wrinkled her nose, pulling off her bobble hat and stepping inside as Cal pulled the door closed behind them.

They stood shoulder to shoulder, or rather side by side, given that Cal was a good six foot two to Violet's five foot four.

'Wow,' Cal murmured. 'I've only ever seen inside it in photographs.'

His words reminded Violet how much the pier was ingrained in the locals, and also reinforced how bizarre it was really that she'd grown up with no knowledge of it at all.

'Do you know what it was used for?' she asked, not yet moving further inside.

He paused. 'Exhibitions, I think? And as a gallery too, for a while in the sixties. If my memory serves me rightly, it was a shopping arcade for a while too.'

'Really?'

Cal nodded. 'Local craft shops, souvenirs, that kind of thing.'

Violet gathered her coat closer around her. She had no idea what she was going to do with the pier, if anything. Her thought process hadn't got much beyond this moment; seeing it, walking in Monica's footsteps, trying to understand its power over her grandmother.

'Shall we look around?'

Violet found herself glad of Cal's suggestion; she'd faltered, held still by the quiet cathedral of the glass pavilion. Inside, it seemed to be separated into various spaces by smoked-glass walls, creating an illusion of rooms, almost.

'This isn't what I expected,' she said, even though she didn't really know what she'd expected.

'I think the walls were put in to create the shop effect,' he said. 'They could probably come down again if you wanted them to.'

Vi nodded, not really taking the suggestion in beyond drily noting it as a male thought process, already assessing the place for DIY. Walking slowly, she led the way through the birdcage from empty room to empty room, saying very little and thinking a lot.

What on earth was she going to do with it? What had her grandmother done with the place when it was hers? She needed to know more, and given the amount that Cal knew already, she was pretty sure that the older generation in Swallow Beach would be able to fill in the gaps. Barty, perhaps. Each square space had smoked interior walls for privacy but the outer wall offered a wide view out over the sea. Standing in the back corner, Violet laid her hands on the cold, dusty glass.

'Don't lean on it,' Cal cautioned. 'You might end up in the sea.'

She smiled, far away. This room offered the best sea-view of all. She couldn't see any land, just wall-to-wall water. Even the grubby windows couldn't dampen the effect all that much; it was serene, like a cabin on a ship out in the middle of nowhere.

'Want me to leave you in peace for a while?'

Vi turned to look at Cal, and as she did, she noticed that some of the floorboards in the room had been painted, much like out on the pier. They weren't blue though. Someone, Monica presumably, had painted them in shades of the rainbow, faded now but still easily distinguishable as red, orange, yellow, green, blue, indigo, and violet. More than that. She'd painted the names of the colours, the same golden swirly letters as before, illuminated by the early morning sun.

Kneeling by them, Vi caught her breath, reading the words one by one until she reached the last. Pulling her gloves off quickly, she swept the layer of dust away with her flat hands, then stilled, staring down at the glittering letters.

Violet.

Her name, written there on the end of the pier by her grandmother all of those years ago.

Hot tears bubbled up out of nowhere; it was so unexpected, and so direct a link, almost as if her gran always knew she'd one day kneel here and find it. Her logical brain understood, of course; her mum hadn't just chosen her name at random after all. She'd always said it was a whim, but now Violet knew different. You couldn't call a girl Orange or Green, but Violet . . . yes. Had her mum remembered this floor on the day she was born, maybe given her a name that made her think of Monica? Vi swallowed down a great gulp of air, sentimental to the brim.

'That's pretty special,' Cal said, hunkering down next to her.

'I can't believe it's here,' she whispered, swiping her hand over her damp cheeks. 'Sorry, stupid of me.'

He stood, holding his hand out and heaving her up too. 'Not stupid at all,' he said, reaching out briefly to touch the blue tips of her hair.

She nodded quickly, feeling out of her depth, then looked up, startled by a scrabbling noise on the glass roof overhead.

'The swallows,' Cal said, gazing up. 'They gather on the pavilion roof.'

Violet watched them flit around for a few silent moments, not quite trusting herself to answer, not even sure what she wanted to say.

'I'm glad you've come to Swallow Beach,' he said softly when she looked back at him.

'You are?'

'You brighten it up.'

It was a compliment that she very much appreciated; she was accustomed to people finding her style a little too quirky, her colours a little too much.

'Thank you,' she murmured, still damp-eyed. She didn't know Calvin Dearheart at all really, yet in that moment she felt as if he knew her pretty well. Maybe that was why she didn't resist when he opened his arms.

'Need a hug? I'm told mine are the best in the business.'

He wasn't kidding. His arms folded around her and held her close but not too tight, his chin resting on the top of her head. He was warmth on the cold morning, and he was reassuringly alive when she felt surrounded by echoes of the past.

'I'm told I'm the best kisser in the business too, if you're interested,' he said, and even though she couldn't see his face she could feel him laughing into her hair.

'Don't push your luck,' she hiccupped, not ready to let go yet, because she'd just had the most rollercoaster twenty-four hours of her life and his arms felt like a safe place to be. And then she caught herself, because how could that be? She was practically engaged to Simon, yet here she was being held by a super-hot stranger who may or may not have just kissed her hair. She tried not to notice the fact that Cal smelt of warm leather and something almost like cinnamon spice, and of running water and of new opportunities.

'I think I've seen enough for now,' she said.

'Home then?'

She nodded, realising it was after nine only when she glanced at her watch. 'Do you need to get off to work?'

Cal kind of shrugged. 'I'm pretty flexible.'

Violet wanted to ask him what he did, but felt as if it might sound intrusive so held the question back for another time. Taking one last look around the pavilion, she led the way back out onto the pier and locked the doors again.

Later that day, fortified by a warm bath and a cupboard full of groceries, Vi perched on one of the breakfast stools and tried to work out where was best to set up her sewing machine. Common sense suggested the spare bedroom, once upon a time her mother's bedroom, as the practical answer. But that would mean moving things, emptying things, changing things, and she didn't want to do that before Della had had a chance to come and see it as it was for herself. Even though her mum had said that she couldn't face coming to Swallow Beach, Violet couldn't face the thought of her mum never visiting her here. She didn't know the full story really, but she got a strong sense from her mum of unfinished business where Swallow Beach was concerned and she hoped that, at some point over the summer, she'd soften and come.

So, with the only spare room not an option, Vi decided to leave the machine where it was on the dining table and work from there. Her eyes moved over the space, working out where the light fell and where she could store all of her accessories and stock. A large walnut and white sideboard stretched across the back wall behind the table; she could empty that out and use it. Decision made, she jumped up and set to work.

Two hours later, Violet sat cross-legged on the floor, damp-cheeked for the second time that day, surrounded by the trinkets and detritus of a life only half lived. Her grandparents' wedding album, black and white, crisp vellum protecting the framed images. Monica's fifties tea-length dress looked like something straight out of *Grease*, sleeveless white lace with a boat neck and layers of net underskirts over impossibly pointed kitten heels. Her dark hair had been styled into an elegant bouffant and dressed with a white band, and despite her winged black eyeliner and wide smile she looked impossibly young and naive. Hopeful, in shiny-eyed love with the tall, suited man standing proudly beside her. Was that really Grandpa Henry? He looked so carefree and youthful, it was hard to even identify him as the kind, world-weary man Vi had known and loved beyond measure.

There were more albums in there too, including one with 'Della' hand-painted on the first page in yellow and silver. It was filled with heart-achingly sweet photographs of Della's baby years, all inscribed beneath with dates and captions. *The day we brought our beautiful baby girl home,* written beneath a photograph of them on the steps of the Lido, the shawled baby cradled in Monica's arms. *Della's first tooth!* underneath a shot of a laughing, pink-cheeked baby proudly displaying one tiny white bottom tooth. A homemade chocolate cake iced with Della's name; it didn't really need the *Della is one!* to place it in time, but the flurry of tiny coloured hearts beside it made Violet's heart hurt. Snapshot after snapshot. *Della can walk! Della's first word – Dadda, of course!*

Violet closed the album and laid it with the others beside a box of tickets and faded receipts from high days and holidays. Monica had probably kept them with the intention of scrapbooking them, but for one reason and another they'd never got that far. They were precious, and they painted a picture of the woman her grandmother had been. Someone who loved her husband and her daughter, someone who – if the pictures were any gauge – laughed often, someone who dripped creativity from her fingertips. Vi found herself feeling more and more protective of Monica with every new thing she learned, and in turn determined to protect her legacy here in Swallow Beach. Her grandparents had been happy here for a while; she was going to do them both proud and try to be happy here too.

Across the landing in the Lido, Cal immersed himself in his work to stop himself from wondering what his new neighbour was doing. He was far too used to having the top floor to himself, it was taking some getting used to knowing that there was a blue-haired mermaid girl living just across the hall from him.

Running the leather collar he'd just finished through his fingers, he methodically checked the stitching, the precision of the buckle, the correct positioning of the studs. Every piece he produced was handmade to order, and his reputation was growing with every satisfied customer, much to his mother's irritation.

Checking his watch, he realised he was already cutting it fine if he was going to make his hastily rearranged date from last night. Clara would be pissed if he cancelled twice, and she was way too attractive to bother waiting around for a third attempt. He'd met her the week before at a convention and they'd hit it off, arranging to meet for dinner in Hastings.

She ticked all of his usual boxes: forthright, striking, not looking for anything serious. He'd done serious and come out not so much with his fingers burned as with his fingerprints incinerated off – these days he chose his female company carefully to avoid complications. Which brought him back to Violet. She didn't tick any of his boxes. Or else she did, in that she was definitely striking, but she was also his neighbour, and more than that, she seemed like someone who needed a friend while she was here. So, regretfully, he'd relegated himself to the friend zone, which was a novel and not all that pleasant place to find himself. Still. It'd be okay, he told himself. There were plenty of fish in the sea. Just not many mermaids.

After an afternoon spent arranging her temporary workspace and a rather unglamorous dinner of cheese on toast,

Violet decided to call it quits and have an early night. She'd called her mum, replied to a text from Simon and tomorrow she planned to get stuck into her next work order. Her whole world seemed to have flipped on its axis since she'd received the letter from her grandpa; she found the idea of getting her teeth into work familiar and soothing.

Turning out the lights, she headed for the bathroom to brush her teeth, and then paused, surprised by the sight of a note pushed underneath her door.

Being neighbourly. Here's my mobile number in case you hear anything go bump in the night. Or run out of milk. Or you're lonely. C x

He'd scrawled his number underneath in the same confident script as his words. Violet couldn't help but smile as she read it twice over, then put it down beside the old telephone. Cal seemed to live his life with his finger permanently on the humour button; given that everything else around her seemed deep and confusing, he was a tonic. She'd heard him go out earlier in the evening, and found the top floor a lonelier place without him across the hall. He wasn't the quietest of neighbours. In fact earlier he'd been making quite a racket at times, hammering and sanding by the sound of it. Perhaps he was a DIY fan.

After a moment's hesitation, she went back into the living room and ripped a page out of her notepad, scrawling on it before opening her front door and making a PJ-clad dash across to Cal's apartment. Her heart hammered in case he came back while she was out there, but all was quiet.

She paused as she passed the huge landing window looking down over the bay. It was gorgeous by night, creamy street lamps dotted along the seafront, the darkness of the sea glinting beneath the clear moon. She could just about make out the shadow of the pier, a spindled outline.

Her feelings for it were already strengthening, especially since finding her name painted there out over the waves. How special. How wondrous, really, as if the past was reaching out and welcoming her to Swallow Beach, asking her to safeguard Monica's memories. She would. Vi didn't yet know exactly what she was going to do with the pier, or even if she'd stay here for more than a summer, but she wasn't leaving until the pier was open again. The intention settled on her shoulders as she stood with her palm flat against the window.

'I'm here now,' she whispered. 'I'm here and I'll take care of you.'

There would be no compulsory purchase order on Violet's watch. The people of Swallow Beach may well have felt that the pier belonged to them, but the truth was that it belonged to Violet now, and to Monica before her. She really hoped that the townspeople would be glad of her presence in the bay, but if they weren't . . . Vi wasn't a girl accustomed to trouble, but looking out over the pier in that quiet, reflective moment, she resolved that she wasn't going to be pushed around. It was too important.

Just after midnight, Cal let himself into his apartment, taking care not to disturb his neighbour. On the whole, it had been a pretty successful evening. Clara was good company, undeniably gorgeous and she'd made it pretty clear that she was up for some fun when he'd dropped her home just now. He hoped he hadn't offended her by tactfully declining her offer to go inside; he didn't even know why he'd taken a rain check, really, aside from the fact he'd been up since five and had a lot on work wise.

Looking down as he locked up for the night, he spotted a white folded sheet of paper on the wooden floor, and for a moment he wondered if he'd overstepped the mark with Violet and she'd returned his letter to sender. Opening it though, he found silver loopy handwriting very different from his own.

Being equally neighbourly. Here's my mobile number in case of an actual, genuine, bona fide emergency. Or if you need someone to take in a parcel. Or similar. Violet. :)

Laughing under his breath, he shoved it in his jeans pocket and turned out the lights.

It was no good. Sleep just wasn't happening. Violet tossed and turned, sliding in and out from under the coattails of sleep, never really sinking much beyond the point where her brain flicked from conscious to unconscious thought. It wasn't all that surprising, really, that her brain jumbled up images of the pier, and her name in golden script, and a dark-haired man laughing into the morning sun. She could almost see Monica on her knees painting the boards, dressed in chic Capri pants, an Audrey Hepburn-esque vision, her dark hair held back from her face by a silk scarf.

Clicking on the bedside lamp, Violet plumped the pillows and sat herself up a little, looking around the shaded room. The mermaids looked passively back at her, their scales glinting in the lamplight, and the outline of the dress-maker's dummy in the bay seemed almost as if someone was standing looking out to sea. Her grandmother, perhaps. The idea wasn't frightening; it was more a gentle tugging sensation, as if Violet was here to do something Monica hadn't been able to do herself.

Giving up on the idea of sleep, she headed for the kitchen in search of a cup of tea.

CHAPTER SIX

Someone was banging on Violet's skull.

'Stop,' she mumbled, pulling the soft throw her mum had given her last week over her head on the sofa. She'd settled there with her cuppa and book in the middle of the night, and she must have finally managed some sleep for whoever it was knocking on her door to have woken her up.

'Oh, crap,' she whispered, her eyes still closed. 'Wait for me.'

She wasn't talking to whoever was at her door. She meant her dream, even though it was already sliding away from her; she couldn't remember the details, just the delicious feeling of enjoyment and she wanted to stay there and enjoy it some more.

'Hello?' a loud female voice fired through the letterbox. 'Anybody home?'

It was the kind of voice you didn't ignore, school-headmistress-like and official. Sighing, Violet untangled herself from the blanket and folded it on the end of the sofa before padding barefoot into the hallway.

'Just a second,' she said, throwing the bolt. 'I'm here.'

Opening the door a few seconds later, she found herself

confronted with a woman whose voice matched her appearance perfectly. Boxy suit, overpowering floral blouse, stout-heeled shoes and an unnaturally red rinse on her helmet of hair. She looked curiously as if she'd come in battledress; Vi looked warily around her to make sure she hadn't arrived with an army of pitchfork-waving locals hiding behind her skirts.

'Rumours are true then,' she said by way of introduction, looking Violet up and down as if PJs after nine in the morning was a crime. Her eyes settled on Violet's blue-tipped hair.

'Word clearly travels fast here,' Vi said, still wishing she was asleep.

The woman didn't introduce herself, just reached into her large black briefcase-style handbag and pulled out a stiff white envelope, holding it out like a bailiff serving up a summons.

'You're cordially invited to a council consultation on the future of Swallow Beach Pier.'

The words seeped in slowly, making Vi's brow furrow. 'A consultation?' She blinked a few times, trying to wake up. 'I'm sorry, I didn't catch your name.'

'I didn't give it to you, dear. I'm the Lady Mayoress of Swallow Beach, and given that you're laying claim to our pier, I suggest you might want to attend the meeting in the parish hall at six sharp.'

That was a lot of words for a girl who'd been asleep five minutes previously to process, and Vi had stopped listening at the clearly antagonistic 'given you're laying claim' bit.

'Excuse me?' She pulled herself up to her full height, which given she was barefoot, brought her up level with Mayoress No-name's violently patterned bosom.

'It's all in the letter.' The silver chains attached to the

woman's large specs rattled as she reached out and tapped the envelope.

'And was this meeting already arranged before I arrived?' Vi asked, battling to bring herself up to speed.

The sudden set of the woman's jaw suggested not.

'I see,' Vi said. 'Well, thanks. I'll think about it.'

She retreated, closing the door on the woman, whose gaping mouth suggested she didn't like the idea of being dismissed before she'd got what she wanted – in this case clearly the upper hand over the bay's newest resident.

'Great,' she murmured, ripping the envelope open as she headed for the kettle. Her eyes skimmed the words after she'd set the water on to boil. *Town meeting . . . suggested uses for Swallow Beach Pier . . . council compulsory purchase application . . .* the words blurred; Violet was shocked to find herself suddenly tearful.

'Bloody sodding hell,' she muttered, dashing the back of her hand over her eyes. She wasn't a crier, and she wasn't going to let this less than warm welcome reduce her to one. It was just a shock to wake up to, that was all. She could always just not go to the meeting, she reasoned. It had clearly been called with the sole intention of putting the wind up her. She could call Mayoress No-name's bluff and stay away. It would likely be just the two of them anyway; given how hastily the meeting had been called, there was every chance no one would even know about it.

A brisk walk along the seafront half an hour later changed Vi's mind about two things. One, every last resident of Swallow Beach would know about the meeting before the morning was out, and two, she was going to the bloody meeting after all. With bells on.

Neon-green A4 placards had been stuck on every

lamppost for as far as the eye could see, and a dozen or more others were tied to the gates of the pier. Vi sunk down onto the low sea wall, watching the signs flap around in the sharp breeze. What was wrong with that bloody woman? Why was she suddenly getting her knickers in such a twist about the pier now, when it had stood silent and overlooked for so many years? Yanking the signs down from her beautiful pier gates, she shoved them in the nearest bin and headed back to the relative safety of the Lido.

'You must be Violet.'

Vi looked up at the grinning blonde girl who'd just opened the entrance door to the Lido.

'I'm Keris from number 2. You met my granddad, I think?'

'Ah, Barty,' Vi said, smiling. 'Yes, yes, we met.' Glancing down, she saw the telltale flash of neon in Keris's hand. 'You heard then.'

Keris nodded, unabashed. 'You've ruffled a few feathers all right.'

'I don't know how.' Violet's shoulders slumped. 'I only arrived a couple of days ago and I've hardly been out of the building. What do people think I'm going to do, bring the town into disrepute?'

'Someone said you're a showgirl,' Keris said, her blue eyes merry. 'I didn't believe them, for the record.'

It was such a false and ridiculous claim that Violet almost laughed along. 'You're kidding, right?'

Keris looked rueful, as if she wished she was. ''Fraid not. Go-go dancer, I heard. I was rather hoping they were right, to be honest, we could do with some excitement around here.'

'Who's a go-go dancer?' Cal appeared, heading down

the stairs two at a time, bringing with him the scent of shower gel, and again, warm leather. 'Morning ladies.'

'Me apparently,' Vi said.

'Great stuff,' he said, rubbing his hands together. 'When's the show?'

'Tonight at six o'clock,' Keris said, handing Cal the neon poster. He eyed it, frowning.

'Oh.'

A look passed between her neighbours, and Vi didn't know them well enough to be able to interpret it. 'What?'

Keris put her hands up, backing away towards the door. 'I'm just running out to work. I'll leave this one to you, Cal.'

She leaned in and kissed him quickly on the cheek. 'See you guys at the meeting.'

Vi watched Barty's granddaughter skip off down the steps towards the pavement, bouncing with energy. She seemed around Violet's age, and even though she'd met her for only five minutes, Vi felt hopeful that she'd just made a new friend.

'She's nice, Keris,' Cal said, watching her leave. 'You'll like her. Everyone does.'

Vi digested his words, thinking about the way Keris had kissed him just now.

'Are you trying to change the subject?'

'Not exactly . . . I—' his mobile interrupted him, loud in the pocket of his jeans. 'Sorry, Vi,' he said, apologetic as he pulled it out and glanced at the screen. 'I need to take this. Customer.'

He lifted his hand in a distracted goodbye, handing the poster back as he turned and left in the opposite direction to Keris, leaving Vi alone and perplexed on the top step of the Lido.

'See you later,' she muttered, watching him head across to a black jeep parked over by the sea wall.

'Violet?'

She swung back to find Barty standing in his open doorway.

'Hi,' she said, glad to see his familiar face.

'Thought I heard voices,' he said.

'Keris and Cal. You just missed them.'

'And you? Have you any grand plans today?'

'Well, I hadn't,' she sighed. 'But it seems I'm expected to go to a town meeting about the pier this evening.'

She held the poster out for Barty to examine, watching his face carefully. Very few people had known she was here – just two, actually, Barty and Cal. She liked them both, but it would appear that one of them had been talking about her arrival in the bay, or else how would anyone know?

'Oh dear.' Barty leaned against his doorframe, downcast. 'I rather think that might be my fault, Violet. I mentioned your arrival in passing last night at Zumba.'

The idea of Barty at Zumba had Violet half laughing despite herself. 'Zumba?'

'Don't knock it till you've tried it,' he said. 'You haven't seen anything until you've seen my hip gyrations. Snake-like, if I say so myself.'

Vi looked down at her boots, smiling. 'Will you come to the meeting?' She swallowed. 'Please?'

His eyes softened. 'Of course. We'll go together, shall we? I'll be the envy of the place.' He checked his watch, regretful. 'I better get on, tea dance at the town ballroom at eleven. Need to polish my dancing shoes.'

'You have a better social life than most twenty year olds,' she said, shaking her head. Swallow Beach had a ballroom?

'Life in the old dog,' he said, waggling his eyebrows as he stepped back inside his flat and closed the door.

All neighbours off about their business, Violet trudged off up the stairs, screwing up the neon poster as she went.

Surrounded by red feathers and gold sequins, the radio on quietly in the background, Vi rediscovered her happy place. She had an order in from a theatre in London for a set of eight identical military-styled corsets, all embellished in gold and red with matching feather headdresses. Completing the first one had been a work of art, but thankfully the company loved it and had given Vi the green light to go ahead with the whole order, one of her most ambitious to date. She'd borrowed her grandmother's tailor's dummy from the bedroom, setting it up in the corner of the living room dressed as a military showgirl to serve as a consistent reminder to ensure they all matched. It looked fabulous, and given how kitsch the Lido apartment was, not even that much out of place.

'I'm going to call you Lola,' she said, positioning the dummy to best show off the costume. 'Barry Manilow himself would be impressed.'

Everything about her work soothed her. The low hum of the sewing machine, the tape around her neck, the feel of the feathers as she sorted them by colour and size to ensure a spectacular finish. Tall ostrich plumes to work into headdresses, shorter dyed marabou feathers for the corsets. Black grosgrain ribbons, gold buttons . . . She had everything sorted into boxes and the open drawers of the sideboard, and for a few blessed hours she forgot all about Swallow Beach, or the pier, or that damn meeting. Much as she'd come here in search of adventure, what she was actually used to was peace and simplicity, both of which were in short supply around here.

When someone knocked the door just after one, she debated whether to pretend she wasn't home. What if it was another angry local come to tear a strip off her?

'Violet, open up. I've brought lunch.'

Cal. And more to the point, given that Violet had yet to eat, Cal with food. Laying her work down carefully, she stepped over the sewing machine's electricity cord and went out to open the door.

Cal looked her up and down, taking in the tape measure around her neck and the red feathers tucked into the pocket of her work apron. 'Busy?'

She nodded. 'Working.' He was dressed as he'd been earlier, so probably just returning. 'And hungry, so you're welcome.'

He followed her inside. 'You mean you only want me for my burgers?'

'There's burgers in that bag?' she said, sniffing. He wasn't lying, and her stomach grumbled in appreciation.

'Best burgers for miles,' he said, distracted, his eyes moving over her bright, busy workspace. 'What *are* you doing?'

His appreciative, interested eyes found Lola standing to attention in the corner.

'Ooh,' he said, putting the burger bag down on the breakfast bar. 'You didn't say you had company. I'd have brought extra food.'

Vi rolled her eyes. 'Meet Lola.'

'Is she a go-go dancer, same as you?'

'High kicks like you wouldn't believe,' Violet said, opening the food bag flat to dispense with the need for plates because she'd forgotten to buy washing-up liquid. Burgers and fries, and he'd even thought to supply strawberry shakes. 'My kind of food, thank you.'

He perched on one of the stools. 'Guessed as much.'

She wasn't certain if being thought of as a burger kind of girl was a compliment or not.

'So,' he said, unwrapping the waxy paper from around his burger. 'Is this what you do?' He nodded towards her temporary workspace, which, now her machine was set up and her accessories displayed, seemed to have taken over half of the living room. 'Make costumes?'

Violet nodded. She couldn't speak, because she was experiencing burger nirvana.

'Oh my God,' she mumbled.

'I know, right?' Cal high-fived her across the breakfast bar. 'I did tell you.'

'Yeah, this is me,' she said. 'I've been working for myself for a while now, I love it.'

His eyes strayed to the dressmaker's dummy again. 'Bloody good at it, by the looks of our Lola.'

It had taken Vi quite a while to accept compliments about her work without automatically shaking them off. The fact was that she'd worked damn hard to be good at it, so she wasn't going to apologise for it.

'Thanks. I'm pretty proud of it. I make dancers' costumes, the occasional wedding dress, even, but theatrical and club stuff mainly.'

'You should be proud.' He nodded, looking at her again now. 'And your family? Are they cool with what you do?'

That was an unusually perceptive question; some of the outfits she made were incredibly skimpy and designed to show off the wearer's body to best effect. Thankfully, her parents didn't have any issue with it – she'd have had to take their feelings into consideration while she lived under their roof and worked in their garden.

'Yeah, they're not stuffy about things like that.'

He huffed under his breath, screwing up all of the empty papers into a ball. 'What?' Vi asked.

'You're lucky, that's all.'

It was Vi's turn to be inquisitive. 'I guess I am. Why do I get the feeling that you understand?'

He sighed, his face bunched up. 'It might be easier to show you, rather than tell you.' Scanning the kitchen, he found the bin and shoved their rubbish in. 'Come on. It'll only take five minutes.'

Intrigued, Violet searched around the floor for her shoes.

'Don't bother,' he said. 'We're only going across the landing.'

'You work from home too?'

He nodded, leading her across the landing. 'You haven't heard the noise?'

'I just assumed DIY,' she said.

He laughed softly, unlocking his front door. 'Not quite.'

Cal's apartment looked to be the same layout as hers, a small hallway with doors leading off it. That was where the similarity ended though; his was clear of clutter and kitsch, lots of white and neutral greys to make the most of the light and space. It wasn't cold – he'd added a few touches of colour to avoid that – but it was a world away from her place across the landing.

'These places are all about the views, aren't they?' he said, nodding at the living-room bay window. 'I tried to keep it un-distracting in here, because I can't compete with what's going on out there.'

'My grandmother clearly didn't feel the same way,' Violet laughed.

He led her through one of the other doors, and she found herself in what would be the spare bedroom in her own apartment, or Della's yellow bedroom. This, however, wasn't a bedroom. It was a busy workroom, masculine and far more cluttered than the rest of his place, everything jammed in.

'What do you make in here?' she asked, surprised, taking in the cutting equipment, the workbench, and what looked like an industrial overlocker. Rolls of leather. Hammers, scissors, tools. It looked like a beefed-up version of her own set-up, though she was pretty sure there weren't any feathers or sequins.

'My family have been leatherworkers for more generations than I can count back,' he said. 'Saddles, equine equipment mostly.'

'Wow,' she said, glancing around for evidence of a saddle and finding nothing. 'Can I see? I used to love ponies as a kid.'

He shrugged. 'I don't work for the family business any more,' he said. 'I branched out on my own, much to my mother's disgust.'

'Oh, that's rough,' she frowned. 'So do you have to compete with them for work?'

The ghost of a smile passed across his face. 'You'd know how funny that was if you knew my mother.'

'So what are you working on at the moment?' she asked, intrigued.

He paused, and then bent to retrieve something from the lower shelf of his workbench. He held a long sturdy box in his hands when he straightened.

'These.'

Violet stepped closer as he shook the box lightly to get the lid off, looking inside as he held it out for her to inspect.

'Are they . . .'

He finished her sentence for her. 'Floggers. Yes.'

The box contained about a dozen of them, slender

midnight-blue leather handles with a wrist strap, long fronds of tassels. Cal turned and picked up another box, opening it up to show her its contents.

'Collars,' she said, her eyebrows raised as she looked at the collection of black studded rings. 'I wouldn't like to see the dog big enough to wear those.'

'You won't. They're designed for six-foot men with a submissive side.'

Violet's mouth formed a perfect O. Floggers. Collars. She was sensing a theme.

'So you make . . .' She tailed off, unsure how to categorise his line of products.

'Sex toys. Floggers, whips, cuffs, collars, handcuffs, harnesses, masks.' He reeled it off like a supermarket shopping list. 'I do bespoke too, if people are looking for something unusual.'

'I'm genuinely lost for words,' Violet said, half laughing.

'It's just another branch of leatherwork,' he said. 'And a bloody lucrative one at that. The family business was struggling – that's how I got into this originally, trying to think outside the box to bring new business in. There's a big crossover between the equine and sex industries: crops, whips, stirrups, spurs. It wasn't that big a leap.'

'But your parents don't agree?' Violet was starting to understand the rift.

'Just my mum,' he said. 'My dad died when I was three, a horse riding accident.' His melancholy shrug said please don't offer pity, so she just nodded and held her tongue. 'My mother has been more than vocal about the fact that she thinks all of this is a disgrace. Dragging the Dearheart name through the mud, apparently.' He shook his head. 'These products are officially unwelcome in the factory.'

Violet picked up one of the navy floggers, appreciating

the fine leatherwork and the contrasting scarlet stitches. 'You're seriously good. This is gorgeous work.'

He swallowed. 'I've trained for years at what I do.' He put the lid back on the box of collars, looking down for an inch of space to set it down. 'And business is booming. I'm going to have to move my workshop into the main bedroom at this rate and sleep in the box room like a moody teenager.'

'There's really no chance of healing the family rift?'

'Not unless I go back to making saddles for a living, no.'

They looked at each other across his workbench.

'Well, we're going to go down well at the meeting,' Vi said. 'You make sex toys and I'm practically a go-go dancer.'

'The Lido, otherwise known as a den of iniquity,' Cal laughed. 'You should probably quit hanging around with me. I'm the black sheep of Swallow Beach thanks to my—' he broke off to pick up a flogger and thwacked it against the workbench, 'proclivities.'

Vi nodded. 'And you should probably swerve me too. In the summer months I wear nothing but hot-pants and feather bras.'

He raised his eyebrows. 'Roll on summertime, I say.'

'I don't, really,' she said.

'That's a crying shame, Violet.'

Once again, she wasn't certain whether or not they were flirting. They seemed to dance right along the line between friendship and more, even though both knew that, as neighbours, it was a line to stay on the right side of.

'Although I have to say, I don't strut the seafront in a harness and gimp-mask, either,' he said. 'Just so you know.'

'So we're both pretty normal, despite our frankly salacious line of work,' she said, trying not to let herself imagine Cal in fetish gear.

'Don't tell anyone though,' he said. 'Far more fun to be talked about.'

Violet wasn't sure she agreed there, but then it appeared that he'd had far more practice at it than she had. If she'd known she was walking into a town with attitudes buttoned up tighter than Queen Victoria's corsets, she might have thought twice about moving here at all.

'Will you come to the meeting?'

The same look crossed his face as downstairs earlier with Keris, one that suggested there were things Violet didn't know.

'Barty's coming,' she said. 'We could go for a drink afterwards, my shout?'

He sighed. 'How can I say no to a mermaid?'

Violet smiled, complimented, reminded of her bedroom across the hallway. 'You can't?'

He picked up his overalls from the back of a chair. 'I'm going to strip off now. You should probably go before you're overcome with unstoppable lust.'

For a second, she didn't move, and in that same second, they eyed each other more seriously than either of them expected. Then he reached for the hem of his T-shirt and started counting backwards from three, so Violet shot out of the apartment, shouting that he should meet her and Barty in the lobby to go to the meeting later as she left.

'And thank you for lunch too!' she called belatedly, slamming his door as she headed back to her side of the building. Full of jangling nerves, she sat down to work, her mind on the man across the hall doing the same, and more ominously on the meeting in the parish hall about her pier.

'It's mine and you can't take it from me,' she muttered into the quiet room. 'Don't worry, Gran. I've got this.'

CHAPTER SEVEN

Some people might have chosen to dress conservatively, to present as plain and respectable a presence as possible in the circumstances. Violet, however, wasn't some people. Her clothes were her armour, and she chose to go into battle wearing a scarlet dungaree mini dress over a long-sleeved T-shirt and stripy tights. None of it matched with her hair.

'You look fabulous!' Keris said, already in the lower lobby when Violet made her way downstairs. Barty threw a jaunty wave over his shoulder at her as he locked his door. He was dressed as he'd been on the morning Violet first met him, long coat and fedora. His granddaughter shared his tall frame, and had an infectious energy about her that Violet found herself drawn to and encouraged by.

'Cal's running late.' Keris glanced at her phone. 'He texted just now to say he'll meet us there.'

Vi nodded. She'd tapped on his door a couple of minutes ago and found him out, and although he hadn't expressly agreed to come to the meeting with them, she'd felt her heart sink because she wanted him there on her side. She paused also to momentarily wonder at the relationship between Keris and Cal again; they seemed pretty close.

Looking from Barty to Keris, she put her chin in the air. 'Come on then. Let's do this.'

Violet offered to drive, but Barty said he'd rather stretch his legs and it was only ten minutes along the seafront, so why bother? Besides, he said, he wanted to walk in there with the two best girls in Swallow Beach on his arms, so Violet had slipped the car keys into her bag and hooked her arm through the one he offered.

It turned out that it wasn't far, and by the time they arrived he'd had them both laughing with a story about a new woman who'd moved into the local residential home and tried to feel his bum at the tea dance that afternoon. Maureen, by all accounts, was a frisky one for a woman in her nineties.

'Best feet forward, girls,' Barty said, removing his fedora as he held the door open for them to go in ahead of him. Violet followed Keris into the wooden-clad hall built on the side of the church.

'Keep your coat on, the heating never works in here,' Keris said, leading them through a set of double doors into the main room, which looked like pretty much every other local church hall up and down the land. Scuffed wooden floor, magnolia walls, plastic chairs piled around the edges. Except some of those chairs had been hastily dragged down and arranged in lines, and a gathering of perhaps twenty or so people were assembled there. Vi scanned the faces for Cal, but he wasn't there. She wasn't surprised, but she really hoped he'd try to make it, even if he was late; she needed as many people on her side as possible.

'Usual suspects,' Keris whispered, saying a few hellos as she led them to an empty row of chairs in the safety of the middle of the gathering.

Curious eyes turned to look at Violet as she settled into her seat next to Keris. She tried her best to meet their eyes and smile; Della had taught her the value of first impressions and she badly wanted these people to warm to her.

'Showtime,' Barty said, sliding into the row on Keris's other side, nodding towards a side door at the front of the hall. Following his nod, Violet found herself looking at the floral blouse of Swallow Beach's Mayoress, her official mayoral chains rattling around her neck as she placed her huge briefcase on a side table and made a show of unsnapping the catches. Shuffling her folders, she took her place at the lectern. Given that most people were looking at her there really wasn't any need to bang the gavel, but she gave it several good thumps just for effect anyway.

'Order in the room please,' she said. 'Order in the room.'

The general hubbub hushed, and Mayoress No-name laid the gavel down slowly and looked around from face to face until she found Violet and narrowed her eyes.

'Psyching you out,' Keris muttered. 'Don't look away first.'

Violet wasn't about to.

'Thank you all for coming at short notice tonight, it's good to see so many concerned faces here.'

Vi's eyes moved around the room, trying to work out the mood. Thankfully they didn't seem like a lynch mob; she and Keris were the youngest there by a long chalk.

'As everyone who has been here for any length of time knows . . .' she paused here to look down her nose at Violet, 'our beloved pier has played an integral part in our community for almost two hundred years.'

She nodded, falling silent to let that grand fact sink in.

'And again, *as those of us who've been residents for more than five minutes know,* its continued closure has affected our town tremendously.'

'Ouch,' Keris whispered, leaning in. 'I can feel Glad's barbs and I'm only sitting next to you!'

Vi swallowed hard. 'Glad?'

'Short for Gladys. Everyone calls her Glad though. God knows why, because I don't think anyone's ever glad to see that woman, she can be a right pain in the arse.'

A woman sitting in the row in front turned round and lifted her eyebrows, but the look on her face suggested that she didn't wholeheartedly disagree.

'I can't remember the pier ever being open, Glad,' someone down the front piped up. A low murmur of consent bubbled around the room, and the Mayoress raised and lowered her hands like an orchestra conductor appealing for quiet.

'Well I can,' she shot back. 'As can anyone else over the age of fifty.' She squinted towards them. 'Barty?'

Keris and Violet turned to look at him, as did most of the heads in the room. Barty lifted his shoulders, for all the world like a schoolboy who didn't want to tell the truth and land his mates in hot water.

'I'm not a day over forty-five, as you well know, Lady Mayoress,' he said, going for humour to diffuse the spotlight, effectively so given the laugh that rippled around the room. Gladys didn't see the funny side of it, huffing and making a point of opening her file and peering at it over her glasses.

'Swallow Beach Pier has stood proudly on our shore since 1879,' she said, clearly gearing up to read an impassioned speech.

After a second Keris raised her hand, interrupting the Mayoress in full flight. 'That's a hundred and thirty-nine years, Glad.'

Gladys narrowed her eyes. 'And?'

'You said nearly two hundred years, but it's not. It's one hundred and thirty-nine so actually it's closer to one hundred.'

'I'd thank you not to question my mathematics, Keris Harwood,' Gladys said, haughty, and Violet looked down at her boots to hide her smile. Glad cleared her throat, banged the gavel once for gravitas, and then started again.

'Swallow Beach Pier has stood proudly on our shores since 1879, and back in its heyday it was a major tourist attraction, rivalling Brighton.'

'Steady on, Glad,' a man across the aisle said. 'Brighton's bloody massive.'

'Melvin Williams, I'll have you know that our pier once housed a national exhibition of paintings by . . .' Gladys paused and consulted her notes, 'Arthur Bowmore.'

A woman at the back of the room stood up. 'He was my grandfather!'

'There you go then,' Gladys spread her hands. 'Sue Simpson's grandfather, a prolific local artist, held a grand exhibition there in the twenties.' Sensing an ally, Gladys homed in deeper. 'Have you any idea of the breadth of his work, Sue?'

Sue frowned and held her hands out in front of her as if holding a dinner plate. 'About like that?'

Gladys stalled, and then rallied. 'No, no. The number of paintings dear, not the size. Size is irrelevant.' She let out a small peal of laughter.

A woman with a bubble perm sitting beside Melvin

Williams raised her hand. 'I have to come in there, it's my area of expertise.'

Keris started laughing under her breath. 'You'll love Linda and Melvin. Sex therapists. Make the Fockers look tame.'

'Linda Williams, this is neither the time nor the place to lower the tone,' Gladys said, exasperated. 'If I could just get on.'

Linda shrugged as if to say it was Gladys's loss.

'Three,' Sue Simpson said, still standing up at the back. 'He painted three in total, all of his dog, Mindy.'

'Sit down, Susan Simpson,' Gladys growled, her mayoral chains shuddering on her heaving chest. She looked down at her speech again, and then seemed to think better of it, closing her file.

'My point, ladies and gentlemen of Swallow Beach, is that our pier has long lived in the heart of our townsfolk and it should be officially given back to us. We could reinvigorate our town's fortune, rather than line the greedy pockets of a private investor.'

Violet couldn't help herself, she shot to her feet. 'Those would be my pockets that you're talking about, Lady Mayoress, and I'll have you know that they're neither greedy nor private.'

A hush fell over the room, and every eye in the place rested on Violet.

'This isn't how I wanted to introduce myself to everyone, but I'm Violet Spencer, and I very recently inherited the Swallow Beach Pier from my grandmother, Monica Spencer, who lived here in the bay back in the seventies.'

A low whisper rattled around the room.

'I didn't even know the pier existed until a few weeks ago when my grandfather died and willed it to me. He bought the pier, *legitimately*, when it was put up for sale in 1965. He and my grandmother came here on honeymoon and she fell in love with the place; as far as I know they came for a holiday and stayed here for the rest of her life. I know for a fact that she loved this town, and even though he wasn't living here my grandpa has always ensured that the pier has been properly maintained, so I hoped that I'd come here and find a friendly welcome, at least.'

Some people nodded, hesitant to be unnecessarily rude to the blue-haired girl in their midst. Gladys didn't flinch, just stared at Violet, her thin lips puckered cat's-bum-tight.

'I admit that I'm not exactly sure what I'm going to do with the pier yet, but—'

'Exactly! No clue!' Gladys barked, derisory, throwing her hands out in an *I rest my case* gesture.

'But I do want to have the pier open again, if that's possible,' Vi said. 'Make it vibrant to honour my gran's memory.'

Gladys rolled her eyes. 'By all accounts your grandmother was quite avant-garde, Violet Spencer, and I don't mean that as a compliment.'

'What?' Vi's voice shot up, properly annoyed now. 'You didn't even know my grandmother, how dare you speak ill of her!'

'Young lady, the Lido has housed artists and hippies since the 1960s, and it appears that you're keeping its disreputable tradition alive and kicking with your . . .' Gladys's lips turned down in distaste, 'dancing.'

Keris stood up beside Violet. 'Now hang on, Glad—'

'Oh, don't you "hang on" me, Keris Harwood, what with you sending out unmentionables in the post!'

Violet looked at Keris, confused, and Barty got to his feet too.

'I'll have to ask you not to take that offensive tone, Glad.'

There was a gentle authoritativeness to his voice that seemed to have the desired effect; Gladys looked suitably rebuked and held her tongue, settling for a rattle of her mayoral chains.

'I for one am gladdened by Violet's presence in Swallow Beach.' Barty addressed the people rather than the Lady Mayoress. 'I'm sure that once she's found her feet in our community, she'll be brimming with exciting new ideas for the pier.'

'Strip club,' Gladys muttered, earning herself a few frowns from around the room.

'Did someone say strip club? Count me in.'

Everyone turned around at the sound of a new voice in the room, and Cal strolled down the aisle and dropped into the empty seat beside Violet.

'What did I miss?' he asked, looking innocently towards the Mayoress.

Gladys turned puce. 'You know full well that your presence is unhelpful here, Calvin. Please leave immediately. I'm sure your friends can join you in The Swallow when we're done.'

Cal smiled genially but stayed exactly where he was. For a second the Mayoress looked as if she might thunder down the aisle, ceremonial chains swinging, and drag Cal out of the parish hall by his unruly dark hair.

'What *did* I miss?' he asked, when Gladys finally stopped eyeballing him like a bull about to be released.

'The Mayoress hates me,' Vi whispered. 'She thinks the Lido is a beacon for disreputables, and that I'm going to turn the pier into a brothel, or something equally unsavoury.'

'Figures,' Cal muttered. 'She's always been keen to jump to the worst conclusion.'

'You know her well then?'

'Just a bit.' He flicked his eyes to the ceiling and blew out. 'She's my mother.'

Violet stared at him, hoping he was going to crack into a smile to let on that he was kidding. He didn't; instead, Keris leaned forward across Vi and hissed, 'I know she's your mother, but she's getting right on my bloody tits, Cal.'

'No apology needed,' he said. 'She has that effect on everyone. Me included, most of the time.'

They listened as the Mayoress laboured through the speech she'd prepared, doggedly determined to read the whole thing out regardless, putting forward her case for applying for a compulsory purchase order to return the pier to public ownership – under her own expert guidance, naturally.

Violet listened in fraught silence, her jaw clamped tight in case she let out a long string of expletives. Gladys appeared to expect a round of applause as she reached the end of the speech, throwing her arms out and almost bowing as her motley crowd stared at her, taken aback by the fact that she'd adapted Winston Churchill's 'Fight them on the beaches' speech in a frankly alarming way, claiming she was ready to 'fight on Swallow Beaches' in a way that came over as both sabre-rattling and nonsensical.

'Reminded me of Putin for a second there,' Barty said mildly as they stood to leave. 'Despotic.'

'Pub?' Keris suggested.

Cal nodded. 'I'll catch you up.'

Violet watched him disappear through the same door as Gladys, obviously keen for a private word with his mother.

'I take it they don't see eye to eye?'

Keris laughed. 'Understatement of the century.'

'Chalk and cheese,' Barty said. 'Although he was the apple of her eye when he was knee-high. Shame, really, how families change.'

Violet sighed, aware that the comment could equally be applied to her own family. She'd thought them to be fairly dull with no skeletons in the cupboard, yet all the time Swallow Beach had been sitting silently in there without her even knowing about its existence. The vintage apartment, silent and empty save for the monthly cleaner. The beautiful pier, mothballed and unwalked on by anyone but the safety inspectors in all of those years. The Mayoress was right about one thing: it was time for Swallow Beach Pier to come back to life.

'Rum,' Cal said, laying his hand on Barty's shoulder as he placed a drink down on the table in front of the senior statesman of the Lido. It was a more than healthy measure in a tumbler engraved with a B; it was fast becoming clear to Vi that, as much as Barty belonged to Swallow Beach, Swallow Beach belonged to him.

Revived by a large glass of red, she turned to Keris beside her. 'What was all that about you sending unmentionables in the post?'

'Terribly racy,' Barty said. 'Shamed, I am.' He grinned and raised his glass to his granddaughter.

Keris picked up her gin and tonic. 'I run a mail order lingerie business.'

'Do you really?' Vi said, taken aback. 'How did you end up doing that?'

'By accident, really.'

'The accidental knicker-seller,' Cal said, putting his pint down. 'That's the name of her online store.'

'It's not, is it?' Vi said, looking from one to the other.

Keris rolled her eyes. 'Shut up, Dearheart.' She chucked a beermat and Cal caught it, laughing.

'I lived in London for a while,' Keris said. 'Ended up working in one of those high-end lingerie stores and sort of fell in love with it all.'

'And now you sell underwear from home?'

'For the moment,' Keris said. 'Until I can open my own shop.'

Violet started to laugh. 'Your mum wasn't that far off the mark after all, Cal,' she said, finally relaxing thanks to the wine and the company. 'We are a sordid bunch in the Lido, what with you and your floggers and Keris and her saucy knickers.'

'And you and Lola too now,' Cal said. 'You've definitely lowered the tone.'

'Lola?' Keris looked at Violet, startled. 'Do you have a daughter?'

Vi almost spluttered on her wine. 'God, no. No! Lola's the dressmaker's dummy in my apartment.'

'She's a showgirl,' Cal threw in. 'I met her this afternoon, quite the looker.'

'She doesn't even have a head,' Violet pointed out.

Barty and Cal exchanged a knowing glance, and Keris shook her head at Vi. 'Ignore them, Violet. It works for me.'

Their conversation rolled on around her, easing her troubles, making her laugh with stories about the town and its people.

'Glad kills me how she calls everyone by their full name all the time,' Keris said. 'It's like she's calling the register.'

'She always fancied herself as a headmistress,' Cal said. 'Mayoress is as close as it gets.'

'*Lady* Mayoress,' Barty corrected with a benign smile, a good way through his second triple rum. 'I quite like a powerful woman,' he mused, as an afterthought almost to himself.

Keris covered her face with her hands. 'Make him stop, Vi.'

Barty knocked his drink back and reached for his fedora from the empty stool beside him. 'I'll go one better. Leave you whippersnappers in peace.'

Cal stood up even though his pint was fresh on the table. 'I'll walk back with you,' he said.

Barty batted the air. 'You'll do no such thing,' he said. 'I'm a man in my prime.'

Keris smiled at Cal, who picked up Barty's coat and held it open for him. 'You're twice the man I'll ever be, Barty. Let me, you know I'm only doing it to look good for the ladies.'

Barty didn't argue further. 'Don't let anyone drink his beer,' he said, nodding towards Cal's glass. 'He'll be back in five minutes. We'll jog.'

They watched the two men leave, laughing about something as they moved out of earshot.

'He's pretty special,' Keris said, her eyes lingering on the door.

'Hmm. Is there anything . . .' Vi said, tentative despite the wine. 'You know, are you two . . .?'

Keris frowned, and then laughed. 'I meant my grandpa,' she said. 'Did you think I meant Cal?'

Vi half nodded, a little embarrassed. 'You two seem close.'

Spearing the lemon in her gin with her cocktail umbrella, Keris nodded. 'Everyone's close to Cal.'

'I'm not sure I get what you mean,' Vi said.

Keris screwed up her nose, as if thinking how to put it. 'He's a funny one. We dated a few times, years ago.'

She rolled her eyes. 'Disaster, but you know how most of the time you date someone, it doesn't work out, and you never speak to them again if you can help it?'

Vi nodded. Her experience with men was pretty limited, but she couldn't imagine ever being besties with Simon after they went their separate ways.

'It's not like that with Cal,' Keris said. 'And I don't mean just me. He doesn't kiss and tell, and women can't seem to decide if they want to be his mother, his lover or his sister. I ended up in the sister camp, but either way everyone ends up still loving him.'

Vi frowned, perplexed. Calvin Dearheart was probably the best-looking man she'd ever seen in the flesh.

'I'm surprised no one's snapped him up by now, though,' she said, then wished she hadn't because it made her sound interested, which she wasn't.

'Oh, someone did.' Keris nodded. 'He's married.'

CHAPTER EIGHT

'He's married?' Violet couldn't keep the shock from her voice.

Keris looked unsure. 'Well, he was. He married Ursula when they were barely twenty-one, and then she got some modelling job in America and took off without him.'

'But they're still married?'

'Now you ask, I'm not sure,' Keris said. 'It was a long time ago and she never came back, so either way it's dead in the water.'

Violet wasn't sure she agreed. Married was married, whether or not you lived in the same house, or the same town, or the same country.

'He doesn't wear a wedding ring,' she said, sure she'd have noticed.

'Probably lost it. I'd have chucked it off the end of the pier if I was him.' She looked up as the pub door opened. 'Ah, here he is. We can ask him.'

A flush shot up Vi's neck. 'No! God, Keris, please don't. I don't want him to think I was prying.'

'You weren't,' she said. 'Or only a tiny bit, but that's okay. Every woman on the planet asks about Cal.'

Violet was getting a different picture of Cal tonight: charming every woman in town and a wife tucked away somewhere in the world to boot? Was he a womaniser? And he was the Mayoress's son too. The Mayoress who had taken violently against her. He wasn't just complicated. He was a seething mass of trouble wrapped up in an easy smile and dark, sparkling eyes. Violet didn't want to become another notch on his bedpost, however chivalrous he was about it the morning after.

'Safely through his front door,' Cal confirmed, shrugging out of his leather jacket. 'Bloody hero, he is. Been telling me about the boat he was on that went down in the war.'

Keris laughed. 'Not that story again.' She turned to Violet. 'No doubt you'll hear it a million times before the summer's out.'

Vi found herself looking at Cal with different eyes. Married. He'd stood at the altar and promised his forever to someone. That was as big as it got. Perhaps it was amplified in Vi's mind because of Simon's recent proposal; marriage was something she'd thought quite a lot about lately.

'So the plan is to have your own store one day, Keris?' she said, catching the other girl by surprise with her new line of conversation. Keris blinked a few times before she caught up.

'Oh. Umm, yes, one day. The rent though . . .' She shrugged, as if to say she was in a Catch 22 situation.

'Same as me, really,' Vi said. 'I have a workshop in my mum's garden back home, but it's not ideal. And I'm working in the living room here, which is even worse.'

Cal nodded, raising his drink because he was in the same boat.

And that was when it happened – inspiration struck.

'The pier,' Vi said, suddenly.

'*Your pier,*' Cal said, and Keris clinked her glass to his. 'To Violet's pier.'

They toasted her, but she shook her head. 'No. I mean I know what I want to do with the pier.'

The others looked at her, trying to catch her train of thought.

'Work there,' she said. 'The light in there is perfect. You too, Cal. You could work from there, right?' She looked at him, desperate for him not to shoot her fledgling plan down. Turning to Keris, she pressed on. 'What do you think? Could you open up your store in one of the glass units on the pier?'

Keris opened her eyes wide. 'Are you serious?'

Violet nodded. 'For the summer to begin with, but then who knows? If it works, maybe we could stay there.'

Cal looked at her steadily. 'Why don't you sleep on it before you get carried away with the idea?'

She frowned. He reminded her for a moment of her father, cautious. 'You don't think it'll work.'

'I didn't say that,' he said, leaning forward on his stool. 'But you've been in there, Vi. It would need work, and there's more units than just three, you'd need to fill the others to convince the council that it's being put to good use. If I know my mother that'll be the tack she chooses – she'll argue that it should be fully utilised, helping the community.'

Vi pressed her lips together, thinking. 'And I will be. I'll be creating workspaces for small businesses. Yours, mine, Keris's.'

Keris glanced between them. 'Our businesses are kind of connected . . .' she said, trailing off to let them all see where she was going. 'Maybe you could make a thing of that?'

Vi was a step ahead, buoyed by the wine and annoyed by Gladys Dearheart. 'Yes! I could theme it. Lease the units to adult businesses. Nothing too bad – I don't want to prove your mother right, Cal. But there must be other craftspeople who could come in with us?'

'Does it even have electric?' There he was again, Mr Practical.

'Yes, it flipping does,' Vi said, sparkly-eyed. 'Come on, be enthusiastic, this could be great.'

Keris and Vi fell silent and stared at him, and after a long minute a slow smile crept over his face. 'You know how much this is going to annoy my mother, right?'

Vi considered it, and decided she wasn't remotely bothered. 'My pier, my rules.'

'I still think you should wait and see how you feel about it in the morning,' he said.

Vi sighed, dramatic. 'I'm going off you. I thought you were more spontaneous.'

'I am spontaneous. Just not about business.'

'Yeah, I heard that about you,' she laughed lightly.

His dark eyes turned serious. 'Heard what about me?'

Violet flushed, wishing she hadn't said something so throwaway. 'Nothing, forget it.'

Keris jumped up, a sudden movement designed to distract and it worked. 'Come on kids. School night. Time to hit the hay.'

As they left the pub for the short walk back to the Lido, Violet listened to Keris bubble with ideas for the pier, and listened to Cal say nothing at all.

They deposited Keris on the ground floor with a promise to visit the pier the following day, and then walked upstairs in silence. Their quietness was born of two things: one, consideration for other residents – the middle flats of the building were leased as holiday lets so you never knew if anyone was staying there or not; and two, there was a new coolness between them that Vi wasn't sure how to fix.

They hesitated before going their separate ways on the top landing, lit only by moonlight from the picture window.

She broke first. 'I'm sorry if I offended you. I didn't mean anything by it.'

'People talk, Violet,' he said eventually, his voice gravel in his throat. 'It's not always a good idea to believe everything you hear.'

She wondered about his marriage, and thought about what Keris had said about the number of casual affairs he'd had. He was right, she had judged him on what she'd heard, and on inspection found she wasn't very impressed with herself for it. After all, hadn't tonight's public meeting been a classic example of how people could misconstrue and distort the truth?

'You're right. I'm not actually a go-go dancer,' she said, glad when she caught the hint of a smile on his lips in the darkness.

'And I haven't shagged every woman in Swallow Beach.'

'Well, I know that much,' she said, serious again. 'Because I live in Swallow Beach.'

What the actual hell was she doing? She was near enough to see the confusion in his eyes, the battle between doing the right thing and doing the thing you wanted to do playing out there on his face. He swallowed, and then reached out and curved his hand around her neck, drawing her close.

'Go and sleep in your clamshell, mermaid girl,' he whispered, lowering his mouth to kiss the top of her head. 'It's late.'

Violet laid her hand flat against his chest, feeling the steady rhythm of his heart. God, he smelt so damn good close up, that mix of leather and spice and heat and something indefinable. God knew what it was, but it was bloody sexy. He was basically catnip for girls, and right there in that moment Vi was fighting the urge to rub herself against him and see where it led.

Tipping her head back to look at him, she curled her fingers, bunching his T-shirt in her hand.

'It's a bad idea, Violet,' he said. His mouth was close enough for her to feel the heat of his breath.

'Is it?' she breathed. Her heart knocked on her ribs, and her skin burned underneath his hand on her neck. His touch was firm; warm, cradling, his thumb skimming her jaw.

'You'll think so in the morning,' he said.

'I promised myself that I wouldn't be dull when I came here,' she said. 'My life back home is too safe, it suffocates me.' The words tumbled out of her head into the space between them.

She felt his low huff beneath her hand. 'Your life might have been dull, Violet, but you're not. You shine brighter than the fucking moon.'

No one had ever said anything quite so suddenly, joltingly sexy to Violet in her life; she made a noise dangerously close to a whimper.

'If I kiss you, will you stop me?'

He moved his hand a little, enough to drag his thumb slowly over her mouth as he considered her question. She watched him, his eyes lowered to her lips. He was barely touching her, yet it felt more intimate than most of the sex she'd had.

'If I kiss you, I won't be able to stop,' he said. 'So you're not going to kiss me, and I'm not going to kiss you.'

She sighed, disappointment so loud it rumbled out of her. 'I really want you to.'

He laughed softly, dipping his head to her ear. 'Go inside.'

Did his mouth brush her ear? Her skin said yes and yearned for more, even as he lowered his hand and stepped backwards.

'Goodnight Violet,' he said.

Violet sighed. 'Will we ever, do you think?'

He was at his door, and she turned away to unlock hers. Stepping inside, they just stood and looked at each other for a long breath across the moonlit landing.

'Goodnight then,' she said, forlorn.

He nodded once, then stepped inside and closed his door.

Vi kicked off her boots on her way through the hallway, and then face-planted herself on the couch. What the hell had just happened out there? She'd never behaved like that in her life, she'd practically begged him to throw her over his shoulder and have his way with her. She wouldn't have stopped him. Maybe Keris was right; there was something about Calvin Dearheart that made him almost irresistible. She'd gone from being concerned about the fact that he had a wife to not giving a stuff if he had a wife in every port, and all because he'd laid his hand on her neck.

'I'm sorry,' she mumbled into the cushions, unsure if she was apologising to Cal for coming on to him, apologising to Simon even though they were no longer a couple despite what he said, or apologising to herself for jeopardising her chances of truly settling here in Swallow Beach.

Cal leaned his back against the door as he closed it, frustrated as hell. It was one thing making a decision to keep things on a friendship level with Violet. It was another thing altogether having to resist her when she asked him to kiss her. Christ, he'd wanted to. Her mouth was full and warm under his thumb, soft and giving.

He bang his head lightly against the door to knock some sense in, he repeated a simple mantra he could only hope would sink in. *I will not mess around with Violet. I will not mess around with Violet. I will not mess around with Violet.*

As he got into bed, lonely and still frustrated, he tried and failed not to think about the girl sleeping, or not sleeping, across the hallway.

'This place is even better than I've always imagined,' Keris said, standing inside the birdcage on the end of the pier the following morning. 'Our own tiny crystal palace, Grandpa used to call it. He made up stories for me about it, magical fairies and all sorts.'

It touched Violet to think that Keris had grown up with fanciful stories about the pier; she was glad, really, that at least someone had benefited, even if her own childhood had been bereft of Swallow Beach. And how very Barty to bring life to the empty pier via stories. How many other residents of the town included it in their family folklore and history?

'Am I doing the wrong thing?' she said suddenly, turning to Keris and Cal. 'Is everyone going to disapprove?'

Keris shrugged. 'Does it matter?'

The truth was yes, it did.

Cal threw his more pragmatic opinion into the ring. 'My mother is going to disapprove. Her bridge club will most likely join in her disapproval. The rest of the town though, I think you'll find, will just be glad to see the pier come back into use again. Last night's jokes about it being a strip club aside, I don't think you'll run into much opposition.'

Vi nodded, drawing strength from his words. 'We're legitimate business people,' she said.

'We are,' Keris said, turning to gaze out at the sea.

'Just because we cater for the more sensual side of life, it doesn't make us illegal,' Cal said, testing the lights. It was an odd juxtaposition – checking the electrics whilst absently talking about sensuality, one that had Violet turning away and leaning her head against the cool glass for a second of clarity.

She and Keris had met Cal at the pier a little after ten, and although she'd woken up feeling slightly mortified about her behaviour and determined to apologise and laugh it off, now she was in close proximity again, one mention of the word 'sensuality' and she'd strayed straight down the same path. *Reel it in,* she told herself, *for God's sake Violet, reel it in. He's just a man.* Granted, a fairly spectacular-looking one, but also one with a lot of baggage. Wife-shaped baggage.

'. . . I think this one's Violet's.'

She tuned back in, catching the back end of Cal's sentence to Keris.

'What was that?' she said, turning back.

'We were talking about which of the units to use,' she said. 'And Cal said he thought this one had your name on it.'

They were standing in one of the back units with the spectacular three-hundred-and-sixty-degree outlook. Violet's eyes fell to the floor, however, to the rainbow and her name inscribed on the boards.

She nodded. 'Yeah. I'll use this one.'

They walked through the birdcage, assessing which

spaces to use themselves and which to try to find new tenants for.

'Six,' Keris said, standing in the first room, soon to be her new shop. They'd talked about it over the course of the morning, and agreed that, alongside her current stock, Keris would include Cal's leatherwork and perhaps other lines from whoever else rented the other units. 'That's us three and three others. Any ideas?'

Cal nodded. 'I do, actually. I was at an adult convention a couple of weeks back and had a beer with an old mate there who works in a similar line of work. I know he's looking for premises, this would be right up his street.'

'Go on,' Violet said, hoping he wasn't going to say his friend was a gigolo or anything.

'He's an artisan metal-worker. Supplies a lot of the metal elements I use for collars and bondage gear, and some bigger stuff too.' He looked away. 'Cages, shackles, that sort of thing.'

'Cages?' Vi said. 'As in . . . cages?'

Keris pulled a faux scandalised face, and Cal nodded, meeting Vi's eyes again. 'Yeah. Cages as in human cages. For adults that get off on being locked up.'

'Oh.'

She couldn't think of a single appropriate response to that. 'Shall we start cleaning the windows?'

They worked solidly for the rest of the week, cleaning and scrubbing until their arms ached and their knees complained. Even Barty got in on the action, paying regular visits to see how things were coming along. They hadn't put the word out officially about the pier's new use for fear of incurring the early wrath of Cal's mother – it would all be grist to her mill when it came to her proposed compulsory purchase application, and therefore best kept on a need-to-know basis until they were ready to open. Word, it would seem though, got round as far as Melvin and Linda Williams, Swallow Beach's resident sex therapists.

'We came as soon as we heard,' Linda said, tucking a stray dark curl back inside her silk turban. 'We take a room over the chiropodist's in the High Street at the moment, but between me and you the clientele can be quite unsavoury. Let's just say hygiene isn't always top of the list.'

She screwed her nose up to indicate that the smells coming from below their consulting room weren't always complementary to their line of therapy.

'Although, that said, feet can be terribly erotic to the right person. We had one man who orgasmed if he even so much as saw a painted toenail.'

Melvin nodded. 'Terrible for him really, couldn't leave the house in the summer.'

'On account of all the sandals, you see,' Linda said, inspecting Violet's footwear, presumably to see if she was wearing accidentally orgasmic shoes.

'All safe here,' Vi said, wiggling her toes inside her plimsolls.

'So we heard about this place, and straight away we thought, "Where else? Where better?" Didn't we, Mel?'

Linda looked at her husband, who though slightly shorter than his wife, made up for it with his block-heeled boots and backcombed hair.

'We did,' he said. 'We did. And look at this place!'

Violet preened, because now that the windows were cleaned and every inch of the birdcage scrubbed, it was starting to look pretty darn magnificent. She'd shown Melvin and Linda around, and they'd fallen in love with the smallest of the glass studios in the building.

'I'm quite overcome.' Linda brushed non-existent tears from her eyes. 'This place has a good energy about it. Healing.'

'That healing feeling,' Melvin mused, handing his wife a tissue from his trouser pocket. 'Come, let me take you home, Linda.'

He put an arm around his wife's shuddering shoulders and turned to speak to Violet in hushed tones. 'She's a husk. I need to take her home and replenish her.'

Unsure what that might involve, Vi gave him a little thumbs up and a cheesy grin. They were certainly going to fit in around here, she thought, watching them walk back along the deck towards the shore. Then Cal wandered into the room and she wondered instead if Linda and Melvin could explain why her body twanged to attention whenever he appeared.

'Drink because it's Friday?' he asked, a bottle of fizz in his hand. Given her ever-increasing predicament where he was concerned, she should say no.

'Yes.'

CHAPTER NINE

'Beau's going to come over on Monday to check the place out,' Cal said, dropping down on the floor beside Violet in the room earmarked as her new studio. This time next week it would be set up with all of her equipment and stock, but for now it was gloriously empty and pristine, all the better to show off her grandmother's paint-work on the floor. 'He's really keen, space permitting.'

Beau, affectionately known by Violet and Keris as Cage-Guy, was the artisan metal-worker Cal thought would suit the larger of the two empty rooms. As long as he wanted to rent it, that left only one space to fill, the one in the opposite corner to Violet.

They sat with their backs leaning against the wall looking out to sea.

'It's like sitting on the edge of the world, isn't it,' she said, accepting the bottle for first glug. Cal had remembered the wine but forgotten the cups, which they both acknowledged was better than the other way around. He'd remembered to chill it too, Vi noticed, as ice-cold bubbles danced down her throat.

'Are you pleased with how it's all coming together?' he asked, taking the bottle when she held it out.

'God, yes,' she said. 'It's impacting on my work productivity getting things set up, but can you imagine how fabulous it's going to be once we're in?'

'Worth it,' he said. 'I'm looking forward to having my space back at home, it was good timing.' He frowned and twisted to look at her. 'I don't mean your grandpa dying and leaving it to you was good timing, of course.'

She smiled and rolled her eyes. 'I got that.'

Drinking deeply, she put the bottle down between them. 'It was good timing for me, too,' she said. 'I needed to get away.'

'And has it helped? Because in my experience, you can't run away from problems, they have a nasty habit of following you.'

She wondered exactly what he was referring to, but didn't ask. 'This one hasn't. Not yet, anyway,' she said. 'I was proposed to, and I said no.'

'Ouch,' he murmured, reaching for the wine. 'Wrong time?'

'Wrong man, I think,' she said. 'I didn't realise that was the case until he asked me.'

'Poor guy,' Cal said.

'And he doesn't want to take no for an answer, so has sort of said, "Go and do what you need to do and I'll wait."'

'Ah, fuck.' Cal shook his head, his elbows on his knees, the bottle in his hand. 'Is that romantic of him, to you? Or is it stifling?'

Cal's perceptive question caught her unaware. 'I guess, if I loved him and was going to be a missionary in some war zone or something for a year, it would be romantic. But seeing as I don't think I love him anywhere near enough and I've come here to run a sex pier, probably not so much.'

He laughed, shaking his head. 'A sex pier? Is that what you call this in your head?' He handed her the wine.

'No, of course not,' she said, shrugging and half laughing as she took a swig. 'It's just that this wasn't what I'd anticipated when I came here.'

'I see that.'

They looked out to sea in contemplative silence. Violet could feel the alcohol sliding into her bloodstream too fast; a long day working without stopping to eat would do that.

'So, besides running away to manage a sex pier, what did you expect to find here?'

He made it sound as if she'd run away to join the circus. It felt a little like that, in truth. She'd come here in search of excitement, and she'd found that in the shape of mermaids on her bedroom walls and Lola the headless go-go dancer and a hot, disreputable neighbour who made whips for a living.

'I don't think I thought very much about what I might find. I just felt like I needed to get here.' She couldn't really articulate what had pulled her so strongly to Swallow Beach. It wasn't just about escaping a difficult situation, it was more . . . 'A calling, I guess, if that doesn't sound too fanciful.'

'And now you're here, are you glad you came?'

'Have you been taking therapist lessons from Linda and Melvin?'

They sat shoulder to shoulder, their heads against the wall, looking at each other.

'Is that your way of telling me to mind my own?'

She bit her lip. 'I just don't know the answers.'

'Well, I'm glad you're here,' he said.

'You are?'

He grinned. 'My mother needed someone new to moan about. She's bored of me.'

Violet remembered Barty's comment about Cal being the apple of his mother's eye when he was a little boy.

'It's sad that you don't see eye to eye with her,' she said. 'I rely on my mum more than I can tell you.' Della had been on the phone most days, and even though she pretended not to want to know, she was getting more and more curious about goings-on at Swallow Beach. 'Don't you wish things were better between you two?'

'Now who's being the pop psychiatrist?'

She supposed she deserved that.

'So is this spurned fiancé likely to turn up at some point to throw you over his shoulder and take you home?'

She was too loyal to say anything unkind, but the very idea of Simon charging down here to get her was so outlandish it made Violet sigh. He'd never take the time off work, and besides anything else, it'd throw his dodgy knee out.

'I think not,' she said.

Now would be the perfect time to ask Cal about his own experience of marriage; she couldn't engineer a better inroad into the subject if she tried. Yet still she didn't, and if she'd been forced to explain why she'd have had to confess that it was because she didn't really want to know anything that might make her conscience heavy. Cal was part of her Swallow Beach summer fairytale complete with a wicked mother; it just didn't work if he already had his princess, even if she was half way across the globe. For now, Violet just wanted to drink wine with him and enjoy the moment.

'The sun's shining on my name,' she said, nodding towards the painted rainbow on the floor. The sun had dipped low over the sea, casting a rose-gold glow over the birdcage, gilding the words painted on the boards.

'I take it you were named after it,' he said.

She leaned her head against his shoulder. 'I must have been, although I didn't know I was until I saw it.'

He whistled. 'Your mum really didn't tell you much at all about this place, did she?' he said, holding the bottle up to see how much they had left. Very little, it appeared.

'Nothing. You were all a big secret as far as I was concerned.'

She felt rather than saw his laugh. 'I quite like being your dirty secret.'

She lifted her head. 'Not dirty. You had your chance the other night and knocked me back, remember.'

It was the first time they'd actually talked about what had happened on the landing at the Lido the previous week.

He drank from the bottle and then handed it over for Violet to finish. 'You know that's not true.'

'Er, yes it is,' she said. 'I asked you to kiss me and you said no.' She tipped the bottle and finished the wine.

'Do you always have your hair blue?'

She didn't comment on the fact he'd changed the subject. 'No. It's been all colours of the rainbow.'

His eyes shifted to the rainbow on the floor. 'Blue suits you.'

'I looked good in pink.'

'I'll bet.'

'I've been known to dye my pubic hair to match,' she said, trying to keep a straight face.

He laughed. 'Very thorough of you.'

She shrugged. 'A girl likes to be prepared for anything.'

'And are you? Prepared for anything?'

'God, no,' she said. 'I wasn't prepared for any of the things I've found out since I came here. I wasn't prepared for the shock of my grandmother's apartment, or the protectiveness I feel towards the pier . . .' she patted the floor, 'and I wasn't prepared for you, either.'

He raised his eyebrows. 'Go on.'

'Stop fishing for compliments,' she said. 'I won't lie, Cal. You've had a strange effect on me. I think we're good neighbours and hope we'll be good friends for a long time, but then whenever we're together I sort of want all of my clothes to fall off, and that's a bit of a problem.'

Cal made a choking sound.

'And to be honest, I'm a bit humiliated. It's as if you've awoken my inner sex goddess and then told her you don't fancy her.'

'Fucking hell,' he said, scrubbing his hand over his jaw.

'But that's okay too, because I might just be on the rebound from Simon and projecting onto you. I probably don't fancy you at all really and our sex would be hideous, so you don't need to feel bad about it.'

'Right, that's enough,' he said, sudden and exasperated, and then he twisted to face her and slid his hand into her hair until he was cradling her head in his hand.

'You've had a strange effect on me too, Violet. You turn up here with your blue hair and sea-foam eyes, looking like someone who needs rescuing, then acting like a warrior princess, and I tell myself don't go there because she's someone else's, and because we're living next door to each other and that would be massively awkward afterwards, and I don't want to screw it up because I actually *like* you rather than just want to get you naked. And then you go and say stuff about your inner sex goddess and all I can think is I want you.'

They stared at each other, both breathless and giddy from saying too much and drinking too much too fast. She turned to face him too, one hand on the floor holding her upright, unsure what to do with the other until she realised she'd reached out and laid her fingertips on his lips as if to stop any more words coming out.

'Shall we kiss, just to confirm it's hideous?' she whispered, because she'd lost her senses.

He stared at her, his fingers warm and massaging the back of her neck.

'And then we can just relax because we've cleared the air,' she said. 'And go back to being platonic friends again.'

As she spoke, he kissed her fingertips. If she'd stopped to think about it she'd have realised the folly of her words, because even that barely-there touch of his mouth was enough to tell her she was kidding herself. Then he shifted her hand up and kissed her palm, his lashes lowered, tilting his head to let his lips slide down slowly over the pulse point in her wrist. She leaned into the heat of his body, gasping at the touch of his tongue on her skin.

And then he circled his arm around her body, holding her against him, and she tilted her head back as he lowered his. He kissed her slowly, deeply, opening her lips under his own, sighing into her mouth at the slide of her tongue over his. He controlled it, built it, until she snapped and pushed her hands into his hair and took the kiss from sensual to X-rated. He leaned into her until her back pressed against the glass, and she wrapped her arms around his neck and clung to him, scared by how turned on she was.

'You're crying,' he whispered into her mouth, slowing the kiss down to agonising and sweet. 'Don't cry, mermaid girl.'

'It's just that . . .'

'Shh,' he sank his teeth into her bottom lip then kissed it better. 'It's just a kiss. Hardly anything, really.' He wrapped both arms around her, holding her tight.

'I shouldn't have asked you to do it,' she said, still kissing him because she didn't want it to end.

'I think it was the best idea you've ever had,' he said, licking his tongue back into her mouth, cupping her face, stroking his thumbs across her cheekbones. And then they didn't say anything for a few minutes, because the kiss was too intense, too deep, too vulnerable, too fragile and close to be able to withstand conversation.

Cal had known that kissing Violet wasn't going to be hideous. He'd been imagining how she'd taste from the first moment he met her, and his imagination hadn't done her justice. Her skin smelt of fresh bed sheets after a shower and of the beach at sunrise, and the sea-salt on her warm lips gave way to rich, deep sweetness when she opened her mouth for him. He could taste the wine they'd shared, and her excitement, and the way she flipped from being kissed to kissing him was dynamite in his veins.

She was delicious, and for a few minutes he threw all of his reasons not to get involved with her off the end of the pier and just let himself be a man kissing a woman because she was lovely and she'd asked him to. He wasn't the black sheep of the family, or the failed husband, or the perceived Jack the lad. For those minutes, he wasn't any of the labels so frequently attached to him by other people. He was just Calvin Dearheart, a man with a temporary clean slate and it felt so damn good. She felt so damn good. She was *too* damn good for a man like him, but Jesus, when she kissed him like that he lost every rational thought in favour of just wanting more, and more, and more.

'Cal? Violet?'

They jumped guiltily apart at the sound of Keris's voice carrying through from outside the birdcage.

'Shit,' Violet said, wide-eyed and shaky.

'I dropped the bolt when I came in,' he said. 'Don't panic, it's okay.'

She nodded, pressing her fingers to her kiss-swollen mouth. 'I should go and let her in.'

Cal nodded. Fond as he was of Keris, he'd quite like to go and push her into the sea right at that moment.

Standing up, he held his hand out to Violet and helped her to her feet, straightening the neck of her blouse gently. They locked eyes, and he was blindsided by a distinct urge to protect this woman. What from, he didn't even know. It was just . . . primal.

'I've got you.' He ran the blue ends of her hair through his fingers, and a small, curious smile touched her lips.

'I better go and open the door before Keris wonders what we've been up to,' she said, and when she left the room Cal buried his face in his hands and swore repeatedly.

When Violet opened the door, she found Keris wasn't alone; there was a woman with her Vi hadn't met before.

'Violet, this is Lucy,' she said, looking Vi up and down quickly as if she knew what she'd interrupted. 'Lucy's a photographer. We were chatting in the pub last night, and it occurred to me that the pier might make a great photography studio with all the light?'

As she smiled and invited them both in, Violet tried to absorb the information and work out how it slotted in with the adult theme of the pier. Lucy was all curves and curls and smiles, but her eyes were wary as she looked around the birdcage, assessing.

'It's the end studio that's still available,' Vi said, leading them through to the back. Cal wandered out of her room as they drew level, raising his hand in greeting, and again Keris frowned slightly, glancing questioningly back at Violet.

Lucy stood in the centre of the available room. and then broke into a wide smile. 'It's bloody perfect. Being in the corner gives me complete privacy.'

Violet nodded, still not quite getting it. 'Is it portrait photography you do, Lucy?'

Lucy nodded. 'Kind of. Boudoir.'

Ah, now it was starting to make more sense.

'As in . . . bedroom?'

Lucy shrugged. 'As in photographs that make women feel good about themselves, for themselves.'

'I see,' Vi said. She liked Lucy instantly; older by a decade or two, there was a quiet, contained warmth to her that reminded her oddly of her mum. 'Well, it's available for the summer to begin with, and then I'm going to review things at the end to see where we go from there.'

Cal put his head around the doorway. 'I'm off now. See you later, guys.' His eyes lingered on Violet for a few seconds before he left.

'Well, he made my fingers itch for my camera,' Lucy grinned.

'Cal,' Keris said. 'You'll get to know him over the summer, he's in the next one along.'

Lucy put her hand out. 'I think you've got yourself a deal.'

Vi grinned as they shook on it. This was really happening; within a week or two, Swallow Beach Pier would finally hum again with life and laughter. She only hoped her gran would have approved.

*

Walking back up the steps into the Lido a while later, Violet yawned wide. 'Sorry Keris,' she said, blinking a few times. 'I'm not sleeping all that well.'

'Must be all the excitement,' Keris said, holding the door open for Vi to go through first. 'Am I going mad or did I pick up on something with you and Cal earlier?'

Violet shrugged, not meeting her friend's eye. 'Nope,' she said. 'We just had a drink to celebrate the end of the week.'

She could feel Keris eyeing her curiously so threw in an extra yawn to close the conversation down. 'Right, I'm going to go and run myself a bath and see if I can get my second wind,' she said, already heading for the stairs. 'I could do with working a couple of hours after dinner.'

'Sewing?'

Vi shook her head. 'Boring stuff. Insurance paperwork and all that stuff for the pier to run as a business. My dad's got his solicitor doing all of the necessary, he's sent me a load of forms and paperwork to fill in.'

Keris pulled a face. 'Bleurgh. That kind of thing brings me out in hives.'

'Me too. Got to be done though.'

She took the stairs at a jog, waving over her shoulder without hanging around for more. All she wanted was to make it inside her own front door without bumping into Cal, and then lie in the bath and try to work out what the hell had happened earlier at the pier.

Which was why her heart stopped when, just as she was closing her door, Cal opened his and said her name.

CHAPTER TEN

'Hey, Violet.'

Cal watched as Violet stalled, her back turned, her key already in her lock. For a second he thought she was going to go inside and pretend she hadn't heard him. That was exactly what he wanted to avoid, and precisely the reason he'd told himself not to get romantically involved with her in the first place. She turned slowly, like a grounded teenager caught sneaking out of their bedroom window.

'Hey,' she said, her smile too wide.

'I just thought we should clear the air, while it's still today.'

She chewed her bottom lip. 'Okay. Well, shall we just forget it happened?'

'We'd had a drink,' he offered.

'And like you said, it was only a kiss, barely anything.'

'I've pretty much wiped it from my mind already.'

She nodded. 'It wasn't as hideous as feared though.'

Cal didn't know whether to nod or shake his head. 'Not hideous at all. Rather pleasant, all things considered.'

'Quite,' she said. 'Well, I'm glad we got that sorted.'

'Me too.'

Fiddling with her keys, Violet scuffed the toe of her boot against the floor.

'I should, you know . . . go inside. Stuff to do.'

'Yes,' Cal said. 'I'm pretty busy, so . . .'

They looked at each other for a couple of beats, and then Violet turned away and disappeared inside her apartment with a decisive slam of the door.

Cal leaned his head against his own doorframe and looked at the now empty hallway.

'Well, that wasn't awkward at all, was it?' he murmured into the silence.

He was starting to wonder if it had been easier when he'd been the only resident of the top floor. He'd lied just now when he said it had been a rather pleasant kiss. It hadn't been pleasant. It had been like no other kiss he'd ever known, and he'd kissed a lot of women.

Maybe it had been just been a strange amalgamation of setting, wine, a girl he shouldn't kiss . . . that old 'forbidden fruit tastes sweeter' baloney. He'd never actively tried *not* to kiss someone he found attractive before; the novelty had grown old fast. Would it be so wrong? Everything in his rational head said yes. He'd made a decent life for himself in recent years. He'd built his business up from scratch, and he'd picked himself up off the floor after Ursula left. He didn't get involved in the mess of relationships these days, for one really simple reason. He still loved his wife.

Bathed and fed, Violet climbed into bed surrounded by the paperwork from her father's solicitor. Her parents hadn't been at all keen on the idea of her running the pier as a business, it felt far too much like a permanent plan, but nonetheless her dad had made sure that she was properly insured, because that was just the kind of man he was. In some ways he was a lot like Simon, super-reliable and steady as a rock, qualities Violet had a new appreciation for now that her life was so all over the place.

Around the bedroom, mermaids watched as she shuffled the papers in search of her pen. They looked suitably unimpressed with her choice of bedroom activity, so much so that she rolled her eyes at the nearest one.

'Have you stolen my pen to save me from having to do this?' she said, looking at the impassive face of the bare-breasted mermaid perched on her rock. Leaning over the edge of the bed in search of it, Violet peered underneath and couldn't see anything.

'Bugger,' she muttered, sliding the bedside drawer open, even though she knew it would be pointless, because any pen in there would be forty years old and dried up anyway. Feeling tentatively inside, Violet found nothing of practical use, although lots of interest. Aside from the living room sideboard, she'd tried not to mooch too much in the cupboards and drawers because it somehow felt intrusive – which was ridiculous because it was all hers now and she needed to find out how to make a home of it. She still thought of it very much as her grandmother's place. Oddly, never really as her grandfather's – she thought of it only as Monica's, probably because her grandmother's heart was stamped in every painted wall or quirky furniture choice.

So this time, she let herself look through the bedside drawer. Horn-rimmed reading glasses lay on top of a yellowing paperback, something sci-fi by the looks of it. Violet set them on top of the bedside table and looked at what lay beneath it. A hair comb, silver with paste jewels in cornflower blue and peridot green. Scattered bobby pins.

A slim silver tube of moisturiser, long since empty. Nothing of monetary value, but precious to Violet because it was like looking through a window into the past. She'd wait for a special day and wear the hair comb somewhere nice; maybe she'd ask Barty to take her to one of his tea dances at Swallow Beach ballroom. And, at the back, a pretty silk headscarf printed with cherries. She lifted it out, delighted, and found that it had been used as a makeshift wrapper around a book. Or rather, around a small, sky-blue leather diary, year stamped in gold as 1978.

Violet stared at it, gasping softly when she realised the significance. Monica died in 1978. She sat completely still on the edge of the bed, the diary clutched in her hands, all thoughts of dull paperwork chased from her mind. Should she read it? Part of her shouted, *No, you absolutely should* not *read it, it's private and personal.* And because it was both of those things, she battled with the other side of her that desperately wanted to know her grandmother better.

If Monica had written inside the diary, which she probably had, given that it had been carefully wrapped and put to the back of her bedside table, then this was gold dust. A chance to learn about her grandmother from the one person who really understood – Monica herself. She'd just flick through and see if there was anything in there. That's all.

So she did, fanning the tissue-thin pages quickly. Crap. It was filled with entries, and not just 'dental appointment' or 'parents' evening'. Pages and pages of close-knit, sloping writing, all in the same vivid teal-blue ink, as if Monica had a special pen set aside just for diary entries.

Try as she might, Violet wasn't able to resist peeking – she lifted the cover to January 1st and read the first entry, then closed it gently because she couldn't see through her own tears. The entry itself wasn't anything terribly out of the ordinary, but the woman who'd written it jumped out of the page to her so clearly it was as if she was perched beside her on the bed. Her grandmother wrote of the overnight snow that blanketed the beach, and how she and Della had walked into town that morning in the new matching red wellington boots Henry had given them for Christmas, and of how terribly she missed her own mother. Violet didn't know anything really about her great-grandma, but she sure understood what it was like to want your mum. She understood, because right then she'd love nothing more than to curl up on the sofa and watch a movie with Della, a cup of tea on the table and a box of chocolates open between them.

Sighing hard, she lay back on the pillows and clicked out the lights. It had been a long and confusing sort of day; if her fairy godmother had appeared and offered her a pair of ruby slippers, she'd have gladly clicked her heels and said, 'There's no place like home.'

'Good to see you again, Violet.' Beau Hamilton stood and pumped Violet's hand as soon as she walked into The Swallow on Tuesday evening. He was probably around forty, all shaggy hair and crinkly blue eyes. He somehow reminded Violet of an adventurer, someone you might see on TV reporting from the North Pole with ice crystals in his beard. She shook his hand, then introduced him to Keris and Lucy who'd just filed in behind her.

This was the first official meeting of all of the new occupants of the pier, and like all the best meetings, it was being held in the pub.

'Melvin and Linda can't make it,' Cal said, returning

from the bar with full beer glasses balanced in his hands. 'I ran into Mel earlier and he asked me to pass on their apologies.'

'That's a shame,' Vi said, although actually it was probably a bit of a godsend for their inaugural meeting, because fabulous as Melvin and Linda were, they could be pretty overwhelming. Taking a seat at the table between Keris and Lucy, she pulled a folder from her bag and laid it on the table.

'I got a bottle of white,' Cal said, placing it down with some glasses. 'I can change it if you want something else?'

Violet appreciated the effort. 'No, that's fab, thank you.' She glanced quickly at Lucy, who nodded, and at Keris, who cracked the lid on the bottle and shot Cal a thank you smile.

'Okay,' she said, once they were all settled with a drink in hand. 'Thanks for coming, everyone, I wanted us to all get together tonight to meet each other properly. Firstly, I want to thank you all for having faith in me and the pier project, especially given that we've come up against some resistance from certain factions in Swallow Beach.'

She paused for breath, not glancing at Cal when she alluded to his mother's campaign. It was showing no signs of abating; just that morning the local magazine had landed on her mat with a picture of Mayoress Gladys on the front and an outraged quote from the double-page spread. Violet had read it with a sinking heart. Gladys shared her fears for the morals of the impressionable youth of Swallow Beach if the salacious nature of the pier went unchallenged, and she felt it her civic duty to protect her subjects – or something to that effect.

'I want to assure you all that I've made sure all of the boxes are ticked and all of the legal hoops have been jumped through where the pier is concerned,' Violet continued. 'It's insured and good to open as soon as you're ready. I'm going to set my workshop up tomorrow, and as of Thursday I'll be there full-time. I'll make sure the pier is unlocked by seven thirty, and we can talk about times to lock up when everyone's in and got more of an idea. I only live over the road so it's no trouble for me to come over and lock up late on if needs be. I want it to be really flexible and kind of fun, you know?'

Beau raised his glass and the others followed suit. 'To Swallow Beach Pier,' he said. 'I for one can't wait. Let's work hard and play harder, people.'

Vi laughed, clinking her glass. She appreciated Beau's American zest for life. She'd met him only briefly the day before at the pier, but she already knew he was a perfect fit for the pier. He exuded a calm, chilled-out vibe, as if no problem was going to be insurmountable, or no council sticky beak enough to derail things.

Each of them spoke a little about their plans, and it became clear that Beau and Cal often worked together to produce bespoke items for adult clubs both in the UK and internationally. Clear pride ran through their words as they spoke; they were businessmen, and rightly unembarrassed by the nature of the goods they produced. Lucy was next up, pulling her portfolio from her bag to hand around.

'Everyone in there is happy for their pictures to be in my workbook,' she added, because some of the photographs were pretty sensual, and some of the women weren't wearing all that much.

'It's not especially about making women look sexy, although they invariably do,' she said. 'I do what I do to empower women, to encourage them to feel fabulous in their own skin, regardless of size or shape. It's about being confident and bold and not letting anyone tell you who you are or how to be.'

When she spoke about her work, Lucy lit up, full of grit and determination. It was impossible not to see the fire in her eyes, and Violet found herself wondering what fuelled Lucy's fire. All she knew about the other woman was that she was a single mum with a teenage son at the local high school, and she lived in the next town along the coast to Swallow Beach. For now that was enough, but she was keen to know more.

'Maybe you could sit for me some time,' Lucy said, looking from Keris to Violet and back again. 'Get a true feel for how I work.'

Violet's automatic response was to say no, but then she found herself wondering *why not*? And glancing across the table at Cal, she found his eyes on her, looking at her in a way that made her skin start to tingle. Was he imagining her posing in her undies like the women in Lucy's portfolio? Or in his shirt, as it looked like in one of the shots?

'And you, Keris?' Violet said, turning to her friend to change the subject. 'How are your plans for the shop looking?' She knew the answer to the question already, because she and Keris had talked at length about the proposed layout and the website design.

'Good,' Keris said, topping up their wine glasses. 'Being across the front of the building means the shop space is big enough to display a couple of Beau's bigger pieces, and I've picked up a gorgeous vintage glass-topped display case for Cal's things.' She grinned. 'I think it was originally from a sweet shop.'

'Very fitting,' Cal laughed.

Vi let the conversation wash over her, feeling more and more sure that she was doing the right thing with the pier.

She wasn't quite sure how it had all come together so quickly, she was just glad to have these people around her. Safety in numbers.

In bed that evening, she allowed herself to read a few more pages of her grandmother's diary, further into the early weeks of the year. It had been a punishing winter in Swallow Beach, and Della had been unwell so had missed the first week of school. Monica said that she was secretly glad to have her little girl at home for a few extra days, and described how they'd baked animal-shaped biscuits and iced them messily; bright pink flamingos and blue and yellow parrots.

The entries were both beautiful and difficult to read; everyday recollections rendered heartbreaking because Violet knew that her grandmother wouldn't live to see another Christmas in Swallow Beach. Those were possibly the last biscuits she baked with her daughter, the last snowfall she saw, the last new bottle of nail varnish chosen. Violet read the words slowly, feeling closer to Monica with every sentence.

Then, towards the end of January, an entry caused Violet to pause, chilled without really understanding why. All it said was: *Met T again today. I know it's wrong.*

Reading the scant entry over for a second time, Violet shut the diary hurriedly. She shouldn't be reading this. Who was T? Not her Grandpa Henry, that much was for sure. She flicked the lights out and slept fitfully, and although she couldn't remember her dreams, she woke with a feeling of dread in the pit of her stomach, as if trouble lurked just around the corner.

By five o'clock on Thursday afternoon, Violet had transformed her empty workroom at the pier into a light-flooded studio. Beau and Cal had stepped up to the plate to help her move the heavier things, most notably the beast of a sewing machine, which now stood on a sturdy table that had been left behind when the pier was closed up for the last time in 1978. Lola the go-go dancer had also made the journey across from the Lido, and now stood in the far corner, a headless siren in red and gold feathers luring sailors in. All of her materials, feathers and threads had been sorted into a large shelving unit with baskets across the back wall – it was, in short, perfect. Vi stood in the centre, her hand resting on top of the sewing machine, and let a great whoosh of air leave her lungs. She wasn't going to worry about who T was any more. It was history, and not hers to discover or attempt to understand. Who was she to judge?

Wandering from her room, she went to see how everyone else was getting on with their own studios.

'Lucy?' She tapped and waited to be invited in, even though she knew that Lucy didn't have anyone in there yet. Like Melvin and Linda, Lucy was officially opening her studio on the pier after she'd served her month's notice at her old rental. It was kind of nice actually, it meant they could have a soft launch rather than hit Swallow Beach with an all-singing, all-dancing pier.

She knew a handful of residents had grumbled that the pier's new use wasn't more of a community project; an amusement arcade, say, or a mainstream shopping arcade. She took their point, but also she felt strongly that there was nothing shameful in what any of them did and she was happy for anyone who wanted to to come and have a look around. At least this way the pier would be open again. People would be free to wander along the board-walk, to sit on the ornate metal benches set into the sidings, to enjoy the sea. She'd done that exact thing herself for a few minutes every day since she'd arrived here; just sat and looked out towards the horizon, a cup of coffee in her hand. Maybe she could do that; have a coffee machine put just inside the entrance to the birdcage, one of those fancy self-serve ones that offered a million different ways to enjoy your brew. That might work, and it would certainly go some way towards appeasing the locals.

'Come in,' Lucy called, shaking Violet from her daydreams.

Pushing the door open, Violet stepped inside and looked around approvingly.

'I like what you've done with the place,' she said, as if looking at someone's new home rather than workspace. But then Lucy's studio did look quite homely, with a big red velvet chaise begging to be draped over with a good book, and a table and chairs too.

'Props,' Lucy said. 'And somewhere for Charlie to do his homework when he comes by.'

Charlie, Lucy's fourteen-year-old son, had been by a couple of times since Lucy had signed the lease, and on both occasions Violet had been struck by the tight bond between mother and son.

'You're not worried for his moral well-being if he spends time here?' Violet smiled, and Lucy laughed lightly.

'Fourteen-year-old boys today know more than most adults,' she said drily. 'Besides, Charlie's got his head screwed on. He's had to have really, being just us for the last ten years.'

Vi had no idea what had happened to Charlie's dad and didn't like to pry.

'Ian was a bastard,' Lucy said, as if she'd read Violet's mind. 'Handy with his fists, knew where to hit me so it wouldn't show.'

'Oh God, Lucy . . .' Violet said, taken aback.

'I put up with it for too long.' Lucy sat down on the chaise, her eyes fixed out to sea. 'But then I had Charlie, and I had someone else to be brave for. I couldn't let him be taught how to be a man by someone who had no idea how to be a good one. Or worse, let Charlie become his next punch bag.'

Violet sat down beside Lucy on the chaise. 'And that's why you do what you do now for other women.'

Lucy nodded. 'We left one night in the clothes we stood up in and moved three hundred miles away to get away from him. Charlie was three years old, and I was a mess for a long time. Charlie and photography saved me, gave me things to live for.'

'That makes you pretty amazing in my book, Lucy.'

The other woman looked at her. 'It's taken me a long time to be able to tell people what happened. I was ashamed. Ashamed that I stayed for as long as I did, that I'd allowed myself to become *that* woman.'

'Lucy, no . . .'

'It's okay,' Lucy said, patting Violet's leg. 'I don't think those things now. But it's taken a long time, and help from other women who've been through the same. I guess this,' she gestured around her at the studio, 'this is my way of reaching out to other women, all women, regardless of their circumstances, and saying you're enough just as you are. You're fabulous and worthy and enough, just as you are.'

Violet sat in silence and listened to Lucy speak, choked up.

'I'm glad you're here,' she said, eventually.

'So am I,' Lucy said, and for a few moments they sat shoulder to shoulder looking out to sea, peaceful.

*

Leaving Lucy to finish up, Violet moved along to Cal's workshop and found him hard at work, bent over something on his workbench with Beau.

'Industrious in here,' she said, leaning against the doorframe.

Beau gave whatever it was on the workbench a good whack with a hammer.

'There,' he said. 'That's got it.'

Both men stood up and looked her way.

'When in doubt, hit with a hammer,' Beau grinned at her. 'It was my father's lifelong motto, and now mine.'

'I don't think it's one I can adopt in my line of work,' she said, laughing softly. 'Do you guys need me to come back and lock up later or are you winding things up?'

'Ten minutes max,' Cal said. 'We just need to take this through to Lucy. She's going to photograph it for Keris, she needs some "feature pieces" for the pier's website.'

There was an old pine door flat on Cal's workbench, and as the two men righted it Violet realised that it had a complicated-looking leather and metal-work harness attached to the back of it. Putting her head on one side, she tried to formulate the question in her head.

'Don't ask,' Cal advised.

'But . . .' She stared at the restraint system. 'How does . . .'

Cal shook his head, glancing away. 'Seriously. Don't.'

Beau, however, had no such sensibilities.

'Ingenious bit of kit actually,' he said. 'Hands go here, and this bit goes around here . . .' He positioned himself against the door, and put his hands up by his shoulders. 'We do another fabulous one too for folks who have strong ceiling beams. This one is more practical though, because it's door-mounted. I mean, everyone has doors, right?'

He grinned and gave her a double thumbs up from his position flat against the door.

'Umm, yes, I guess,' Vi said, thinking that yes, everyone had doors, but no, not everyone fancied being lashed to the back of them.

Beau stepped away and picked the door up, sliding it under his arm as if it were made of paper.

'I'll take this out to Keris,' he said to Cal. Violet stepped inside to let him past, eyeing the dubious contraption as he went by.

'Not everything I make is quite so in your face,' Cal said, as if he needed to explain himself. 'It's mostly mainstream stuff. You know . . . the things you've already seen.'

Vi nodded. 'Floggers and things.'

'Yes.'

Were floggers mainstream, now? Was it a prerequisite of bedrooms up and down the land to have a whip and a gimp-mask stashed under the bed next to your suitcases and shoes? Vi couldn't imagine that it was. Or perhaps she was out of touch. She couldn't even imagine Simon's face if she'd tried to introduce any of those kinds of things into their sex life; he wasn't at all adventurous. In fact, he wasn't big on spontaneity at all; she'd always tried to tell herself that they were a classic case of opposites attract, but now that they were no longer together, she was more and more sure that that wasn't a strategy that would have worked long-term.

'Settled in?' she said, changing the subject.

'I love it,' Cal said, relaxing into that smile that did odd things to her insides. 'So much space and light.'

She nodded, because she appreciated those same things in her own workshop. The light in the birdcage really was spectacular; she could see why it might have been used as a gallery.

'The light's amazing, isn't it? I can imagine painting here.'

'You paint?'

'Not for a long time,' she said, wistful. 'I used to love it though. I'm not that great at it, but it's joyful all the same.'

'No end to your talents,' he said lightly.

'Oh, there is,' she said. 'I'm terrible at anything maths related. Or science. Or computers.'

'Did you see the website? Keris is nearly done now, looks pretty cool.'

Keris, thankfully, was a whizz with computers, and had taken charge of building the pier's new website.

'I know,' Violet said. 'She's a clever one.'

'Melvin and Linda's furniture arrived earlier,' Cal said. 'I had it put just inside their room.'

Violet nodded. Chatting with Cal was more stilted since they'd kissed; she hoped it wouldn't always feel that way. Maybe if she offered an olive branch . . .

'I'm cooking later, if you're around? Nothing fancy, just pasta . . .' She stopped speaking, because his expression already told her the answer.

'I've already made plans,' he said, looking awkward. 'Sorry. Really.'

She could feel the flush of embarrassment crawling up her neck. 'Hey, don't be silly,' she said, overcompensating with a forced laugh. 'I'm cooking anyway, it was just a thought.'

'Another time?' he said, his dark eyes asking her to say yes.

She shrugged it off. 'For sure.' Backing out of his room, she lifted her hand. 'See you later them. Umm, have a fun night.'

Escaping to the relative safety of her workroom, Violet sat down at her worktable and laid her head against the wood, feeling like a fool.

In his room, Cal seriously contemplated texting Maria and rearranging for a different night. They had a very occasional, casual arrangement, she wouldn't mind taking a rain check. He went as far as to pull his phone out of his back pocket, but then stopped himself as he clicked the screen into life. What was he thinking of? Turning away a gorgeous, funny girl who'd end up in his bed tonight for a bowl of pasta and a strained conversation with the one girl he was trying to avoid being alone with? Shoving his phone in his pocket, he started to pack his stuff away.

CHAPTER ELEVEN

'We're on the front of the local paper!'

Violet met Keris and Barty in the Lido lobby on Monday morning, after a quiet weekend of reading and mooching around the apartment. She'd read the sci-fi novel from her grandmother's bedside table, and resisted reading more of her diary even though she was desperate to. Instead she'd emptied out the kitchen cupboards and delighted in Monica's eclectic taste in crockery and cookware. She'd clearly not been troubled by the idea of a matching dinner service, there wasn't even one plate or cup that matched another. It appealed to Violet's artistic sensibilities, and to her sentimental side, too. It pleased her to imagine her grandmother hunting down the random pieces in charity shops and vintage market stalls, or perhaps picking up a cup or bowl to remind her of a holiday or special place.

She baked a cake too, another thing she used to enjoy but never seemed to find the time for recently. But leafing through Monica's old, well-used orange cookbook, she'd found a recipe speckled with chocolate and decorated with childish blue-crayoned hearts around the page. Clearly a well-loved recipe, and once she'd baked it, Violet understood why. Who knew you could add old-fashioned milkshake powder to a sponge recipe? She'd had to dig around a couple of supermarkets to find the old-style powder still for sale, but it was worth the effort – the resulting cake was delicately pink and strawberry-sweet, topped with chocolate icing; the kind of cake a child would love. Would her mum remember it, she'd wondered, eating a huge slice for breakfast on Sunday morning.

'We're in the paper?' she said, handing Barty a small Tupperware box holding a slice of cake. 'I made a cake,' she said. 'Thought you might like a slice.'

Barty lifted the lid to peep, and his eyes lit up. 'Did you really make this?'

Violet nodded, pleased with herself as he sniffed the box and closed his eyes, smiling.

'Takes me back, that does,' he said, then opened his eyes and unexpectedly kissed her on the cheek.

'None for me then?' Keris said, her mouth downturned for comedy.

'I ate it all,' Violet said. 'Breakfast, lunch and dinner.'

'You're not even joking, are you?'

Vi shook her head, trying not to laugh.

'I hope you break out in a plague of cake-related spots,' Keris grumbled, handing her the newspaper. 'Look at this though.'

Violet scanned the headline. 'Pier opens again after forty years!' Nothing too worrisome there. There were several shots of the pier, one black and white from the pier's yesteryears, another that looked to be from the seventies and one of Cal and Beau struggling through the open gates carrying her sewing machine with Lucy trying to offer direction. She looked closer at the image from the seventies.

'That's my grandmother,' she said, bringing it closer to her face. Monica was standing proudly outside the pier, one of quite a few people in the busy seaside image. She wasn't looking at the camera; in fact she didn't look as if she knew the shot was being taken. She had one hand on the sea wall, laughing up into the face of a man beside her. His face was turned slightly away from the camera so you couldn't see him clearly, but even from that angle it clearly wasn't her Grandpa Henry. Oh God. Was this the mysterious T?

'Is it?' Keris said, leaning over to peer at the picture. 'Bloody hell, Violet! You're her double!'

Violet couldn't take her eyes from the grainy image. 'I know.' Holding the paper towards Barty, she frowned. 'Do you know who that is with her, Barty?'

She passed him the newspaper, and he obligingly took it and peered at it for a moment. 'I'm not wearing my specs so I couldn't be sure darling, but it looks like your grandfather to me.'

Vi sighed. 'You think? His hair wasn't that dark, I don't think.'

Barty looked nonplussed. 'Cameras back then weren't as sophisticated as today. Could just be a trick of the light.'

Taking the paper back, she studied it again. 'Maybe you're right.' Belatedly, she felt that she'd spoken out of turn to question Monica, especially to someone old enough to remember her grandparents.

'Thought I'd walk over there with you, see what you're all up to,' Barty said. 'I might be able to stick my oar in, as they say.' He winked, always the joker.

Violet scanned the rest of the article and then laid the paper down on the hall table. She'd look at it more closely again later.

*

'I've got someone coming to see about fitting a fancy coffee machine just inside the birdcage tomorrow,' Violet said a week or two later, pouring Barty a coffee from the Thermos she'd found underneath the sink back at the Lido. 'Thought people might like to come and sit on the benches and look at the sea for a while.'

They were sitting half way along the pier on one of the ten benches set into the ironwork side-barrier. Barty smiled, his eyes on the horizon.

'It's been a long time since people have been able to come and go on this pier. I didn't realise how much I'd missed it until now.' He sipped his coffee. 'I ran up and down here as a kid, and I shared my first kiss with Elizabeth Robertson a few benches that way.' He jerked his head towards the birdcage. 'Scandalous it was. Older woman.'

'Really?' Vi's eyebrows lifted towards her hairline.

Barty nodded. 'She was fourteen. I was twelve.'

Vi laughed softly, imagining how it must feel to have lived your whole life in such a small community, for your every memory to be woven around a place and its people.

'You must love it here to have never been tempted away,' she said.

He sighed, heavily enough to indicate that she'd hit a nerve. 'Oh, I was tempted. Once or twice I came close, but then I met Florence and had a reason to stay.'

Violet knew from Keris that Barty had lost his wife Florence about a decade previously.

'Did you come here to the pier together?' she asked, hoping that they had.

He drained his coffee, standing up. 'Stories for another day,' he smiled. 'I should get on. Hot yoga this morning at the parish hall.'

Violet found she wasn't surprised. Zumba, ballroom

dancing, yoga . . . *Please let me be like Barty when I'm old,* she thought. *Please let me be here in Swallow Beach, a beloved resident rather than an outsider.*

'Okay?' Cal asked, as she walked past his room when she headed back inside.

She paused. 'Yeah. Just chatting to Barty about his life here.'

'He's probably one of the oldest long-term residents here now,' Cal said. 'My mother's coming up a close second, though.'

His mention of Mayoress Gladys Dearheart made her heart sink.

'Any more rumbles about the compulsory purchase order?' she asked, crossing her fingers that he said no.

'Well, she's planning to come over here tomorrow to see what's happening,' he said, grimacing. 'Sorry, she only texted a few minutes ago to tell me. I can't really say no, given that the pier is open again now.'

'Great,' Vi sighed. 'I might make myself scarce.'

'No, don't,' Cal said. 'If you run, she'll catch the scent of fear and chase harder.'

What an odd opinion to hold of your own mother, Violet thought but didn't say. Had Gladys been a terribly harsh mother to her son? Violet could well imagine that there had been strict rules in the Dearheart household, and almost see a wild-haired younger Cal rebelling every chance he got. He'd probably been quite a handful; there must have been some colourful rows in their household when he hit his teenage years.

'What time is she coming?'

'Eleven,' Cal said. 'Which means eleven. Not five to or five past. Eleven on the nose.'

Violet felt her insides shrivel up a little. 'Okay. I'll tell everyone else. Be here with our game faces on.'

At just before ten o'clock the following morning, Violet was hard at work in her studio, immersed in finishing off the third of the military showgirl outfits. Holding the corset up in front of her eyes told her there was something not quite right about it but she couldn't quite work out what it was.

'Looks fabulous,' Keris said, coming in to see what she was up to. 'Make me one in green? I reckon I'd kill it down the ballroom in that.'

'The ballroom?' All Violet knew about the ballroom so far was that Barty went to tea dances there. Surely Keris wasn't planning to head down there to waltz with the local octogenarians dressed like Lola the headless showgirl?

'Yeah,' Keris said. 'They have things on there sometimes in the summer. You know, Robbie tribute acts, that kind of thing. We should go.'

Violet nodded, distracted. 'There's something not quite right about this,' she said, looking at the corset again. 'Can you see?'

They stood together and stared at it.

'I'm not sure,' Keris said. 'Is it fractionally longer on that side than this?'

Vi bit her lip. 'I'm sure I measured it correctly.'

'Shall I try it on?'

Violet looked up at Keris and found her eyes sparkling with excitement. She *really* wanted to try the corset on.

'Um, okay,' she said. It would actually help to see how the corset looked and moved on a real body. 'You're sure?'

'God, yes!' Keris closed the door quickly and unceremoniously whipped her T-shirt over her head. 'Do you want me to take my bra off?'

Outside Violet's door at that very moment, Melvin and Linda stood staring at each other, agog. They'd arrived a few seconds earlier and decided to come and let Violet know they were in for the morning to set up their consulting room. Finding Violet's door closed, poised to knock, they distinctly heard Keris moan, 'God, yes! Do you want me to take my bra off?' so they thought better of knocking and tiptoed back to make a start on their room instead.

'Jesus God! I bloody love this,' Keris said, standing barefoot in the middle of Violet's room wearing the red feather and rhinestone corset and her black denim mini. 'I was kidding earlier when I said make me one. I'm deadly serious now. I'll pay, Violet. Whatever it costs. I've never felt sexier in my entire bloody life.'

'Violet? Have you seen Keris anywhere?'

Cal tapped the door and opened it without waiting to be called in, and then stood there with his mouth open.

'Bloody hell,' he said. 'What are you two doing in here? Playing dress-up?'

'Did you want something?' Violet asked.

He looked for a second as if he genuinely couldn't remember.

'Oh. Yes, Beau needs to know where Keris wants him to put the display cage she asked him to make for the shop. We've just carted it out of his unit and he's waiting for you to tell him where to put it.'

Keris frowned. 'Er, I'm not sure. I'll come and look.'

'Like that?' Cal said, dubious.

Keris looked down at the corset laughing, her boobs frothing over the top of it. 'Why not? It's not as if I'm not covered up. Besides, I love it. I might make it my new uniform, really give people something to talk about.'

They trailed through the birdcage to the shop at the front and found Beau sitting on the new cage chatting to Melvin and Linda about the fetish scene.

'Ah, there you all ar—' Beau stood up and looked at them, and then he opened his eyes wider than should have been strictly anatomically possible. Violet preened, secretly thrilled that her corset was clearly having an effect on everyone who saw it. It helped that Keris wore it well; confident and sassy with hourglass curves and generous boobs.

'What?' Keris said, pretending she had no clue what was wrong with the big American. 'Did you want me for something?'

'Shut your mouth Beau, you're going to catch flies,' Violet said.

'Beau here was just filling us in on the different styles of cages he makes,' Melvin said, as if he hadn't even noticed the fact that Keris was wearing anything out of the ordinary.

'Where do you want me to put it?' Beau said, looking somewhere over Keris's shoulder rather than in the eye.

Keris put her hands on her hips and surveyed the entrance space of the birdcage. 'Over there, I think?'

'I'm thinking of having the coffee machine put there,' Violet interjected.

Keris fell silent, thinking. 'Here then?' she said, gesturing to a spot on the other side of the entrance doors. 'I want it to have impact when people come in, really showcase Beau's workmanship.'

Vi didn't miss the twin spots of colour that had appeared above Beau's beard.

'Okey dokey,' he muttered. 'Let's move this baby. Cal, give me a hand to lift it?'

The two men lifted it between them, snagging Beau's T-shirt with a loud rip. He put it down again sharpish and looked down; his T-shirt looked as if he moonlighted as the Hulk.

'Jeez,' he muttered. 'I liked this one.'

Resigned, he picked up his end of the cage again and then shuffled it across into place.

'Careful, the door's swinging open,' Violet said, too late because the ornate key Beau had fashioned for the lock fell out.

'Grab that, will you?' Beau puffed, as he and Cal positioned the heavy cage down by the doors.

Violet lunged for it but it skittered away across the boards of the pier. Terrified it was going to go down between the wooden slats into the sea below, she crawled quickly across towards the cage. The key had gone through the bars, so she opened the door and crawled in, reaching for it carefully in case it fell.

'Don't let it fall,' Beau said, squatting down, rubbing his beard.

Vi got her fingertips to it, and as feared, the ornate black jailer's key slid out of reach between the boards.

'Shit,' she muttered, peering down the gap. 'I'm terrified it's going to fall through. Have you got a hook or something? It needs something delicate to go through the pattern, my fingers will knock it out.'

Cal disappeared in search of something suitable, leaving Violet on all fours in the cage, Keris bending over her in the feather corset.

And *that* was the precise moment Lady Mayoress Gladys Dearheart chose to walk through the door, a cameraman with her from the local paper snapping away with furious delight.

CHAPTER TWELVE

'This should do it,' Cal said, walking back through from his workshop with a thin metal rod, then coming to an almost comical halt as he took in the sight of his mother framed in the doorway staring at Violet through the bars of the cage and Keris trying to hide behind Beau's bulk in her feather dancing girl kit.

'What in God's name is going on here?' Gladys practically roared, thundering into the middle of the room. Swinging around to the photographer, she waved her arms, her briefcase perilously close to taking his camera out. 'Get it all on film! Especially that girl in the cage like an animal! Good God, I thought I'd seen it all but this takes the biscuit!'

Cal rolled his eyes, handing Violet the rod through the bars.

'What are you doing now? Poking her? Is that what you're doing, poking her with a stick? Is that part of the ritual? This is illegal, I'm sure of it!' she shouted, then stooped down to look at Violet as if she were an exhibit in a zoo. 'I was right about you, young lady.'

Violet knew she should get out and attempt to smooth

the situation, but on the other hand, Gladys was ten minutes early and she was never early, and if she didn't get that key now it would as good as likely fall through the boards. So instead of doing the sensible thing, gripped with the absurdity of the situation, she clutched the bars and sort of growled.

'Did you just . . .' Gladys backed away. 'She's feral. I knew it. Calvin, enough is enough. This whole thing is a debacle.'

Keris put her hands on her hips to say something indignant, and Gladys turned to her all guns blazing.

'And you ought to know better than to get sucked into a cult like this, Keris Harwood,' she declared. 'Although with a mother like yours, it was always on the cards.'

Keris's face turned the colour of the scarlet feathers on her corset. 'Don't you dare talk ill of my family, Gladys Dearheart. At least we can still stand the sight of each other. I doubt your lot would piss on you if you were on fire!'

Violet felt almost sorry for Gladys for a moment; her eyes shot to Cal for back-up, and to be fair he did look conflicted, but being her own worst enemy Gladys ploughed on and made things a million times worse.

'I said this place would be turned into a place of ill repute, and I was right. You can't come here and peddle your filth to good people like us from the safety of your dog cage, young woman.' She slapped her hand down on the top of the cage for effect, making it rattle.

Beau, who so far had held his tongue on the sidelines, stepped forward in front of the cage.

'It's not a dog cage, ma'am,' he said. 'It's a handmade artisan fetish cage of the highest quality.' He looked over Gladys's shoulder and smiled genially into the lens of the cameraman. 'Available on request in a variety of sizes.'

He'd probably just forgotten about his ripped T-shirt, nor realised that Gladys was eye level with his nipple.

'Call your gigolo off! Keris, now!' Gladys squawked, shielding her eyes from the sight of so much man.

'Are you suggesting I pay men for sex, Gladys?' Keris said, her boobs jiggling around because she was hopping mad.

'If the cap fits!'

Melvin and Linda hovered in the background, and at this Linda raised her hand tentatively. 'I think I can interject here. Keris most certainly isn't paying any man for sex.'

Keris nodded at the support from an unexpected source.

'I know this,' Linda nodded, 'because I recently found out that Keris is in fact a lesbian.'

All eyes swung to Linda, who put both hands up and smiled. 'Not that that's anything to be ashamed of or applauded, it just is what it is and I thought it might help diffuse the gigolo confusion.' She adjusted her silk turban. 'As you were.'

'I'm going to need a lot of therapy to get over this,' Gladys muttered, backing towards the door.

'Our rates are very reasonable,' Melvin said, withdrawing his business card from his shirt pocket and holding it out. Gladys narrowed her eyes, and he tucked it slowly away with a shrug. 'Classic case of sexual repression,' he muttered as an aside to Linda.

Gladys stomped off down the pier, her sensible heels clattering, just as Lucy appeared, her camera around her neck.

'Any sign of that coffee machine yet? I could kill for a cappuccino.'

Later that night, Violet curled up on the bed and cried. She cried with frustration, and with annoyance, and because she felt well and truly out of her depth in just about every aspect of her life. Bloody sodding Gladys Dearheart had got exactly what she wanted that afternoon; if the rest of Swallow Beach hadn't been taking the Mayoress seriously up to now, they'd listen up once she backed up her wild claims with photographic evidence of depravity on the pier. What had she been thinking of, growling?

Honestly, she felt like a complete and utter fool. She'd retired with the rest of the team to The Swallow for a restorative drink after work, and despite the fact that they'd all seen the humorous side, she was finding it harder to raise a smile. But then it wasn't their pier; they weren't responsible for honouring Monica's memory. She felt so shoddy, as if she'd somehow disrespected her grandmother.

'I'm sorry,' she whispered, and her fingers curled around something underneath her pillow. Monica's diary. She held it against her heart, trying to feel closer to the woman who'd written it. Just knowing that Monica had held it, touched the pages, made her feel slightly better, a little more connected. And then, although she felt some misgivings about invading her gran's privacy, she opened it and started to read. She just hoped her gran would understand she was reading it to feel closer to her rather than to snoop.

February had blown in on a cold wind, Monica said. She missed Della now she was in school full-time, and Henry was away so much on business that she was unbearably lonely sometimes. She knew it was no excuse, mind – and although she didn't specify what for, exactly, Violet had the distinct impression that it was to do with the mysterious T. Was he the guy in the newspaper photograph? Despite Barty's suggestion of a trick of the light, Violet had studied the image again and decided the man in the photo was slightly too tall, and definitely too dark-haired to be her grandpa. Was Barty lying, she wondered? Not that she thought he'd have a malicious reason to do so, more that he might be protecting a friend, or just felt that the past was best left undisturbed. Or maybe he simply didn't know, and genuinely thought it could be Henry.

T gave me a shell bracelet today, Monica wrote on Valentine's day. *He made it himself from shells on the beach. Isn't that the most romantic thing ever? I can't seem to stay away from him, even though I know it's dangerous for all of us.*

Violet closed her eyes, her heart breaking for both Monica and her Grandpa Henry. She was in no position to judge her grandmother – who really knew anything about other people's marriages? But it was becoming more and more clear to Violet – her grandmother had been having an affair before she died in 1978.

At just after midnight, Violet's mobile vibrated on the bedside table. She wasn't sleeping yet, and reached for it, concerned that something might be wrong at home. But the message wasn't from her mum – it was from Cal.

You asleep, mermaid girl?

She lay in the dark, reading and re-reading his words. No. Not yet. You? She smiled softly as she sent it.

Don't let today upset you. It won't make any difference in the grand scheme of things.

Vi sighed, finding it hard not to feel the weight of the day on her bones. Just feeling a bit rubbish about things tonight she sent.

He didn't reply for a few minutes. In fact he didn't reply at all – he tapped on her door lightly, just loud enough to hear. Violet looked down at her PJs, a bit panicked.

'Hang on,' she whisper-shouted. 'I'm coming.'

Opening her door a minute later, she found him barefoot in jeans and a T-shirt.

'Special delivery,' he said, holding something out to her. 'I made it for you to say sorry for my mother being a right real pain in the bloody arse.'

She looked down at the delicate ribbon of leather in his hand. Heather-grey, set with five tiny seashells interspersed along its length.

'Oh my God,' she whispered. 'Cal . . .' He didn't know of course. He didn't understand how spookily reminiscent this was of Monica's diary. 'It's so pretty.'

Stepping back, she opened her door a little wider. 'Come in for a while?'

He looked once behind him towards his door, and then made up his mind and followed her into her hallway.

Violet led him through to the lounge. 'Coffee?' she said. 'Or I have some brandy.'

He nodded, standing in the bay window. 'Brandy.'

She poured them a couple of good measures, and then sank down on the sofa with one leg curled underneath her. She'd pulled her hair up hastily into a band on the way to answer the door, and her black, wide-necked pineapple-print top kept sliding off her shoulder.

'Thanks,' he said, coming to sit on the sofa beside her, accepting the tumbler she held out.

The brandy scorched her throat, deep rich heat that helped calm her nerves. 'Thank you for the bracelet,' she said, looking down at it on her wrist. It really was lovely.

'It was the closest shade to violet I could find in my stock,' he said, almost bashful.

His thoughtfulness touched her. 'You don't need to

apologise for your mum,' she said. 'It's not your fault, and I didn't do myself any favours,' she sighed, regretting that growl for the hundredth time.

'I thought growling was inspired, in the circumstances,' Cal laughed softly. 'You surprised me.'

'I surprised myself,' she said, a tiny smile hovering on her lips for the first time since it happened. 'God,' she said, louder, covering her face with her hands. 'What a complete farce!'

And then, finally, she saw the lighter side. Her shoulders started to shake, and Cal looked down and pushed his hand through his hair, laughing.

'My mother called me several times afterwards,' he said. 'Ordering me to pick up my ball and come home because I'm grounded, or words to that effect.'

'And will you?'

He rolled his eyes. 'What do you think I said?'

'I think you probably tried to be diplomatic?'

Cal sighed. 'There is very little point in trying to be diplomatic with my mother,' he said. 'I've learned over the years that it's best to be direct to the point of bluntness.'

'I don't want to make things difficult for you,' she said.

He nodded. 'She *sure* wants to make things difficult for you.'

'Yeah, I got that. We did kind of play into her hands today, to be honest.'

Cal started to laugh. 'Beau's T-shirt!'

'Keris in that bloody corset!' Violet gasped, laughing with him. 'Your mum couldn't have come at a worse time if she'd tried. In fact, I blame you. You told me she's always exactly on time. I wouldn't have let Keris out in that corset if I'd thought your mum might materialise early.'

Cal tried not to smile. 'Especially with you and Keris being raging lesbians now, too.'

Vi covered her cheeks with her fingertips. 'Melvin and Linda really didn't help the situation, did they.'

'Life certainly isn't dull in Swallow Beach since you arrived,' he said.

She twisted her bracelet around on her wrist, studying the shells. She couldn't believe she'd only been in Swallow Beach for five weeks, it felt like far longer. 'I didn't anticipate my arrival would make such headline news.'

'Oh, you'll be headline news in the local *Chronicle* this week, all right. On the front page in a fetish cage, I should think.'

A sudden thought occurred to Violet. 'God, I really hope my family don't get wind of this.'

He drank deeply from his brandy glass, contemplative. 'And your sometime boyfriend? What will he make of things?'

Violet cringed. 'Simon would be absolutely mortified if he knew. In fact I think he'd back your mum's compulsory purchase order just to preserve my modesty.' She reached for her brandy on the table and sipped it. 'Simon's not my sometime boyfriend. It was over before I came here. For me, anyway.'

Cal reached out and touched his finger against the leather ribbon around her wrist. 'It suits you.'

'I really love it,' she said, and she meant it.

His fingers stroked the skin of her wrist, tracing the line of the bracelet. 'I know we said we wouldn't kiss each other again, but I think I'm going to kiss you now.'

'We did say that,' she whispered, looking at his mouth and wanting it on hers. 'Shall we call it extenuating circumstances?'

He reached out and held her jaw, dragging his thumb over her lips. 'It *has* been one hell of a day.' His voice was low in his throat, his dark eyes turned on. Violet swallowed hard, a little breathless.

'Cal . . .' she said.

In reply, he slid his hand into her hair and drew her face to his, cutting off any more words with his kiss.

'Don't say anything else,' he whispered. 'And for God's sake don't say stop.'

She couldn't have if she'd tried. Her brain wasn't able to form any other words than *yes*, or *Cal*, or some kind of animalistic growl not dissimilar to the one she'd let out that morning. Maybe Gladys was right, she was feral. What was happening to her? She knew the answer to that question, Calvin Dearheart was happening to her. He was happening to her mouth, and he was making her heart beat twice the speed it should, and he was pressing her back against the sofa cushions with the weight of his body and God, it was delicious and delirious and heady.

'You're my favourite new neighbour ever,' he said, breathing fast and shallow.

'Am I your only new neighbour ever?' she half laughed, then gasped when Cal's hand slid inside the back of her top. She was braless, and his hand stroked slow and sure up her spine, moulding her body into his, shockingly close. It was a line crossed; this wasn't just kissing. It was more, and then it was a lot more when he slipped his hand around between their bodies and touched her breasts, her nipples, the warm curves and dips of her body.

Neither Simon nor anyone else had ever made her feel so quickly, intensely turned on, it was almost painful pleasure when Cal moved his tongue inside her mouth as he rolled her nipple. She arched, and his other hand moved up her back, pressing her deeper into him. They slid from talking to feeling, from thinking to wanting, from wanting to needing. She reached down and dragged her top up over her head and he did the same, then closed his eyes and groaned when their skin pressed together hot and seductive.

For a few long minutes, they made out like nineteen year olds on the backseat of a car, wondrous, gasping, hot as hell. He kissed her body, she raked his shoulders. He dipped his head and trailed his tongue across the edge of her PJ trousers, then moved back over her until she lay pinned beneath him on the sofa with her leg hooked around his thigh. There was no hiding how much he wanted her, the evidence strained against his jeans and pressed between her legs. She wanted to be naked, and she was about to tell him so when her phone started to ring on the coffee table.

CHAPTER THIRTEEN

'I need to check who it is,' she gasped, because everyone knew that late-night phone calls were often portents of bad news. Cal looked at the table, tortured, and then leaned across and grabbed Violet's phone for her. Even as he picked it up, he knew the mood had been broken, and then when he glanced at the screen and saw the name flashing up, he knew he was screwed.

Simon.

Handing it to her, he sat up and turned away from her to avoid the guilt in her eyes.

'Simon.' She said his name too softly. 'Is everything okay?'

He could tell from the way she reacted to his response that there was no emergency to deal with, and from her hushed-tone response that her ex had phoned just to hear her voice. Cal didn't blame him. Was he wooing her? Was he telling her that he couldn't live without her? Was he begging her to come home? Cal didn't want to listen, and knew she'd probably rather he wasn't here while she had this conversation. Picking up his T-shirt, he scrubbed his hands over his face and then quietly left her to it.

'I've got Friday off work,' Simon said. 'I thought I'd come and see you, make a weekend of it.'

Violet felt hideous. He couldn't have called at a worse time if he'd tried, it was as if he somehow knew what she was doing and had called to make her feel guilty. He couldn't have of course, but the guilt piled in hard regardless. She shouldn't be messing around with Cal, both because she was fresh out of a long-term relationship and because the end of her relationship with Simon had been ambiguous at best. It wasn't really fair of Simon to expect her to just drop everything and spend the weekend with him, but then in true Simon style, he'd made sure to give her enough notice. Gah.

'I've got loads of work on,' she said, trying to be diplomatic. 'Besides, I'm hoping to come back and see Mum and Dad in a couple of weeks. Shall we wait until then, have dinner or something to catch up?'

Part of her felt terrible, and the other part felt pissed off with Simon for inviting himself here. She'd been pretty clear that she wanted a break, in fact more than that. She'd been pretty clear that they'd broken up, but clearly he was sticking to the idea of her coming home at the end of summer and deciding that, actually, she wanted nothing more than to waltz up the aisle. It wasn't going to happen. She knew that even more clearly than before.

'You won't notice I'm there,' he said. 'I'll bring my laptop and can carry on with some work. I've got a new line of frozen fish to upload to the supermarket stock-ordering system anyway, that should keep me busy.'

'No,' she said, summoning up all of her courage. 'I don't

want you to come here, Simon. Please don't. I'm sorry to be so blunt, but I don't want you to come to Swallow Beach. I was honest about coming here for the summer to be on my own, and I know you said you'd wait but I don't want you to. It's not fair on either of us, Simon.'

He fell silent on the other end. 'Is it because I mentioned the fish? Because I can leave work behind for a couple of days if it bothers you that much.'

'No,' she said, exasperated, reaching for her PJ top because it felt inappropriate sitting here half naked. 'Of course it's not because of the fish.'

'So it's just me, then,' he said, forlorn, and her heart broke a little for him – because he was right. For a while he'd seemed like he could be the most important person in her life, but coming here had served only to solidify her conviction that he wasn't the right man for her forever. Maybe she'd been drawn to him because of the safety of familiarity; he reminded her of the people she loved, of her logical, practical, list-loving parents, and of her calm, steady Grandpa Henry. But she realised now that romantic love wasn't like that at all; it was illogical and impractical, tearing up lists and scattering them on the wind.

When she went back to bed after Simon had hung up, she placed Monica's diary on the pillow beside her, looking at it in the shadows, wondering if her gran had felt as churned up and disloyal as she did. Turning on the night-light, she began to read.

Before T, I'd have scoffed at the idea of being able to love two people at the same time. Yet I do, I honestly and truly do. I know it sounds self-indulgent and like a convenient mechanism to let myself off the hook, but believe me, loving them both is anything but convenient. I've turned this thing every which way in my head; wondered if maybe I couldn't have loved Henry enough to be able to let T into my heart too. Should that be the decider? I must love T more, or else I would have never allowed the affair to happen? Jesus, how pious. If I've learned anything from this it's that there is no logic to love.

Violet wasn't the only restless resident at the Lido that night. Cal sat in the armchair in his bay window, his eyes on the beach, his mind anywhere but. He was a groom on his own wedding day, in love with the brown-eyed girl in white. He was the man she'd left behind, and he was the man who had never had a chance to fall out of love with her, because she had disappeared.

He didn't wear his wedding ring any more because people asked too many questions, but that didn't mean he didn't still love his wife. To the rest of Swallow Beach, Ursula was history, someone who used to live there. To Cal, though, she was unfinished business, the woman he'd loved, the woman who for all he knew still loved him and would come home. He wasn't waiting, officially. But unofficially, even though he didn't even acknowledge it explicitly to himself, he sort of was.

On the ground floor, Barty pulled the long silk smoking jacket Keris had given him last Christmas closer around his willowy frame, the newspaper in his hand. He looked for a few moments at the old photograph of Monica on the front, then threw it on the fire and prodded it with the poker to make sure it caught.

'I think we should have a bit of a grand opening,' Violet said. She was walking arm in arm with Keris to unlock the pier. 'You know, let people come and use the pier again. Sit on the benches, look out to sea, satisfy their curiosity that it's not actually a brothel, take the wind out of Gladys's sails. The coffee machine should be installed on Friday.'

'Damage limitation?' Keris grinned. They were all waiting to see how bad the piece about the pier would be after Gladys's visit.

Violet shrugged. 'A bit. But also because I want the town to love the pier again.'

They came to a halt outside the pier gates and Vi rummaged in her bag for the keys.

'Here we go . . .' She stopped speaking, her head on one side because something was different. The usual chain and padlock was there, but also a new, shiny silver chain above it, clamped in place with a heavy-duty brass padlock.

'What the . . .?'

Reaching out, Violet gave the offending thing a good rattle but it was locked tight.

'Who the bloody hell thinks they have the right to do something like that?' she said, fury bubbling in her gut.

'If I had to guess,' Keris said, 'Gladys?'

'But she has no right, this place is mine by law,' Violet said, trying to work out what to do.

'Morning ladies.' A deep voice rumbled behind them.

'Beau,' Violet said, exasperated. 'I'm sorry about this, I can't open the gates. Someone added a new chain and padlock overnight.'

'Bizarre,' he said, peering close. 'Want me to chop it off for you?'

Of course, he'd have the tools to get it off.

'That'd be great,' Vi said, relieved to have an easy solution.

Take that, Gladys Dearheart; it'll take more than a bit of metal to slow me down for long.

'I'll need to climb over the gates and go the workshop for the tools,' he said. 'Stand back, ladies.'

Keris and Violet did as suggested, and Beau took a loping run at the gates and kind of vaulted them.

'Jesus.'

Lucy wandered up, raising her camera out of instinct and catching Beau with one leg slung over the top of the gate. He spotted her and assumed a muscle man pose, giving her a photo worth taking.

'What's going on?' she said, as the three of them stood watching Beau jog off along the pier.

Vi pointed to the new chain. 'Someone decided to make it hard for us all to go to work this morning.'

'The Lady Mayoress, by any chance?' Lucy said.

Violet and Keris both shrugged, but their identical, knowing expressions said they agreed.

'Shall we march up to the mayoral office and dump it on her desk?' Keris said.

'Probably exactly what she wants,' Vi sighed. 'I bet the photographer would just happen to be around too.'

They watched as Beau reappeared with a set of bolt-cutters and made short work of slicing the chain through from the other side. Violet shook it free and unlocked the normal padlock, pocketing the keys as she picked the offending chain and lock up off the floor.

'Come on. I'm going to go and chuck these off the end of the pier.'

'Hi,' Cal said, putting his head around her door an hour or so later.

The sight of him made her heart skip a beat as she looked up from her sewing machine.

'Hi,' she said softly, taking her foot off the pedal and pushing her hair out of her eyes.

'I heard about the chain on the gates,' he said. 'I'm sorry if my mother was responsible.'

So that was how they were going to play it, by pretending last night had never happened.

'No major harm done. Beau saved the day.'

Cal nodded, then held her gaze for a moment.

'About last night,' she said.

'Don't,' he said, cutting in. 'It was my fault.'

'It wasn't anyone's fault, it just happened,' Vi said, slightly hurt by his tone, by the way he obviously felt what happened between them was a mistake to be apologised for.

He frowned, and then he sighed, and then he nodded. 'Okay.'

And then he closed her door, leaving her staring at it and feeling as frustrated with him as she did with his bloody mother. One way or another the Dearhearts were driving her nuts.

Violet sat in the chair in the bay window of her mermaid bedroom and watched the sun come up, rose-gold fingers of light across a deep purple sky. It was Saturday morning, the day she'd invited the local community to come and see the pier for themselves. The weather forecast was for a bright May day, cakes had been baked and bought, and the new coffee machine installed and ready to dispense cup after cup of designer coffee. Who wouldn't fancy a slice of Barty's carrot cake and a stroll along the pier? He'd been a great help in spreading the word at all of his various clubs; Violet couldn't have asked for someone more practised at banging the jungle drums.

'Sorry Gladys, no rain today,' Vi murmured. She was sure the Mayoress would know all about the open day by now and had no doubt been hoping rain would blow in and spoil play. She'd been well and truly thwarted on that score; the last weekend in May promised blue skies and sunshine.

From Violet's bedroom window she could see the pier, the early morning sun slanting off the glass birdcage balanced out over the sea. At this time of morning the swallows gathered; she could just about make them out. The sight of them always touched a place in her heart; she could well imagine that Monica had drawn pleasure from them too. Much had changed in Swallow Beach since her grandmother's day, but the sight of the swallows would have been just the same. It was a comforting thought to start the day on.

'Okay, let's do this,' Keris said, trying to whip them all up into a frenzy of excitement.

It was just before eight in the morning, and the occupants of the pier were gathered bright and early in Keris's shop at the front of the birdcage, which was looking rather splendid now that she'd worked her magic. The old wooden and glass display case looked fabulous stocked with Cal's work, and Beau's cage was now inhabited by a taxidermied fox, which looked terribly avant-garde. Beau and Cal had cleverly worked together too to create a new line of leather jewellery and accessories especially for the shop: ribbon and shell bracelets and necklaces similar to the one Cal had given Violet; funky silver rings Beau had fashioned from a box of old cutlery found in the birdcage; little delicate glass and fretwork replicas of the birdcage; and belts, key rings and purses. It was a great idea – give the public something they could actually buy for themselves or as momentos and gifts.

Lucy had done her bit too, taking wonderfully atmospheric shots of the pier at dawn and sunset, of the beautiful old gates and of Swallow Beach town itself. She'd made them into prints and postcards, and Keris had used them to create a breathtaking display on one side of the shop. And to top it all off, Lola the headless showgirl stood proud in one corner, allowed a one-day pass out of Violet's studio just to add a little extra open-day pizazz.

'Coffee's good,' Beau said.

The newly installed machine was quite a hulk of a thing in chrome and green, but with a bit of coaxing it produced a cracking cappuccino and a killer espresso in cups liveried up with Swallow Beach Pier. Violet loved them a disproportionate amount for a throwaway cup; they suggested established, here to stay regardless.

The plan for the day was for everyone to be hard at work in their studios, business as usual, except with an open-door policy for visitors to wander in and see what they were up to. Barty was spending the day with them on cake duty, perched on a chair at a trestle table just outside the birdcage entrance doors. It had been his idea: an elder statesman of the community acting as the welcome committee to sweeten them up.

'And the carrot cake is rather excellent, even if I do say so myself,' Barty said, preening in his Hawaiian shirt and fedora.

'Someone's coming,' Lucy said, squinting along the pier back towards dry land.

'God, there is as well,' Violet said. 'Quick, stations everyone!'

They all scattered, leaving just Keris, Barty and Violet in the shop.

Barty put his arm around Violet. 'Curtain up, then.' He gave her shoulders a bolstering little squeeze. '*Bonne chance*, darling.'

Violet nodded, a lump in her throat as he headed outside to welcome the first of the open-day visitors. *Bonne chance*. It was the exact same phrase her Grandpa Henry had used in his letter willing her Swallow Beach Pier.

It was just after eleven in the morning, and Violet was almost drunk on delight. There had been a steady flow of visitors all morning, and none of them had seemed especially resistant to the new use of the pier. Perhaps it was because many were friends and acquaintances of Barty's from his numerous clubs; his nude drawing class were particularly appreciative. Mavis, the Rubenesque life model, went so far as to become Lucy's first booking of the day after half an hour spent lying on the chaise in the photography studio.

Violet turned over the corset she was working on, threading the scarlet ribbons methodically through the eyelets down the back as an older woman came in and walked across to Vi's worktable, her weight borne on a stick painted red and white like a barber's shop light.

'I see the rumours are true,' she said, leaning against the table, eyeing Violet keenly. 'Good God. It's as if she's come back to haunt us.'

Vi looked up and smiled, and the woman leaned in closer for a good look at her face and then backed up a little, as if she wasn't keen on what she saw.

'I don't think she'd have wanted you to come here,' she said quietly, her gaze locked on Violet's. 'Monica knew, you see, in the end. She knew that for all its beauty, this pier can be a cruel mistress.' She spread her hands to the sides, moving them up and down like weighing scales. 'It gives, it takes away.' She picked her stick up again from where she'd rested it. 'There. I consider my debt repaid.'

Startled, Violet opened her mouth to speak and then closed it again because the woman turned her back and walked away, clearly in no mind to elaborate or explain. What on earth had that been all about? Her mind raced. It was obvious that the woman had known Monica; Violet laid her work down carefully and headed to her doorway just in time to see Barty touch his hat at the woman as she passed his table on her way out.

'Who was that woman, Barty?' she asked, walking outside to stand beside him, turning her face up towards the warmth of the sunshine.

'Why?' He lifted the brim of his fedora and looked at her over the top of his sunglasses, his eyes guarded. 'Did she say something to you?'

Violet frowned. 'I think she knew my grandmother.'

Barty lowered his hat, preventing Vi from being able to read his expression. 'She's certainly old enough,' he muttered. 'Got a good ten years on me, in any case.'

Violet caught the tang of dislike on his words. 'Who is she?'

'Her name is Hortensia Deville.'

Well, there was a name Violet wasn't likely to forget. 'I got the impression she isn't very fond of the pier.'

Barty sighed. 'Possibly not. She did sell it, after all.'

CHAPTER FOURTEEN

'Really? She was the woman who sold the pier to my grandparents?'

Vi scanned the far end of the pier, wondering if it was too late to run and catch up with Hortensia Deville. But then . . . what would she say if she did? What did she actually want to know?

'She said something like the pier can be a cruel mistress. What do you think she meant by that?'

'Violet, indulge me, I'm a very old man,' Barty said, even though his Hawaiian shirt and Ray-Bans suggested otherwise. 'I strongly suggest that you put that woman well and truly out of your mind. Hortensia's always had a theatrical bent; played a bloody good Lady Macbeth in the local am-dram production in the eighties, mind you.' He paused. 'And that notwithstanding, she dabbles in the occult.'

'*What?*' Violet squeaked. 'In what way?'

'Oh I don't know.' He batted the air and Violet got the distinct impression he was being deliberately vague. Then he laid his hands on the table and pretended to shake it. 'Is there anybody there?'

Violet folded her arms, squinting against the bright sunlight. She wasn't stupid; Barty was trying very hard to make light of it, but there was something about his posture, the stiff set of his shoulders and his refusal to look her in the eye that made Violet's gut feel as if there was a python writhing slowly in there. Something wasn't quite right here, and it was obvious that Barty wasn't going to let her in on what it was.

She smiled at a couple of teenagers coming towards her, and then belatedly realised that one of them was Charlie, Lucy's son.

'Hiya,' she smiled. 'Your mum's in her studio, go on in.'

He nodded, chewing his lip as he glanced back towards the land end of the pier, his dark hair flopping in his eyes. 'There's something you should probably see back there,' he said. 'Or should I say, someone.'

Vi strained her eyes along the pier but couldn't see what he was talking about.

'Honestly, you should go and look.'

Charlie and his mate disappeared inside the birdcage. Leaving Barty at his welcome desk, she set off along the pier at a pace.

'I should have guessed,' she said, more to herself than anyone else as she stood beside the open iron gates to the pier and watched Gladys Dearheart. She'd set herself up on a red-and-blue-striped deckchair slap bang between the gates, briefcase across her knees, and she was making it her business to heckle everyone who tried to pass either side of her with a loudhailer.

Violet watched as a couple in their forties approached, her in a black and pink sundress, him in jeans and Converse.

'I see you, Meghan Montgomery!' Gladys yelled, making

the woman jump. 'And you a primary teacher as well! And don't think I don't see you trying to hide behind your wife's skirts, Alan Montgomery Junior!' The guy sighed and looked at his Converse, his arm around the woman, presumably his wife. 'What will your boss at the council offices think of you fraternising with the enemy?'

Violet leaned on the gate and sighed. As far as she knew, no one at the council other than Gladys thought ill of the pier, but it was enough to make the Montgomerys think twice. They faltered, prompting Violet to jump forward and smile.

'Please, come and look,' she said, reaching out a hand, leaving them no choice but to shake it. 'I'm Violet, and I'm so thrilled to be able to share the pier with you. Please, have a wander, feel free to enjoy it.'

'Don't be fooled, Meghan Montgomery,' Gladys yelled, making the couple pause, staring at each other. 'It's the wooden bridge to sin city!'

Violet looked up at the blue sky and counted to five in her head before smiling broadly. 'There's coffee and cake.'

'Coffee, cake and *sex*!' Gladys roared, loud enough to make the driver of a passing white van slow down and shout, 'Yes please love!' out of his open window.

Gladys shook her fist, and the Montgomerys took advantage of her momentary distraction and shot off along the pier.

'Look, Gladys,' Violet started, walking across so she didn't have to shout.

'Lady Mayoress Dearheart to you,' Gladys shouted through the loudhailer, even though there was no need.

Vi managed to refrain from rolling her eyes. 'Lady Mayoress Dearheart,' she said, through gritted teeth. 'I'm sorry about what happened when you came the other day, it was most unfortunate. We were—'

'Unfortunate for you that I caught you in flagrante, you mean.' Gladys sucked her teeth, not unlike Hannibal Lecter. 'Hussy.'

'You really don't need to speak to me with the loudhailer, I can hear you perfectly well without it,' Violet said, ever so slightly testy because Gladys was drawing a bit of a crowd now.

'I'm performing my civic duty,' Gladys shouted.

'Is that what you were doing when you illegally chained our gates together too?'

The Lady Mayoress glowered, feigning blustery innocence. 'Chained your gates? Don't put ideas in my head, harlot.'

Ideas? Violet didn't challenge her because a public slanging match was the last thing she needed, but she shot Gladys an *I'm wise to you* look that she hoped got the message across.

'I'm afraid I'm going to have to ask you to leave now,' Violet said, admirably calm given the circumstances.

Gladys cackled as if terribly amused. 'You can't make me leave. This is a public pavement.'

Violet looked down at the ground. 'You're not on the pavement. You're on my pier.'

Gladys peered over the arm of the chair, then back up at Violet, mutinous. 'By all of three inches, young lady.'

Vi crossed her arms over her chest, holding her tongue. They eyeballed each other for a good ten seconds, and then finally Gladys snarled, and half shuffled, half dragged the legs of her chair forwards until she was no longer on the wooden edge of the pier.

'Don't do it, Brian Hancox!' Gladys yelled, twisting suddenly in her chair towards an older guy who was trying to inch onto the pier without anyone noticing.

Unfortunately for Violet, Gladys clearly had a much stronger hold on Brian Hancox, because he veered back onto the promenade and walked away, rather like he'd been caught stealing flowers from someone's front garden to give to his wife.

Melvin and Linda ambled up the pier arm in arm to see what was happening. Violet smiled, glad of their friendly faces, even if they did exude a slightly eighties *Dynasty* glamour. They were probably the least busy of the occupants of the pier for open day; sex therapy wasn't really the kind of business people wanted to chat idly about.

'Look, Gladys. You're harming Cal's business as much as anyone else's by behaving like this,' Violet said, and the thunderous look it earned her from the Mayoress confirmed that she'd hit a raw nerve.

'It's not a *business*,' Gladys hissed, putting down the loud-hailer now she was talking about her own son. 'It's a hobby.'

Melvin cleared his throat. 'Actually Glad, sex aids are a very relevant part of relationships today,' he said, adjusting the knot of his tie. 'We often recommend a basic bondage kit to spice up a lacklustre bedroom routine.'

Linda lowered her Jackie O glasses and winked at Gladys, then cracked an invisible whip against Melvin's slack-clad backside. He jumped, and they both smiled broadly as if they'd demonstrated their point perfectly.

Violet stifled a laugh, and Gladys pressed her head so far back into her body that her neck disappeared.

'Closed!' Gladys yelled, back on her loudspeaker again now. 'This pier is officially closed as of this very minute, by decree of the council!' She was every inch the pantomime baddie, although her crowd refrained from booing or hissing.

'You know you can't do that, Mum.' Cal appeared, taking both Gladys and Violet by surprise.

'Now wait right there, young man,' Gladys blustered at the sight of her son, putting her briefcase and loud-hailer down to stand up and chastise him as she most likely had for most of his teenage years. As she got to her feet and planted her hands on her hips, Melvin took the opportunity to fold her deckchair up quick smart as Linda picked up the loudhailer and looked in the wrong end of it.

The smattering of people who'd stilled to watch started to clap with delight, and Gladys mistook their applause as support for her cause.

'Thank you,' she said, bowing as she swung her arm out to encompass them.

'They're clapping us, not you, daft bat,' Linda said into the megaphone, more loudly than she probably intended to, causing everyone to stare, most notably Gladys, who swung slowly round to find Melvin clutching her deckchair and Linda looking at the megaphone with surprise. She paused, taking it all in, and then looked from face to face. Melvin, Linda, Violet, and then Cal.

'I suppose you're enjoying this,' she said, her red helmet of curls quivering. Violet couldn't help but momentarily feel sorry for Gladys; she'd gone from pantomime baddie to spurned mum.

'I'm not, actually,' Cal said, low and calm as he gathered his mum's chair and loudhailer from Melvin and Linda. 'Come on. I'll carry these back for you.'

For a horrible moment it looked as if the Lady Mayoress might cry, but then she pulled in a long, deep breath, snatched up her briefcase and strode off without a word.

Cal looked at Violet.

'Sorry,' he said, shrugging even though his face suggested his mother's behaviour had got under his skin. 'I'll be back in half an hour.'

The rest of the day flew by without further incident. Barty's carrot cake was a roaring success, and the benches set along the pier were rarely ever unoccupied. The locals came, couples, families and elderly groups keen to share yesteryear memories about the pier.

Violet's heart swelled with pride whenever people spoke fondly of Monica and Henry; she might be a relatively new addition to Swallow Beach, but she wasn't a stranger to the older generation; she was Monica's granddaughter. She lost track of the number of people who exclaimed on her similarity to her grandmother, and every time it happened a tiny gossamer stitch wove Violet and Monica closer together across the years. Two artistic, impulsive brunettes with eyes almost the exact shade of the sea that surged beneath the pier they loved.

'Any dinner plans?' Cal said, as they trudged up the stairs to the top floor of the Lido. They'd finally locked up the pier just after seven thirty, and Violet was sore-faced from smiling and her feet were killing her; she'd walked for miles that day, back up and down the wooden boards of the pier.

'Bath, scrambled eggs and bed,' she said, feeling for her keys in her bag. 'Rock and roll, eh?'

Cal shrugged, looking out of the landing window towards the beach. 'Sounds like a good Saturday night to me.'

Was he being sarcastic? Violet wasn't sure. And then she was, because he looked down at her and said, 'Come to mine? I'll throw a glass of wine and a movie in with the scrambled eggs.'

She looked at her door. Silence and solitude lay beyond it, which she kind of needed after such a full-on day. She'd planned a bath, an easy dinner and an early night. But then she looked at Cal, and his dark eyes invited her for a different kind of evening, and suddenly she wasn't tired after all.

'Let me just go and grab a quick shower.' Then she sighed, because she remembered that she didn't have a shower. 'A bath, even.'

'You can use my shower if you like?' he offered, then rushed in with, 'I mean that in a totally non-pervy way, just because you don't have a shower in there.'

It was a bit of a ridiculous conversation, and they both laughed a little.

'I could bring my PJs to change into afterwards,' she said, because actually a hot shower sounded heavenly. Exotic as her grandmother's bathroom was, the tub took forever to fill and washing her hair was a nightmare with a cup in the sink. 'I've never been to a slumber party.'

'Me neither,' he grinned. 'Do I get to pick the movie?' he asked, narrowing his eyes.

'Only if you have popcorn,' she said. A TV was another of the things that her apartment lacked. This was shaping up into a pretty decent Saturday night plan.

'Okay,' he said, drawing the word out as he pulled his keys and his phone from the back pocket of his jeans.

'I'll just go and . . . you know . . . do things,' Violet said, nodding towards the door.

'No rush,' he said, casual. Light. 'Just friends having scrambled eggs.'

'And a movie,' she nodded.

He touched his fingers to his forehead, a tiny salute, then turned and headed for his door.

'Come over whenever you're ready,' he said, then disappeared inside.

Cal listened for Violet's door to close, and then opened his again and took the stairs two at a time. He needed to buy eggs and wine and popcorn.

In her own apartment, Violet picked up the mail and made a much needed cup of tea, flicking open a hand-addressed envelope as she reached for a mug. An electrician's business card fell onto the work surface, and the brief letter asked her to keep the sender in mind if she ever needed any work done. Vi folded it and slid it in the kitchen drawer with the menus and other business flyers. She admired anyone enterprising enough to run a small business and always tried to employ them where she could, hoping for cosmic karma to inch her closer to her long-held dream of providing costumes for the Moulin Rouge.

Picking up her cuppa, she wandered through to the bedroom to drink it in the armchair looking out over the bay. It seemed forever since she'd sat there just that morning watching the sun come up. It was after eight thirty in the evening now and the day was fading, the sun low and gold over the sea. It was an ever changing view; Vi wondered what it would be like in winter, tried to imagine this sun-bleached scene blanketed in snow instead. It wasn't easy; Swallow Beach seemed to be the kind of place that existed only for summertime. Or maybe it was more that Violet saw her stay there as only temporary after all, her Amish Rumspringa summer. Picking up her grandmother's diary from the small round table beside the chair, she began to read the entry from May 27th, exactly forty years previously.

CHAPTER FIFTEEN

I'm meeting T tonight. Henry has taken Della to visit his mother for the weekend – he didn't ask me to go and I didn't push it, because in truth I wanted the time alone. It's not my fault that Doris doesn't like me. I could try harder I expect, buy her some leather gloves or a hat, but I don't think anyone would ever be good enough for her darling son so I've given up.

I'm praying for the strength to say no to T, we both know it's wrong but we're powerless. It's as inevitable as the tide.

Violet sipped her tea and closed the diary, laying it in her lap with her hand resting on the cover. Her grandmother shouldn't have written this down. Had Grandpa Henry ever read it? Had he found out about the mysterious T? God, had she met him herself today on the pier? She cast her mind back over the day as best she could but it was a blur of faces and memories, no one leapt out at her as especially odd. Beyond Gladys, of course – and Hortensia Deville too, for that matter. Maybe she'd ask Cal about her, see if he could shed any light.

Gathering her things together for the most unlikely of slumber parties, she let herself out of her apartment and headed across the landing.

'Hello neighbour,' Cal said, opening the door. 'Come in.'

Vi smiled and followed him inside, glimpsing the room that used to be his workroom through the open door and pausing to exclaim how much bigger the place seemed now he'd reclaimed it as living space again. He nodded, chatting about his redecoration plans as he led her through to the living room. Vi nodded in the right places, accepting the glass of wine he poured for her and trying to feel relaxed and grown up instead of nervous and slightly hysterical. He'd changed already into old faded jeans and a T-shirt, and his hair was still slightly damp from the shower. He looked at home, barefoot with a bottle of beer in his hand.

'You go and grab a shower,' he said, when they both lapsed into silence.

'You're sure you don't mind?' she said, because it felt slightly weird now she was here.

'Honestly, go for it,' he said. 'I'll go and crack a few eggs.'

There was very little Vi could think to say to that, so she did as he'd suggested and headed for the bathroom.

Cal's place was different in every way to Violet's. Sleek lines and dark wood, white tiles and ink-blue towels, and not a gilt loo-roll holder or mermaid in sight. It was masculine, but calmingly so, quite Zen-like in comparison to Violet's glitzy glam pad. Locking the door, she stood still for a moment. It was a bit odd stripping naked in Cal's home, even if the door was bolted – she'd checked it twice to make sure.

Telling herself to just think of it like going to the communal shower block on a campsite rather than intimately as Cal's bathroom, she stepped out of her clothes and under the shower. Five minutes later, she wondered why she'd ever contemplated saying no. It was absolute bliss letting the powerful jets rain down on her skin, and joyful to wash and condition her hair without bending forwards over her grandmother's small, shell-shaped bathroom sink. She'd brought her favourite lotions and potions with her, and by the time she stepped out of the bathroom again in her PJs with a towel around her hair, she was a relaxed and rejuvenated woman.

'You have quite the PJ collection,' Cal said, glancing up from the armchair when she walked through into the lamp-lit living room. He had the newspaper spread out on his crossed knee and glass of red wine in his hand, a man at one with his surroundings. There was a jolting intimacy to the situation, him relaxing, her fresh from the shower, a couple about to eat a casual dinner and catch a movie.

It didn't escape Violet's notice that she felt strangely peaceful here with Cal; the bathroom Zen filtered all the way through his well-kept home and seemed to seep from the man himself too, tonight. Over in her own apartment she was surrounded by theatre and colour, and by memories and diaries and watchful mermaids. She loved it, but she hadn't realised until that very moment how difficult it was for her to relax amongst all of that visual and emotional noise. Here, there was quiet. Here, there was space. And here there was a man raising his eyebrows at her favourite slouch-wear, which just happened to be super-soft grey jersey-knit leggings with a matching top dotted with pale blue stars.

She'd ummed and ahhed over underwear, because who normally wears underwear with their PJs? But then, who normally wears their PJs to dinner with their neighbour? So she'd erred on the side of yes, you should most definitely wear knickers and a bra in company, especially when your PJs aren't remotely baggy and it would be glaringly obvious that your boobs were swinging free and unfettered. That would probably be seen as suggestive.

'It's not a slumber party unless you're in PJs,' she said, looking pointedly at his jeans and T-shirt.

He glanced down, and then back up. 'I don't own any pyjamas.'

Ahh!

'Oh,' she said, looking at the ceiling and trying not to imagine him sleeping naked.

'I could always . . .?' he gestured down at his outfit, half laughing.

'No,' she said, too fast and too sharp. 'You're good as you are.'

He folded the newspaper and stood up. 'I'll make some eggs.'

Violet sat at the small dining table nursing a glass of wine as she watched Cal move around his kitchen. She'd offered to help but he'd shooed her over to the table, and to give him his due he seemed perfectly at home in the kitchen. Vi was mildly surprised. He seemed more of a takeaway or dinner-out guy; she couldn't imagine him spending many nights alone in here cooking.

'Do you cook much?'

He shrugged, tipping the whisked-up eggs into the butter sizzling in the frying pan. 'Not massively. Enough to get by. Breakfast stuff mainly.'

'You mean there isn't going to be three courses?'

'Toast. Eggs. Wine. There you go, three courses.' He looked along the kitchen counter. 'Oh, and popcorn for dessert. That's four.'

'Practically gourmet,' she said.

He looked pleased with himself as he slid the toast and eggs onto the plates and carried them across.

'*Voila,*' he said, taking a seat opposite. '*Oeufs.*'

'All this and you speak French, too,' she said. 'So much talent for one man.'

He nodded gravely. '*Où est la piscine?*'

Violet swallowed her eggs, summoning any random schoolgirl French she could think of. '*Sous la table.*'

He leaned back and glanced under the table. 'The swimming pool is under the table?'

Violet pushed her glass towards him. '*Plus de vin, s'il vous plaît?*'

Cal topped her glass up. 'Do you like to swim, mermaid girl?'

Violet pushed her eggs around her plate, because the intimacy of his nickname made her stomach flip. 'Yes. I love the water. I just don't get to go much these days.'

'Me too.'

They cleared their plates, both hungry after their long day.

'So, what kind of movie do you fancy?' she asked, laying her cutlery down. 'Action? Funny? Weepie?'

He looked horrified at the idea of a weepie. 'Definitely a no-tissues-required option.' He paused, and then looked freshly mortified. 'I mean as in a tear-jerker, not, well, as in porn.'

Violet paused, and then shook her head, catching up with his teenage-boy-style mistake. Picking up the plates, she put them in the sink, grabbed the popcorn and then led the way back through to the living room.

'That was one of the weirdest movies I've ever seen,' Violet said, eating the last of the popcorn from the bowl between them on Cal's oversized leather sofa.

'*Hot Tub Time Machine* is an all-time classic,' Cal said. 'I can't believe you've never seen it before.'

Violet shook her head. 'Never even heard of it.'

'Everybody needs a bit of random comedy sci-fi in their lives every now and then,' Cal said, laughing.

Vi couldn't argue. 'Up to my arrival in Swallow Beach, my life didn't include much in the way of random in any aspect,' she said.

'And now it's one big random party?'

She looked down into her almost empty wine glass. 'Something like that.'

He looked at her levelly. They were on either end of the sofa, feet up.

'Is that a good thing or a bad thing?'

'Good, in the main, I think,' she said. 'Although it scares me most of the time.'

'Really? Life here scares you?'

She snorted. 'Have you seen where I live? Have you seen your mother blocking me at every turn? Have you seen that hulking great pier out there that I'm now solely responsible for? My life here is big, and bewildering, and it scares the pants off me ninety percent of the time.'

Cal placed his empty glass down. 'And right now? Are you scared right now?'

She sighed, relaxed by the wine and the company. 'Am I scared right now? Yes, a little bit.'

'Of me?'

She rolled her eyes. 'Yes. Of you.'

He leaned forwards. 'Come closer.'

She hesitated, then slid her wine glass onto the table and moved forwards to the middle of the sofa. To him.

'You scare me a little too,' he said, smoothing his hand over her hair. 'I'm careful who I spend time with, Violet, because I don't want to get in over my head. I'm sure you've heard all about the fact that I was married.'

His honesty and openness took Violet by surprise. 'Was?'

Cal played with her fingers, linking his own through hers, though it seemed more for distraction purposes than as a come-on. 'Was. And in truth, I still am.'

Vi nodded, finding it hard to swallow her disappointment.

'Ursula left without a trace. I thought we were forever, and she just took off without looking back when the bright lights of America beckoned.'

Violet looked down at their hands. 'You don't wear your ring.'

He shook his head, a derisory sound in his throat. 'I felt like a fool after a while. What kind of guy still wears his wedding ring several years after his wife left him?'

Heavy-hearted, Vi squeezed his fingers. 'One who still loves his wife?'

He didn't rush to deny it. 'Something like that, at the time. It's hard to end something without knowing why, or what you did wrong. We were so young, we probably shouldn't have married at all.'

'And you haven't heard from her since?'

Cal shook his head. 'Not a thing. I know she's alive and well through her brother, but that's as much information as I'm allowed. It's taken me a long time to get my head around it, Violet.'

'And have you?'

'I've had to learn to live with the situation. I expect one day she'll send a letter asking me for a divorce, that she'll fall in love with someone else and finally decide to cut our ties.'

It was hard to read his words, to decipher the emotion behind them. 'Do you want that too?'

He looked into Violet's eyes for a few quiet moments, and she held her breath waiting for him to answer, because it mattered.

'You know what I really want right this very second?' he said. As he spoke, he ran one fingertip over her collarbone.

He was going to kiss her and she wasn't going to stop him. She wanted it every bit as much.

'What do you want, Cal?'

The trace of a smile ghosted his lips, and that trademark Cal spark lit his eyes.

'To go skinny dipping.'

CHAPTER SIXTEEN

'I can't believe I let you talk me into this,' Violet whispered. She'd been so startled by his out-of-the-blue suggestion that she hadn't said no, and he'd taken her nervous laugh as a yes, tugging her down the stairs after shoving a couple of clean towels under his arm. They were on the beach now, in the midnight shadows of the pier, the sand cool beneath their feet.

'Ah, give over,' he said, dropping the towels down in the sand. 'Aren't you a little bit excited?'

He pulled his T-shirt over his head and grinned, his eyes and his teeth bright against the tan of his face in the darkness. The beach was deserted; Violet knew from watching it from her bedroom window that Swallow Beach was always silent in the small hours.

Was she a little bit excited, she asked herself? Or was she totally terrified? A heady mix of both, in truth.

Cal stepped out of his jeans and dropped his clothes in a heap on the sand. 'You don't have to if you've changed your mind,' he said. 'We can just go back, no harm done.'

She looked into his open expression and knew he meant

it, but she couldn't help but think he'd be a bit disappointed in her if she bottled it. And more to the point, she'd be disappointed with herself. This, this was what she'd come here for. Excitement, adrenalin, self-discovery. Was she going to discover that she really was a church mouse, that scurrying on home to her parents and Simon was actually the right path for her in the end? The thought was enough to make her pull her PJ top over her head, then gasp a little as the cool summer-evening sea air touched her skin. She'd chosen her underwear with more care than strictly necessary for a slumber party; dove-grey and nude silk, pretty but not in your face. Cal held her gaze, not looking down.

'How brave are you, mermaid girl?' he whispered, and then he stepped closer and slid his hand into her hair, kissing her; the briefest heat, the suggestion of his tongue. And then he stepped away, laughing, turned his back, dropped his shorts and made a naked dash for the sea.

Violet made a snap decision. She threw her clothes off in a hot panic, not stopping to think about the fact that she was naked as she lowered her knickers to the pile of clothes next to Cal's, and ran for the cover of the water as if her life depended on it. There was no moon, just ink darkness and ice-cold water and then Cal's hand in hers tugging her deeper in.

'Oh my God!' she gasped, her teeth chattering. She was up to waist-height already, her other arm clamped across her boobs.

'It shelves really gradually,' he said, facing her, covered from his hipbones down. Violet's eyes were adjusted enough to the darkness to be able to see the lean lines of his body, the dark hairs on his chest tapering down. She wondered if he did this often and who with.

'I grew up here, Violet,' he said, as if he'd read her mind. 'I've been in and out of this water since I was barely old enough to walk.'

She was glad of the cover of night. All of her senses were screaming, *It's cold, I'm naked, he's sexy, I'm freezing, I'm turned on, I can't believe we're doing this.*

'I don't think I want to go any deeper,' she said, hanging back when he backed out a little more.

'I won't let anything happen to you,' he said, and out of nowhere a flood of emotion filled her chest. He really shouldn't say things like that if he didn't want women to get overly attached to him.

He held his other hand out, and she had a choice to make – if she took his hand, she bared her breasts. She'd come this far; she was naked in the sea with him, and the truth was that a part of her wanted him to look at her. So, holding his gaze, she lowered her arm and put her hand in his. It felt like more than a simple physical act – symbolic, as if she was stepping out of her own shadow, finally becoming the woman she wanted to be instead of the woman everyone had always expected her to be.

'Ready to dip down?' Cal whispered.

'After three,' she murmured.

He nodded. 'One. Two. Three.'

They submersed themselves fully, and then broke back up through the surface, gasping.

'It's so cold,' Violet said, letting go of Cal's hands to wipe the seawater from her eyes. He did the same, rivulets of water coursing down his body.

'You look like Poseidon,' she said, hot on the inside even though her skin was ice-cold.

He traced his hands down from her shoulders to her

fingertips. 'My beautiful mermaid,' he said, swallowing hard, his eyes on her face, her body, her breasts.

Violet couldn't say for sure if she stepped nearer or if Cal pulled her closer, but his arm slipped around her waist and he lowered his head, kissing her sea-salt lips slowly, deliberately, his mouth a shock of hot on cold.

Pure lust slithered through Violet's bones. She wasn't cold any more. She was burning up, and when Cal's warm, sure hand covered her breast she wound her arms around his damp shoulders and pressed herself against him, loving the answering appreciative moan low in his throat. She felt unearthly, as if they were outside of usual human rules, just the two of them and the sea.

Cal's hand tracked the line of her spine, sweeping down over the fullness of her backside, and without conscious thought Violet let the buoyancy of the water lift her, catching her leg around his thigh until he held her against him. He kissed her again, harder then, his chest rising and falling heavily under hers, his hands underneath her, cupping her.

'Oh God,' she said, breaking off their kiss to bury her face in his neck because he was exploring between her legs, tender fingers, kissing her hair, saying her name as she moved over him, wrapped herself around him. She was his mermaid, and he was her man of the sea, strong, her rock to anchor herself to. And she did; her arms around his shoulders and her legs around his waist, knowing there was only one way this was going to go and wanting it to happen.

'Violet,' he said, his lips roving her hair, her eyelids, her jawline. She kissed his shoulders, tasting the salt on his skin, and then he lifted her high enough to kiss her breasts, his tongue a hot shock over her cold, hard nipples.

When he lowered her slowly down his body again, she clung closer still, her mouth on his ear.

'Don't stop now, Cal. Please don't stop.'

It was enough. He wrapped his arms around her, one hand in her hair, the other banded around her hips as he lowered her onto him, taking the sound of her gasp into his mouth when his body locked inside hers, an intimate thrust of hard heat, a rush of delicious relief that it had happened.

'Fuck.' He shuddered, holding her down on him.

Seawater shimmered on his lashes when Violet opened her eyes and looked into his, and for a moment they held perfectly still, not even breathing. If she could have pressed stop there and then, she would have, because there had never been a moment in her life when she'd felt more womanly or powerful or sensual. But then she'd have needed to press go again, and then fast-forward, and then rewind and play again in slow motion, because she wanted Cal in all of those ways; fast and then slow, and then again and again.

She might have said those things, she couldn't remember forming the words, but she heard his murmured, ragged replies, his hands all over her, the rhythm of his body moving steady and sure and then more urgent, his grip on her sexy and then fierce and almost protective when she started to shudder, her cries muffled against his shoulder. He held her, watched her, kissed her hard as she came, and she kissed him back, wild, their roles reversed as his hips jerked and his dark eyes flooded with animal, primal release.

'Jesus, Violet,' he whispered, holding her weight in his arms, his body still inside hers. It was a moment of beauty, her head on his shoulder, their eyes closed, their bodies cooled by the seawater.

'You're part of Swallow Beach forever now,' he said, his breath warm on her ear as he stroked her back.

She didn't have any adequate words; what had happened between them in the sea had felt like magic; ethereal, spellbinding. He carried her from the water to their clothes, setting her down and wrapping a towel around her shoulders. They dressed, snatching looks at each other, and when she straightened, dressed again, he reached for her hand and pulled her closer.

'No regrets?' he said, his eyes searching her face as he finger-combed her hair.

She smiled, almost shy as she turned her face into his palm. 'None. It was perfect.' She saw his throat move as he swallowed. 'How about you?'

He cupped the back of her neck and pressed a kiss against her forehead.

'It was more than I expected it to be,' he said. 'You're under my skin, mermaid girl.'

From his words, Violet couldn't discern if that was a good or a bad thing; he sounded conflicted. She knew enough of him now to understand him a little.

'Look, Cal. It was . . . well, it was unplanned, and it's happened, and it was far too lovely to say it shouldn't have happened. But you're not in over your head, and neither am I. We're neighbours, and we're friends, and what just happened out there stays out there, in the sea, in some place that isn't real.'

It cost her to say those words. It cost her to detach emotion from the physical act, but she knew it was what he needed to hear. She had her own fears and hang-ups, but he had his too and right now she was taking care of him the way he'd been taking care of her ever since she'd arrived at Swallow Beach.

He studied her face as she spoke, his fingers still in her damp hair.

'I don't think so,' he said, and then he lowered his head and kissed her, slow and sweet and full of the emotion that Violet had denied existed. 'I didn't bring you to the beach for this. I didn't plan to have sex out there, Violet, I promise, but your body and mine . . . you and me . . . I don't know what it is, what this is. I don't want to lead you on.'

His words were a plea: *Don't fall for me, because I can't fall for you.*

So that hurt. 'You're not, Cal. You're not leading me on. You've told me you have a wife, and you've told me you might even still love her. I'm not a child. I made the choice to have sex with you. I even asked you to, out there in the sea. You haven't done anything wrong; we haven't done anything wrong. We're consenting adults, and we had sex. Please let's not beat ourselves up or ignore each other for days after this, okay?'

As she spoke, Violet's mind wandered to her grandmother's diary back in the Lido, to the secrets she'd kept and the lies she'd told. If there was one thing she was going to learn from Monica, it was that secrets and lies can tear you apart from the inside.

'Let's go home,' she said, holding her hand out to him, in charge of the situation because he needed her to be.

He looked at her, and then he took her hand and kissed the back of it. 'I'm glad you came here, mermaid girl.'

Violet smiled, even as her throat thickened with tears. 'Me too.'

He slung his arm around her shoulders as they tracked up the beach, damp and tired, and they didn't speak much as they let themselves quietly into the Lido and made their way up the stairs. On the first landing, Cal snagged Violet's hand and pressed her against the wall, kissing her in a deep, languorous way that made her sigh his name against his lips.

'Come to bed with me,' he said, resting his forehead against hers. 'I don't want to let you go tonight.'

'Yes,' she said, because there wasn't a thought in her head or her body to say no. Her hand moved over his skin beneath his T-shirt as she opened her mouth under his lips, taking his kiss in, his tongue over hers, intimate and personal. She wanted him in a way she'd never wanted anyone, her heart and her body wanted him in a euphoric way that made her want to cry and laugh and come apart over and over.

They took the remaining two flights of stairs, her hand in his, her heart banging behind her ribcage.

It was only when they turned to take the final flight of stairs up to the top landing that they saw someone sitting on the top step.

Violet noticed them first and slowed, surprised, and then Cal stopped altogether, dropping her hand like a stone as the long-limbed stranger unfurled herself into a standing position. Even before anyone spoke, Violet knew.

'Hey Cal,' the woman said, all smokey eyes and bed-head blonde hair. 'Long time no see.'

Vi looked at Cal, but he didn't look back. His eyes were trained on the woman at the top of the stairs.

'Ursula.'

CHAPTER SEVENTEEN

Back in her apartment alone a few minutes later, Violet took a hot bath and then headed into her bedroom with a coffee liberally laced with brandy. What a tangled mess she'd got herself into. Cal had been like a deer in headlights out there on the landing, powerless against Ursula, all waif-like and exuding waves of charisma Marilyn Monroe would have been proud of. She'd smiled at him, and he'd looked from her to Violet, fear and turmoil in his dark eyes, and she'd known. She'd known what was going to happen next, and she didn't want to wait around to see it play out.

'I need to grab my keys,' she'd said, and he'd looked at her as if she wasn't making any sense. 'Cal. Open your door so I can get my stuff?'

He'd frowned, fishing his keys from the plant pot where he'd chucked them for safekeeping on his way out of the Lido earlier.

Ursula had laughed, said something about how she'd wished she'd known they were there, she'd have let herself in. Cal didn't come inside as Violet dashed around gathering up her belongings in her arms, clothes and shampoo and lotions, like someone grabbing things to run from a crime scene. It was a little like that; she felt seedy, fleeing the scene like a humiliated lover when the wife turns up. She hadn't looked back, closing her door and flinging all of her stuff on the hall floor in a fury of frustration and temper. She felt a fool, and she felt let down, and she felt hurt, because what had happened out there on the beach deserved better.

Propping herself up against the pillows with the soft glow of the lamp to soothe her, she picked up Monica's diary and held it over her heart as she sipped the hot, comforting coffee.

'It's this place,' she whispered, to the mermaids around the walls, to her grandmother, to herself. 'It's got a grip on me too, I can feel it pulling me under.'

Opening the diary, she began to read.

T didn't come to me last night. I waited for him in the birdcage, but he never came. He wanted to, but she needed him at home, he said when I saw him this morning. I'd moved heaven and earth to be there. I'd lied to the people I love, and he didn't show because his wife needed him more. How can he know that? How can he compare her needs with mine and deem me less important? I know the answer, of course. Because she is his wife, and I am someone else's.

Oh God, Henry. In my lowest moments I want to confess all, to throw myself at his mercy, but I can't, because what will happen then? I'm a selfish, selfish woman. I want all of the things I already have – Henry, Della, my beautiful pier, our life here in Swallow Beach. But then when I'm with T . . . I didn't mean for this to happen.

Henry is my husband, my pragmatic, kind hero who

indulges my flights of fancy. But T . . . When I'm with him I'm violently alive, punch-drunk on him. I'm as luminescent as a firefly, I'm a mermaid on the rocks, a siren calling him to me.

Tears hovered on Violet's lashes as she read the latest entry. Her grandmother was right; she *had* been selfish to allow herself to be caught up in a love affair with someone else's husband, someone other than her own husband.

She read and re-read Monica's sloping handwriting, knowing that she was reading a warning as if it had been written in advance just for her. She was punch-drunk on Calvin Dearheart. She'd felt all of those same emotions tonight out there in the sea with Cal. Luminescent, siren-like, punch-drunk on him. Her grandmother's life had spiralled out of control because of secret love and unstoppable lust, and she hadn't survived it. Right now the man Violet had had sex with in the sea a mere few hours ago was across the landing with his wife, the woman he'd already told her that he still loved.

For the first time since she'd arrived in Swallow Beach, Violet wanted to go home.

Sunday dawned grey and cool, a fitting contrast to the wall-to-wall blue of the previous day, and a fitting accompaniment to Violet's frame of mind. She'd slept fitfully and woken with a banging headache, rising at dawn to take a couple of pills and crawling back under the blankets until midday. Someone had knocked on her door just after ten – she hadn't even entertained a thought of getting out of bed to answer it. She'd just pulled the blankets over her head and curled up on her side and gone back to sleep.

At two o'clock she sat in the chair in the bay window and

watched the sea, ominous and grey today, not at all the mystical, magical place where she'd given herself to Cal. It looked threatening, swirling around the legs of the pier, throwing flotsam and jetsam up on the shore in vicious bursts. It was a place of all or nothing, of feeling like the centre of the universe and then as insignificant as a leaf on the wind, as strong as the steel girders of the pier and then as fragile as the glass roof of the birdcage pavilion.

Violet watched the beach, the occasional dog walker or jogger tracking left to right or right to left, feeling overwhelmed and a little broken by the place, and then in turn protective and attached, and then a small part of her wished she'd never even heard of Swallow Beach. It was a place that consumed people like her, people like her grandmother. She understood now why her grandfather had walked away from here so soon after Monica had died; he'd taken Della away to save her from the spell. He'd probably been terrified that he'd lose his only child to the place as well as his beloved wife. And now she saw why Della had been afraid of her only daughter coming here – she knew the power of Swallow Beach, that beauty can be smoke and mirrors, that a pretty face can hide an ugly heart.

A little after five, she pulled on her jeans and a jumper. She had no milk, and nothing for dinner beside a couple of eggs, and the thought of scrambled eggs made her kick the fridge and then apologise to the lovely old fifties-style larder. It took a couple of minutes hovering inside her front door to make sure all was quiet out there on the landing before she dared set foot outside, and then she tiptoed across to the stairs and made a run for it so as not to risk encountering Cal or Ursula.

She needn't have worried. She made it to the shops and

back without seeing anyone she knew, and prepared herself a bowl of soup and a sandwich, the kind of dinner her mum used to make her when she was a kid if she was off school ill. Lying on the sofa underneath a blanket afterwards, she dialled her mum and then cancelled the call before it connected because she knew she'd burst into tears at the sound of Della's voice. She wanted her mum in the most basic sense; she craved her comfort and familiarity. Opening her laptop to click through photographs instead, she wrapped the images of her family around herself like a metaphorical security blanket. Birthdays, Christmases, a lifetime of love. She needed to remember that she had a life before Swallow Beach, and it was still there waiting for her to finish her Rumspringa and go home again, if she wanted to. She could sell this place, the pier too, even. She could go back to her workshop in her mum and dad's garden, and back to Simon and his engagement ring.

But then wasn't it selfish of her to think that way? Maybe she was even more like her grandmother than she knew. It was a stark thought; not because she judged Monica harshly for the decisions that she'd made, but because her own life seemed to be eerily hurtling along the same tracks towards disaster. There was no pretty way to dress up the fact that she was involved with a married man. It had been pretty easy to ignore Ursula when she was just a name from the past, but now she was here, a model-esque LA kind of girl in denim cutoffs and messy hair, as if Sienna Miller had wandered in and claimed Cal as her own.

Hearing his door open an hour or so later, Violet hovered by the window to catch sight of him. She wasn't prepared for the sucker punch of seeing them together – Ursula still in those cutoffs to show off her suntanned legs, but this time sporting Cal's oversized hoodie as protection against the wind.

They weren't holding hands, but Violet watched with sickened fascination as Cal reached out a hand to steady Ursula when she stumbled, and how Ursula took the opportunity to link her arm through his afterwards as they walked away. Were they going to The Swallow? Would they trade memories and get to know each other again over lasagne and wine, would Ursula be exclaimed over and remembered and welcomed home? The thought had her turning from the window and heading for the kitchen in search of the largest glass of wine she could lay her hands on.

'There's someone here to see you, Vi.' Keris looked apologetic as she put her head around Violet's door at lunchtime on Monday. Violet had told Keris just enough for her to know that she'd appreciate solitude at work today. Cal and Beau were both out for the next couple of days at a trade show in London, a fact Violet found herself relieved by. She'd made sure not to run into Cal since Saturday night, and ignored the text he sent on Sunday asking if she was okay. She didn't ignore him to be ignorant, she just wasn't in the mood to lie and say she was fine when she wasn't.

'Who is it?'

Keris didn't have a chance to answer, because Ursula appeared behind her and pushed the door open.

'Me,' she said, wandering into Violet's studio, wearing Cal's hoodie even though the day was too warm to warrant it.

Keris shot Violet a silent look of apology, and Violet just shrugged while Ursula wandered over to get a closer look at Lola the headless showgirl.

'This stuff isn't too bad,' she said, turning to look at Violet when Keris closed the door.

Violet looked steadily at her visitor, fighting her urge to poke her eyes out. 'Is there something I can help you with?'

Ursula's eyes travelled over Vi's workbench. 'You could make me one of these, I suppose. Mates' rates, seeing as we're neighbours and all.' She perched on the end of Violet's worktable, crushing a few scarlet feathers under her white jeans. 'Something skimpy.' Her sly eyes sparked. 'Sexy.'

'I'm afraid I don't take such small commissions,' Vi said through gritted teeth, smiling even though it actually hurt her face.

'Shame,' Ursula said, careless as she played with a pile of buttons on the bench. 'I look good in red.'

'I'm sure you do,' Vi said, needled because she had no doubt Ursula looked good in every colour of the rainbow.

'I wondered if you knew what time my husband is due back from London,' Ursula said, watching her carefully.

Violet dug her nails into her palm beneath the table. There was no mistaking Ursula's tone when she called Cal 'my husband'. Territorial. Cat-like.

'I'm afraid I've no clue,' she said, and then instantly regretted adding, 'Didn't he tell you?'

Ursula looked at her, a knowing half smile on her mouth. 'We didn't have much time for talking this morning,' she said. 'You know how it is.'

What the hell was that supposed to mean? Did Ursula know about them, or was she just stabbing around in the dark to try to find out if there was anything between Violet and Cal? She must have her suspicions after seeing them together so late on Saturday night. Violet could only hope and pray that Cal had kept their fleeting romance secret from his wife. God. *His wife.* She'd had sex with this woman's husband on Saturday night. There was no way to square that with herself now that Ursula was back on the scene. It didn't matter that she'd been out of the picture at the time. She was here and real now, her cat eyes missing nothing as she watched Violet fidget in her seat.

'Right,' Vi said, non-committal, because no, she didn't know how it was to wake up next to a man like Cal.

'Cal said you're moving on at the end of the summer.'

Ouch. That one hit the target. He must have said that, because it was too specific to be guesswork.

'Possibly,' she said, shrugging in a *who knows* kind of way. 'I'm keeping my options open.'

Ursula fiddled with her hair, sliding the band from her ponytail and running her fingers through her blonde waves until she looked beach-ready – more Malibu than Swallow Beach.

'Just as long as you don't think Cal is one of your options,' she said, plain as that.

So the gloves were off.

'I don't think that's any of your business,' Violet said, earning herself a sarcastic laugh from Ursula.

'It's not my business if you've got designs on my husband?'

'You weren't here,' Vi said, overplaying her hand.

'And now I am.' Ursula held her left hand out, showing Violet the wedding band on her third finger. 'So back off, lady.'

Vi folded her arms across her chest and decided she'd had more than her fill of Ursula Dearheart.

'I'd like you to leave my pier now,' she said, keeping her voice steady.

'And I'd like you to leave Swallow Beach,' Ursula said, sliding down from the bench, scattering feathers on the floor. 'I wear his jacket, and I wear his ring, and I wear his name.'

Violet crossed to the door and opened it, staring the other woman down. Ursula was right. She held all the cards, but she'd be damned if she let her see that she'd got her on the ropes.

'I'll tell him you came by,' she said, attempting dismissive, knowing that Ursula would prefer to keep her visit between them.

'And I'll tell him you're mistaken,' Ursula said, sauntering past her, Amazonian. 'Do yourself a favour, little girl. Pack up your button box and go home.'

Much as Vi wanted to, she resisted the urge to slam the door behind Ursula. Breathing too fast, she crossed the room to the glass wall looking out over the sea, resting her head on the window pane, breathing in, breathing out, slow and steady, trying to pull herself together.

'I'm in too deep, Gran,' she whispered. 'Is this how you felt too?'

A tear slid down her cheek and she dashed it away, angry with herself for being weak enough to cry. Cal's bracelet caught her eye, still strung around her wrist, and she slid it off, feeling foolish for wearing it. Glancing at Lola, she wrapped the bracelet around the mannequin's wrist and went back to work.

CHAPTER EIGHTEEN

At just after five, someone tapped the door again, and this time Vi was relieved to see Linda's silk turban and dark glasses appear.

'Darling, I have five spare minutes for you,' she said, beckoning Violet by curling her index finger in a mildly disturbing come-hither way.

Vi resisted the urge to glance behind her in the hope that Linda was talking to someone else.

'I could really do with putting another hour in,' Vi said, nodding regretfully towards her sewing machine.

Linda waved her concerns away with a flap of her jewelled hand.

'It's time. Come now.' And then she turned and walked away on a waft of jangling bracelets and fluttering harem pants, leaving Violet with the option of being rude or doing as she was told. Sighing, she laid her work down carefully and headed over to Linda and Melvin's consulting room.

'Come in,' Linda said, throaty, when Vi tapped lightly.

Stepping inside, Vi found that she was being treated to

the full works. Linda and Melvin had brought in Chinese wooden screens to block out a lot of the natural sunlight, and fat, creamy candles filled a shallow bowl on the low table in the centre of the room. Incense was burning somewhere and low chime music emanated from a hidden speaker; it really was quite relaxing after the stress of the last few days.

Linda bowed slightly, then indicated that Vi should lie on the couch with a flourish of her arm. When Vi started to object, Linda lowered her dark glasses and gave her the eyeballs until she caved in and did as she was told. In truth, the room was inviting and she was knackered, so she didn't fight all that hard.

'There there,' Linda said, taking a seat in her counsellor's recliner on the other side of the coffee table. It seemed a strange thing to say, as if she was soothing a child, but Violet breathed in deep and closed her eyes.

'I see you're struggling, Violet,' Linda said, quiet and still, completely at odds with her usual effervescence.

Vi opened her eyes and stared at Linda, who had now taken off her dark glasses, probably because she wouldn't have been able to see a thing if she kept them on in there.

In response, Linda indicated that Vi should close her eyes again by drawing her fingertips down over her own closed lids. After taking a second to look in wonder at Linda's extraordinarily long red fingernails, Vi did as she was told and closed her eyes again.

'Violet darling, I sense romantic turmoil seething in you. It's rolling off you in bigger waves than the beach at high tide.'

This time Vi didn't open her eyes, because she knew she wouldn't be able to hide the fact that Linda was spot on.

'I'm just stressed with all of the changes in my life this summer, Linda.'

'Of course you are,' Linda said. 'You've had a lot to contend with. Take three deep breaths for me, Violet. Peace in, aggravation out. Peace in, aggravation out.'

'Peace in, aggravation out,' Vi repeated, filling her chest with air. 'Peace in, aggravation out.' She blew out a long, slow breath. 'Aggravation in, peace out.'

Linda coughed, and Violet sat up and huffed, her head in her hands.

'I can't help it, Linda,' she said. 'I'm so bloody aggravated by that woman that I want to fold her long arms and legs up into a long box and post her back to America on a slow service. She's like a bloody praying mantis.'

'Ah, now we're getting somewhere,' Linda said. 'Let it all out. This is your safe place.'

Violet found that, once she started, she couldn't stop. 'I didn't come to Swallow Beach looking for romance, Linda. I came here to find out about my grandmother, and to find myself, I suppose, in a non-hippy-clap-trap kind of way.' She bit her lip. 'No offence.'

'None taken,' Linda said smoothly, twisting her long pearls. 'I look at you Violet, with your blue-tipped hair and your eclectic style – no offence,' Linda added, and Violet opened one eye to glance down at herself. She'd made her short blue and green sundress from some left-over fabric she'd bought once for a commission of peacock corsets, and her nail polish was bright green, and her feet were bare because she preferred it for working. Was it the tiny black cat tattoo sitting on her anklebone that gave Linda the impression that she was eclectic?

'None taken,' she said.

Linda nodded. 'I look at you and I see a woman in love.'

Violet opened her eyes and stared. 'I'm not in love. I haven't known him long enough to love him, Linda, but I do feel *something* for him, and now it's over because the woman he loves has come home like a bad penny.'

'You love him.'

'Will you stop saying that?' Vi said, exasperated.

'You have to acknowledge your heart or you'll damage your valves,' Linda said, enigmatically. Violet frowned – she was fairly sure that Linda was on dodgy medical ground there.

'Trust me, I know,' Linda said. 'Melvin was in a long-term relationship with his colleague at a travel agents in Brighton when we first met. I was in the market for two weeks in the Canaries at the time. He took one look at me and gave up his lifetime twenty-percent cruise discount like it was nothing.' Linda nodded slowly, clearly of the view that that was the kind of sacrifice people made when they were in love. 'When you know, you know, and I think you know.'

'You should be a politician,' Violet grumbled. 'I don't *know that I love him*, for the record. I thought I loved my ex-boyfriend up to a few months ago, and then he proposed and I realised that actually I probably didn't. And then I've come here and Cal is all gorgeous and handsome and luring me into the sea for sex, and now I don't know if I love him, or I lust him, or if in fact I'm just on the rebound and don't anything him at all really.'

Linda's eyes bulged. 'You had sex in the sea with Calvin?' She picked up a booklet off the table and fanned herself.

Vi dropped her head into her hands. 'Don't tell a soul I told you that,' she said. 'It was before Ursula was a real person, obviously.'

Linda clicked her tongue. 'We need to send Ursula packing.'

'Is that your therapeutic advice?' Violet said. 'Because it doesn't sound very scientific.'

Linda fluttered her hands in the air. 'Love isn't a science. It's here in the air. Love particles.' She leaned forwards over the table, presumably for confidentiality purposes. 'The air around you is practically crimson, Violet.'

Vi frowned, because Linda seemed to be talking in riddles. But, more pressingly, she was in imminent danger of going up in smoke. Vi leaned forwards to bat Linda's chiffon scarf away from the candles, but she was a second too late and the fringes started to singe.

'Linda, you're on fire.'

Linda nodded, taking the compliment in her stride, unaware of the danger. 'Thank you. I just understand the mechanics of the heart, Violet. It's my gift.'

'No, Linda, you're on actual fire,' Vi said, louder, and in a panic she reached for a glass of water on the table and threw it over Linda, who gasped as if she might actually dissolve. The candles and incense spluttered out too, throwing the room into deep grey shade.

'I'm so sorry – your scarf was on fire,' Vi said by way of explanation, gesticulating at the charred tassels.

Linda's mascara slid down her cheeks, making her look like a Pierrot clown.

'It's a sign,' she whispered. 'There's a force here on this pier, Violet. I felt it the moment I first stepped on the boards, and I feel it right this very minute.'

Vi stood up, shaking droplets of water from her dress. 'I don't think I know what you mean.'

'I think you do,' Linda said, so low it was practically a growl.

'I genuinely don't,' Vi said.

Linda unwound her ruined scarf from around her neck.

'Love is like water, Violet. It finds its way through the cracks and ravines. It doesn't give up. It's just there.'

Thoroughly confused, Violet backed towards the door.

'Well, thanks for that,' she said, disjointed. 'And I'm sorry about your, er, your scarf.'

Linda lowered her glasses over her ruined eye makeup. 'Just doing my job, Violet. My hand is guided by the unseen.'

Closing Linda's door, Violet wondered if Linda's hand was guided by the unseen bottle of rum she kept stashed in her handbag.

Vi drove along the graceful sweeping road of tall, red-brick villas in Darley Terrace, squinting to make out the numbers on the doors until she spotted number twenty-four. Easing the Traveller to a stop by the kerb, she looked up at Hortensia Deville's gothic home, mildly perturbed by the intricate gargoyles peering down at her from the eaves. It wasn't the most welcoming of houses from the outside; Vi only hoped that Hortensia would be more welcoming of her unexpected visitor than her stone guardians.

The door opened as Vi walked up the garden path.

'I expected you'd come,' Hortensia said, leaning heavily on her walking stick.

Vi stepped sideways to avoid a nettle bush invading the paving stones. Hortensia's garden wasn't exactly a jungle, but it definitely erred on the side of unkempt.

'You did?'

'Crazy old lady turns up and mutters bizarre warning,' Hortensia said, walking away slowly down her hallway. 'You wouldn't be Monica Spencer's granddaughter if that didn't bring you running. Come in.'

Vi stepped inside, flicking her eyes around the mahogany-clad hallway. It was pleasant enough, in a horror-movie kind of way. Gloomy. Yesteryear. Hortensia used the end of her stick to push open a door, and seconds later they were in a small back living room lined with bookcases.

'I take it you've come for a sitting.'

Vi frowned. 'Well, no,' she said. 'I just wanted to talk to you.'

Hortensia sighed, leading Vi over to a small round table under the window.

'Come. Take a seat.'

This wasn't really going to plan. Violet had hoped that Hortensia would be surprised but not displeased to see her, and that she'd perhaps fancy a chat over tea and biscuits. Instead, Hortensia produced a bottle of gin and a cigarette in a long holder as Vi did as instructed and perched on the chair opposite her.

'You've come because you wish to talk to your grandmother,' the older woman said, pouring herself a ruinously large gin, raising disappointed eyebrows when Vi declined a glass.

'Talk to my grandmother?'

Hortensia took a slow drag on her cigarette, then blew a plume of thin smoke in the air.

'They've told you I have the sight, so you're here to see if I can summon Monica.'

'What?' Vi sighed and shook her head. 'That isn't even a little bit true. I haven't been talking about you, except to ask Barty who you were on the open day,' she said.

'That old goat,' Hortensia huffed. 'Always fancied himself as Hamlet, but he's wooden as hell; he'd have given Long John Silver's peg-leg a run for its money.'

She laughed under her breath at her own joke, then drained half of her glass and fixed her eyes on Violet.

'Your grandmother is standing behind you.'

Vi jumped violently, twisting in her seat and finding nothing behind her but a Chihuahua snoozing on an overstuffed dark rose velvet chaise.

'You're hardly going to be able to see her, are you darling? Do try to keep up.'

Vi was beginning to realise that this wasn't Hortensia's first gin of the day.

'And I'm not drunk,' she said. Reaching for her box of cigarettes, she flipped it open and held it out, looking over Vi's shoulder. 'Ciggie, Monica?'

Hortensia pulled the same disappointed face as before as she snapped the lid back down, muttering under her breath.

On the one hand, it was powerfully alluring to think that her gran might be in the room, and a big chunk of Violet wanted to believe it and ask a million questions. But on the other, Hortensia was slurring her words slightly and had her cardigan on inside out, so it was hard to cling onto the idea of her gran's ghost paying them a timely visit.

'Are you sure?' she said, adding a little smile to soften the doubt.

'Unless I'm seeing double,' Hortensia said.

That didn't seem entirely unlikely.

'She's worried about you.' Hortensia screwed her face up as she stared hard behind Vi and fiddled with her hearing aid, making it whistle. 'Wants you to choose a different path.'

Vi sighed. It was all so generic, and Hortensia had just drained her gin and refilled her glass.

'A different path? What does that mean?'

'Who knows,' Hortensia said, flicking her ash into a plant pot. 'She's telling you to check your diary. Always was too enigmatic for her own good, that girl.'

And with that, Hortensia went face down on the table, out for the count.

Vi sighed, and sat listening to the steady tick of the mantle clock. She knew it was fanciful to think her gran had ever been there, but a small part of her brain believed that she was. Hortensia had mentioned a diary after all, even if the context was wrong.

'Gran?' she said. 'Are you here?'

Quite what she'd have done if she'd received any kind of positive sign, she didn't know. She didn't of course.

Feeling foolish, she put Hortensia's cigarette out, moved the tumbler of gin out of harm's way, and let herself out of the house.

Violet was in danger of turning into a prune. She'd spent every evening that week wallowing in the bath, music loud on her phone so she couldn't hear any comings and goings out on the landing. She knew enough to know that Ursula was still staying with Cal; she'd glimpsed her blonde head coming and going on the street below. Cal had been working off site and she'd ignored his daily texts, until this morning. He'd asked if they could talk tonight, and she'd finally replied with a terse I'd really rather not in the hope of putting an end to things. Maybe it was because of Monica's diary, but she was trying to learn from her grandmother's mistakes and not let her heart be ruled by a married man.

It had been over a week since they'd hooked up but tonight at least, she had plans. It was Friday night and she had a date; a dinner date with a rather distinguished man in his eighties. She'd bumped into Barty downstairs that morning and invited him up for a bite to eat, hoping to take her mind off Cal by hearing more about her grandparents from someone who actually knew them at the time. She'd made shepherd's pie, splashed out on a decent bottle of red, and she painted a welcoming smile on her face for him when he knocked the door right on time.

It wasn't Barty.

'Cal,' she said, her heart starting to race. 'I thought you were someone else.'

His eyes moved over her, taking in the slick of mascara and lip-gloss, her skinny jeans and pretty pink and black blouse. 'Did you? Who?'

Vi looked at the floor, suddenly unwilling to confess that her effort was just for Barty. 'Does it matter?'

He sighed, then nodded and looked away towards the beach outside the landing window. 'Can we talk?'

She was glad of a genuine reason to say no. 'I can't, Cal.'

'Can't or won't?'

'Does it even matter?' she said, needled, keeping her voice low in case Ursula was in his apartment, already hating the extra layer of illicitness it added to things. 'Your wife came home, Cal. It changes things.'

'This isn't her home, she never lived here,' he said. 'Please, Violet,' he said. 'Talk to me.'

She shook her head. 'I've got nothing to say to you.'

'Well I've got plenty to say to you,' he said, quiet and urgent, glancing over his shoulder like any self-respecting unfaithful husband might.

'I don't want to hear it, Cal,' she said, making a point of glancing at her watch.

He stared at her, breathing a little too fast.

'Fine. Don't listen to me,' he said, then he stepped in to her and kissed her hard on the mouth, making her gasp, making her ache. Relief and frustration rushed through Violet's bloodstream undammed. Relief at the taste of him, frustration because he was turning her into someone she didn't want to be.

'I won't be the other woman,' she said, choked up, wanting him with every traitorous bone in her body as he backed her against the door, his hand in her hair, his mouth agonisingly gentle now as he kissed her slow and deep.

'I wouldn't let you be,' he whispered. 'Don't go out with someone else tonight.'

It was thrillingly possessive. 'You have no right to ask that of me,' she said softly.

He held her face between his hands, looking into her eyes even as they heard footsteps heading up towards the top floor.

'Don't you think I know that?'

They stared silently at each other for a few long seconds before he stepped back, pulling himself together, giving her a moment to do the same before her date arrived. Barty chose that moment to appear at the top of the stairs, clutching his chest and rolling his eyes.

'I hope you have something suitably strong in there to revive me, young woman, those stairs are enough to kill a lesser man.' He leaned on the bannister. 'If I didn't do Zumba twice a week I'd be a goner.'

Cal looked at Barty and then back at Violet. 'I'll leave you to it,' he said, something like relief in his eyes. 'Enjoy your evening.'

Vi watched him go, dully aware that she'd never felt more akin to her gran.

'Someone looks as if he's swallowed a hornet,' Barty said, following her through into the apartment. And then he paused, and laid his hand on his heart as he looked around, taking it all in.

'Just as I recall it.' He shook his head, a nostalgic beam on his face. 'You haven't changed a thing?'

Vi shook her head. 'Not yet at least. It still feels more like theirs than mine.'

'These things take time,' Barty said, patting the dining table like an old friend as he walked into the living room. 'She had fabulous taste, didn't she.'

'My grandmother?' Vi said, pulling a chair out for him and pouring him a glass of red.

Barty didn't answer straight away. His eyes had settled on the collection of framed photos on the sideboard, some with their colour faded, some black and white.

'You're so like her, it's uncanny.'

Vi placed the shepherd's pie down in the middle of the table. 'Will you tell me about her?' she asked, ladling food onto the plates. When Barty's face fell, she added, 'Please, I don't have anyone else to ask.'

She sat down and added roasted veg to their plates, picking up her cutlery.

'She was an enigma,' Barty said, looking at the photographs again. 'Full of energy and movement, like a Picasso brought to life.'

Vi considered his words, startled by the description. 'That's a lovely thing to say,' she said.

Barty lowered his gaze to his food as he loaded his fork. 'Your grandfather was chalk to her cheese. Quiet, stoic.' He ate slowly, thinking. 'What she needed probably, an anchor to stop her from floating away.'

'Were they very in love, do you think?' Vi said, desperate to hear a good account of her grandmother.

'Oh, I'm sure they must have been,' Barty said, drinking his wine. 'They had your mother, after all.'

Vi nodded. 'She won't come back here,' she said. 'My mum, I mean. She doesn't want anything to do with this place.'

Barty frowned. 'She was just a child when it happened,' he said. 'Too young to lose a mother.'

'Do you know what happened to her?' Vi said. She was finding Monica's diary more and more stressful to read, because in the back of her mind she was aware that every entry drew her nearer towards the fateful night of Monica's death.

Barty didn't reply, just laid his cutlery down and swallowed more wine.

'I mean, I know she fell from the pier and died on her birthday, but I don't know any more than that. How it happened, or why.'

For the first time since she'd known him, Barty looked his age.

'It's not my place,' he said, his hand shaking slightly.

'Please Barty. There's no one else I can ask,' Vi said. 'I found her diary,' she added, almost a whisper. 'I think she might have been having an affair.'

She reached for her wine, feeling horribly disloyal talking about Monica like that, especially in her own living room.

'Child, don't ask me any more,' Barty said. 'She isn't here to speak for herself. Some things are best left in the past.'

Violet nodded, almost relieved that Barty was old-school enough to preserve her grandmother's privacy. She craved details of Monica because she felt such a deep affinity with her on so many levels, but in another way she felt as if she was poking a stick in a hornets' nest. She was damn lucky to have inherited this place and the pier, she should just count her blessings and either settle down here or sell up and move on. But still something needled away at her, even if she couldn't quite put her finger on what it was.

'Am I like her?'

She wanted him to say yes, and she wanted him to say no. There seemed an inevitable affinity between Monica and Violet across the decades, and sometimes in the middle of the night she was scared by the knowledge that Monica hadn't survived Swallow Beach.

'In some ways, yes. In features, of course. And you have her charisma too.'

Vi half laughed. 'No one has ever called me charismatic in my whole life, Barty.'

He shrugged. 'Charisma isn't always about being the one who shouts the loudest or looks the slickest, you know,' he said. 'She had a presence, like a principal ballet dancer.'

Barty certainly painted a picture of an interesting woman.

'I wish I'd known her.'

'I'm sure she would have adored you,' he said. 'Don't judge her harshly for her choices, Violet. Your grandpa was a fine man, but if I recall correctly, a rather absent one for much of the time.'

Vi nodded, because his words echoed Monica's diary. 'Oh, I know,' she said. 'I'm not, really I'm not. It's great to hear your memories of her though, because she feels like such a big presence in my life now, which is weird when I didn't even know anything beyond her name before I came here.'

'You were brave to come here,' he said. 'It's what she would have done too.'

Vi smiled softly. 'Everyone at home thought I was crazy. Still do.'

'Maybe you are a little crazy,' he said, raising his glass to hers. 'But far better to be crazy than dull, darling. Your gran had a truly adventurous spirit.'

A sombre question hovered on Vi's lips. 'Did you go to her funeral?'

It felt important to know that Monica had a fitting farewell, hopefully a celebration of colour and vitality.

Barty's face fell. 'I didn't, my darling,' he said. 'I couldn't. There wasn't one.'

Violet sat for a long time after Barty left, a mug of coffee going cold in her hands. She was in her bedroom, curled into the armchair in the bay window as she so often was when she couldn't sleep, a blanket over her legs.

He'd elaborated a little more about the funeral, or lack of it. As far as he could remember, there had been an inquest after Monica's death, and although the people of Swallow Beach expected a funeral to follow, Henry packed up his belongings and he and his daughter had left town. Everyone had assumed that a funeral was to be held elsewhere, and of course Monica's many friends had asked to be kept informed, only to receive a very short missive via Henry's solicitor in the form of a notice attached to the pier gates. Barty couldn't remember the exact words, but it was something to the effect of Monica's funeral having taken place, a small private affair held in Shrewsbury.

How odd. Probably Grandpa Henry just couldn't face the idea of a big funeral, but it was such a shame that Monica hadn't been properly mourned and honoured. Was it evidence that her grandfather had uncovered Monica's affair? Had they argued on the day she died? The whole business felt murky and dark, as unfathomable as the pitch-dark sea out in the bay.

Closing her eyes, she made a silent promise to Monica. *I'll keep your secrets, Gran, and I'll make you proud.*

CHAPTER NINETEEN

'Violet, there's a problem and only you can solve it,' Beau said, making a beeline for her when he arrived for work the following Tuesday morning.

'Should I be nervous?' Vi said, smiling through the mouth full of pins she was using to adjust the corset laid out on her workbench.

Beau shook his shaggy head, his bright blue eyes glittering. 'Not unless the idea of hosting a gala award ceremony on the pier makes you nervous.'

Picking the pins out one by one, Vi stuck them back in the felt sunflower pincushion and put her head on one side.

'Run that one past me again?'

He came further into her studio and dropped down on her sewing chair. 'Picture it. The sun's out, the pier is laid with gorgeous tables, a dance floor here outside the birdcage . . .'

She nodded slowly. 'And all this would happen because . . .?'

He grinned. 'Because the Good Sex industry awards

board just got word that their usual venue in London has been closed down due to health and safety, and they need somewhere else at short notice. Somewhere quirky, somewhere fitting for the event.'

'The Good Sex awards? Is that really what they're called?' Vi said, distracted.

Beau threw his upturned hands out to the side. 'We have a sense of humour in our line of work. What can I say?'

'But why on earth would they want to have it here?'

'Because a certain handsome American who's up for an award suggested it?'

'You suggested it,' Vi said. 'But what about . . .'

'Imagine Cal's mother's face,' Beau said, trying to cajole her into agreeing.

'When is it?'

'The third Saturday of July.'

'That's next month! In fact, it's less than four weeks away, Beau,' she said.

'Hence the urgency,' he said, as if she'd proved his point.

'I don't think so,' she said, doubtful. 'What if . . . I don't know, what if it rains, or . . . what if people get drunk and jump naked from the pier like loons? Lady Mayoress Dearheart would have a field day.'

'Loons?' Beau laughed. 'Who cares what people think? I'll make sure no one is drunk and disorderly and I'll put an express order in for glorious sunshine.' He made it sound so easy. 'Come on, Violet. Be adventurous. Say yes.'

His choice of words pulled her up short. *Adventurous* was the exact word Barty had used to define her grandmother.

Slowly, she started to nod. 'I'm still worried about the weather,' she said. 'But go on then.'

Beau planted a big kiss on her cheek and gave her a bone-crushing bear hug. 'You're a star,' he said.

'Don't make me regret it,' she said, and he shook his head, raising his eyebrows as if to say, *What could possibly go wrong?*

Vi sighed, alone again, praying she hadn't just made a humungous mistake.

'I'm going away for a couple of weeks.'

Violet looked at Cal impassively and shrugged. 'Have a wonderful holiday.'

She'd gone to great pains to avoid being alone with him, but everyone else had already left the pier for the evening on Thursday when he came and leaned against the door-frame to her room.

'It's not like that,' he said, looking at the floor.

'You don't need to explain yourself to me.'

'I want to,' he said.

She crossed her arms. She'd caught the occasional glimpse of Ursula coming and going over the last week and had steered well clear of them both.

'Go on then.'

He fell silent, wrong-footed to be granted an audience after she'd repeatedly shut him down since Ursula's arrival.

'I want to say sorry,' he said.

'For what?'

Cal rubbed the space between his eyes as if he had a migraine, and Vi didn't rush in to help him out.

'I never expected Ursula to come back,' he said. 'Please believe that.'

'I believe you.' Violet held herself perfectly still, her chin raised. 'There, you're off the hook. Go and pack your suitcases.'

A pulse flickered in his cheek and his eyes blazed. 'I'm not trying to get off the hook. That's not fair, Violet.'

She hated that the sound of her name on his lips made her resolve tremble.

'What do you want from me, Cal? A no-hard-feelings pat on the back, a shake of hands, an agreement not to say anything to your wife?' Vi couldn't hide the sharp edge from her voice. 'Fine. Your secret's safe with me – I'm not exactly proud about what happened either, for the record.'

'I didn't say any of those things,' he said softly.

'But there's no denying that everything has changed now she's back, is there?'

He looked down, his jaw clenched. 'I didn't think she was ever coming home.'

Home. And there it was, the nub of it. Swallow Beach was Ursula's home. Keris had filled her in on the colourful history of the town, including how four generations of Ursula's family had lived there cheek by jowl with the Dearheart clan, always dueling to hold the prized mayoral office. Ursula and Cal were sons and daughters of Swallow Beach, and Violet was an interloper. She'd never felt more like a third wheel in her life, and it seethed in her gut, a hot mess of hurt and anger and frustration.

'So this is what, a second honeymoon?'

He shook his head, looking out to sea. 'Of course it fucking isn't.'

'But she's going with you?'

Cal scrubbed his hands over his face. 'I have to try, Violet. I don't know what the hell's going on, and a big part of me wishes she'd just stayed the hell away, but she's here and I have to deal with it.' He looked at her, agonised. 'I didn't want to lie to you, or lead you on.'

Shame washed red hot over her cheeks at the idea that he felt pity for her.

'Just go, Cal.'

'I—'

'Have fun,' Vi cut across him. 'Don't forget your sun cream.'

She turned her back on him and started to sort through the new delivery of feathers on her workbench, and she didn't turn back around again until she heard him leave the birdcage to go home to his wife. She'd never felt more like her grandmother, and it made her as miserable as sin.

Life didn't get any easier with Cal out of the picture. In fact, Violet's Dearheart issues went from bad to worse a couple of mornings later when, despite attempts to intervene from Keris, the Lady Mayoress steamed her way along the pier and into Violet's studio.

'Gladys,' Vi said, taking her foot off the sewing machine pedal. 'What can I help you with?'

'I have it on good authority that you're organising an orgy on the pier in three weeks. Did you honestly imagine you'd get that past me?'

'An orgy?' Vi said, nonplussed.

'I think she means Beau's awards ceremony,' Keris said, hovering by the doorway.

Ah.

'Awards ceremony my eye,' Gladys said, looking at her clipboard. '"A night of good sex",' she read, curling her lip with distaste as her voice dropped an octave, as if the words were summoned by the devil. 'That's what your advert says, bold as brass.'

'My advert?'

Gladys sucked air between her clenched teeth and smacked her clipboard down for Violet's examination.

Clipped to it was a glossy A5 flyer for the awards evening, and someone, Beau presumably, had indeed advertised a night of good sex. Great. She made a mental note to throttle the affable American with one of Cal's whips the next time she saw him.

'It's tongue in cheek, Gladys.'

'Lady Mayoress Dearheart.'

Vi refrained from rolling her eyes, just. 'It's a perfectly legitimate awards ceremony. They're using the pier as an emergency venue, that's all.'

'By *they,* you mean all manner of perverts and smut peddlers, I take it?'

'By *they,* I mean people like Cal,' Violet countered, and Keris high-fived the air behind Gladys, who was looking as if she'd swallowed a lemon.

'I'm sure you're more than well aware that Calvin's salacious sideline was just a distraction, he needed something to keep him busy while Ursula was overseas on business.'

Violet's eyes doubled in size. *Overseas on business?* Was the woman deranged?

'And now she's returned and things will get back to how they should be, you mark my words.'

Vi couldn't decide if Gladys really believed the stuff she was spouting or if it was just wishful thinking.

'And he's told you that himself, has he?' Vi hated herself for not being more dignified and keeping the question inside her head.

'As good as,' Gladys shot back. 'He's a Dearheart. He needed to sow his wild oats, and now he's ready to return and plough his furrow.'

'You've lost me,' Vi said, wondering if she was one of Cal's wild oats.

'I think the Lady Mayoress means she wants Cal

to plough Ursula's furrow,' Keris said, a wicked glint in her eye.

'Don't be so disgusting, Keris Harwood, I said no such thing,' Gladys said, pushing her glasses up her nose.

'You sort of did. And I don't think you're right, because Ursula's a horror and would make his life hell. Surely you don't want that for him?'

Vi looked between the two of them.

'I'd thank you not to speak ill of my daughter-in-law,' Gladys said, looking down her nose, but even Vi could hear the lack of conviction.

'Ah, come off it, Glad. You boycotted their wedding.'

That was news. Vi decided that she'd had enough; her fuse was growing shorter every day lately.

'Did you come for anything specific, Gladys, or just to stir trouble?'

Keris looked at Vi, wide-eyed at her uncharacteristic bluntness, and Gladys turned slowly to look at her too.

'I came to officially inform you that in light of the imminent threat to civil order,' she tapped Beau's leaflet, 'I'm filing the compulsory purchase order application with the authorities this afternoon on grounds of gross public indecency.'

'It's an awards ceremony,' Vi sighed.

'With live sex. This is Swallow Beach, not Amsterdam.'

The Lady Mayoress snatched up her clipboard and huffed out, elbowing Keris out of the way as she went. Violet didn't follow her. Gladys wasn't interested in listening to the truth; she'd spotted an angle she thought might work to turn the locals against the pier and she was going to run with it as far and as fast as she could.

'No fire-eaters. Absolutely *no* fire-eaters, Beau, I mean it.'

Beau put his hands up and laughed, clearly enjoying

winding Violet up. They were having an impromptu lunch meeting in the sunshine on the pier; Keris had just returned from a sandwich run and they were all making the most of the afternoon sunshine.

So far Beau had suggested synchronised divers off the edge of the pier, a naked contortionist and now a troupe of fire-eaters he knew from Kent. Violet knew that he was winding her up after she'd taken him to task over his flyer, but she was struggling to laugh it off because Gladys wasn't without local influence or importance.

'I'm just kidding,' Beau said. 'It'll be a classy affair, I promise.'

'Like that Tom Cruise movie,' Lucy said, unwrapping her chicken salad.

'*Cocktail*?' Violet guessed.

Lucy shook her head. 'No, the one with masks and spanking.'

'You could be the official photographer for the evening, Luce,' Beau said, offering her half of his Kit-Kat. It hadn't escaped Vi's notice that Beau and Lucy were developing quite a close friendship, and Charlie seemed to have a bit of a hero-worship thing going on for the American too. He hung out in Beau's workshop more than his mum's whenever he came by the pier after school lately, his big infectious teenage laugh carrying around the birdcage like a breath of fresh air.

'There better not be masks and spanking, I mean it Beau.'

'Chill out Vi,' he said, shoulder-bumping her. 'Cal's mother's all hot air.'

'You didn't say that when she chained the gates together,' Vi said.

'Or when she set up a one-woman picket line on open day,' Keris said, lying back on her elbows and turning her face up to the sun. 'Who needs Portugal when we have days like this one.'

It was a reference to the fact that Cal was in Portugal, with Ursula of course. They'd been there for a week now; a bolt of fury streaked through Vi's body at the thought of them rekindling their love in the sunshine. Would he make love to her in the sea? A tiny part of Vi's heart turned black at the thought of it.

Was this how it felt to be in an affair with a married man? Forever fantasising about what he was doing, if he was happy, if he and his wife were at that very moment hanging from the chandeliers. It was a deeply unsettling state to be in. Violet couldn't even imagine how much harder it had been for her grandmother with the added complication of her own marriage as well as her lover's, not to mention the fact that she had a child in the mix to think of. Vi could only imagine that T must have been one hell of a guy to be worth all of that risk.

Up on the beach they could see the day unfolding; families with young children paddling, older couples reading the paper, serious sun-worshippers grabbing a few rays. Lucy raised the camera that was always present around her neck and fired off a few shots; it looked like a quintessentially English seaside postcard.

None of them saw the lone figure watching them, the incoming danger.

CHAPTER TWENTY

There was only one funeral directors in Swallow Beach. The old doorbell chimed as Vi pushed the door open on Garland and Sons a couple of mornings later, and a short, balding guy in his thirties appeared behind the desk. He favoured her with a small smile, welcoming and suitably sympathetic, clearly an expression he'd perfected across the years.

'Can I help you?'

Vi swallowed, unsure if he could. 'I've come about my grandmother.'

'Ah,' he said. 'Has she passed away recently?'

'Well, no, not exactly,' Vi said, biting the inside of her lip. 'She died in 1978.'

'Oh,' he said, frowning, as well he might. His mind was probably racing, trying to decide if she was a crackpot. 'I'm sorry for your loss.'

'Would you guys have been here back then?' she asked.

He pulled across one of their suitably sombre leaflets and tapped the front. 'Proudly serving Swallow Beach and the surrounding area since 1906, madam.'

'Okay,' she said. 'Then you might be able to answer my question. My gran died here in the town in 1978, and I'd like to know what happened to her body.'

The guy frowned. 'Is it not on record with your family, madam?'

'There isn't really anyone I can ask,' Vi said.

It was almost the truth. She could ask Della, but she feared the reaction it might provoke. Her mum called at least twice a week for a chat, but Monica was the one subject that had quickly established itself as off limits.

'1978, the year of the winter storm,' the guy said. 'And what was your grandmother's name, please?'

'Monica,' Vi said softly. 'Her name was Monica Spencer.'

He inclined his head in a benign way and asked her to take a seat, and after some minutes returned bearing a large, dusty ledger.

'My apologies for the wait,' he said. 'The archives are in the cellar.'

Vi didn't let herself imagine what lay in the cellar of a funeral directors. It was cool in the shop despite the summer warmth outside, welcome respite in some ways, slightly disturbing in others. She watched as the guy, Stuart according to his nametag, turned the large parchment pages slowly.

'Do you know the date she died?'

Vi hadn't read that far forward in the diary. 'Not precisely, but I know it was towards the end of July, beginning of August.'

He nodded, running his finger methodically down the neatly inked words, and then finally he stopped.

'Monica Spencer,' he said, reading her name aloud with an air of finality. 'Yes, here she is.' He looked up. 'What is it that you'd like to know?'

Vi picked at a loose thread on the knee of her jeans, suddenly full of nervous trepidation. 'Do you have a record of what happened to her?'

He read the ledger in silence, and then slowly raised his eyes. 'We do, madam.'

'And?' Vi held her breath.

'I'm sorry to say that her cause of death is listed here as suicide by drowning, madam.' He consulted the notes. Blood tests showed a significantly high level of alcohol.'

It came as no surprise, but even so it was starkly saddening to hear it officially.

'I expected it to say that,' she said, because Stuart looked almost as distressed as she felt. 'Does it say what happened to her body?'

He looked down again, nodding slowly. 'She was cremated.'

'Here in Swallow Beach?'

Stuart frowned, reading the entry. 'It's highly unusual. We'd normally have the mechanics of the funeral recorded here,' he said, indicating a box in the ledger. 'The cars ordered, flowers, readings. But in this case it seems the body was cremated privately.'

'What does that even mean?' Vi asked, dread rising in her stomach.

Stuart looked as if he wasn't really sure what to say. 'In basic terms, it means there wasn't a funeral as such, just a disposal of the body.'

Vi's face must have fallen, because he coughed and looked contrite. 'Forgive my speaking in such bald terms. It appears that your grandmother's cremation was conducted without fanfare,' he said, trying to frame the same information in a more palatable way.

Vi dashed a rogue tear from her cheek. 'I see,' she said, even though she didn't. 'And her ashes?'

Stuart looked relieved to move the conversation along, returning to the entry concerning Monica's death. 'Ah.'

'Ah what?' Vi said, staring at him.

'Listed as uncollected,' he said.

'No one collected my grandmother's ashes?'

He shook his head, scrutinising the book. 'I'm afraid not.'

'So they're . . .' She could hardly bring herself to ask. Did places like this hold onto uncollected ashes indefinitely? Or did they throw them out after a while, unwanted and unceremonious? It was a terrible thought.

'They'll be here in the cellar,' Stuart confirmed. 'We will have preserved them safely, madam. It's rare for remains to be unclaimed, but I'm aware of a small collection preserved in the cellar. I expect your grandmother's is one of those.'

Relief washed cool through her body. 'Thank you,' she said. 'Could you check please?'

Stuart stood up. 'Of course. If you'll excuse me for a few minutes.'

Alone in the screamingly calm reception area, Vi tried not to dwell on the fact that her poor grandmother had been disposed of so insignificantly. Why on earth had Grandpa Henry allowed it? Even if he'd discovered that Monica had been unfaithful, Vi found she was furious with him for leaving Monica here alone for all of these years.

Stuart returned after a few minutes, a black plastic container in his hands. It looked too ordinary as he placed it down, Monica's name and the date of her death recorded in typed ink on the label. A handwritten addendum had been added in faded green ink.

'Request received from next of kin to retain ashes indefinitely.'

'Is that it?' Vi whispered.

'It is,' he said, in a practised, gentle voice. 'Would you like a few minutes?'

Vi frowned. 'Well, naturally I'd like to take the ashes, please.'

He nodded. 'Of course, madam. Do you have the death certificate?'

Vi shook her head. 'Of course not.'

He looked troubled. 'But you are the next of kin?'

Again, Vi shook her head. 'Strictly speaking, my mother would be the next of kin, but she doesn't live locally.'

'Ah, in that case, and regretfully, may I add, I'm unable to release the remains to you.'

'But no one else is going to collect them,' Vi said, tearful. 'It says so right there on the label.'

'So it would seem,' Stuart said, trying to be helpful. 'Could you speak with your mother, ask her to get in touch? Or if you can provide a death certificate and proof of your relationship with the deceased, that might be enough.'

Vi looked at the black canister, forlorn. 'Could I have a few minutes alone after all?' she said.

Stuart looked unsure, as if she might do a runner with the ashes. 'Certainly,' he said, after a beat. 'Come this way.'

He led Violet through to a small, understated side-room with a low coffee table and chairs, obviously feeling more able to leave her alone somewhere she couldn't easily abscond.

'Would you like a cup of tea?' he asked, kind now.

'No, but thank you all the same,' she said. It wasn't his fault he had to follow protocol. It wasn't every day someone turned up to collect ashes forty years too late.

'Just come through to reception whenever you're ready,' he said, confident now he was back on his usual ground. 'There isn't any hurry.'

He placed the black container down on the table and bowed his head over it momentarily, then left the room with a quiet click of the door.

Alone, Violet found she didn't know what to say or do next. Should she pick it up? Reaching out, she closed her fingers around it and then faltered, drawing her hand back.

'Come on Violet,' she whispered, addressing herself in third person because she needed to be her own cheerleader. 'Barty said you're brave. Be brave now.'

Taking a deep breath, she reached for the canister for a second time, and this time she didn't pull back. She closed her fingers around it, and then something unexpected happened. She burst into tears.

'Oh Gran,' she said, wiping her eyes with her sleeve. 'This is all so hard. I wish you were here for me to talk to, I feel as if you're the only person in the world who'd understand what I'm feeling. Thank you for the apartment. It's given me a place when I didn't know where mine was, but I don't know if I belong here in the way that you did.' She pulled in a deep, shuddery breath. 'I love the pier, but it scares me. Did it scare you too?'

Far from feeling wary of the ashes now, Vi clutched the black canister to her, wrapping both arms around it and folding her body over it protectively, because this was as close as she'd ever be to Monica.

'I know about T. And I have a good idea of how awful you must have felt too, because I've somehow managed to get myself into the same position. I love a married man too, Gran.'

As her mouth formed the words, her heart began to

race. She hadn't acknowledged out loud to either herself or anyone else that she loved Cal. She'd only known him a few months. Was it too soon? Even as she asked herself the question, she knew the answer. The truth was that she'd been a little in love with Calvin Dearheart from the first moment she met him, and now, after all they'd shared, she was a whole lot in love with him. He made her laugh, and in that moment he made her cry her heart out.

Violet sobbed for her grandmother, left unclaimed here for forty years like a mislaid coat. And she cried for herself, because she'd come here to find out who she was and she'd ended up feeling more, not less confused. And most of all she cried over Cal, the man she loved and couldn't be with.

Handing the black canister back to Stuart was more difficult than she'd imagined it would be. She'd dried her eyes and tried not to look like a weepy mess before she returned to reception, but then when he held his hand out for Monica's ashes Vi clung to them, fresh tears in her eyes as she lifted the canister to her lips and pressed a kiss against the lid.

'I'll come back for you,' she whispered. 'I'll put things right.'

Violet threw her overnight bag into her beloved Morris Minor Traveller early on Friday afternoon, then paused to look out at the pier, shielding her eyes from the sun with her hand. Keris was going to lock up for her that evening so she could get on the road in the hope of stealing a march on the Friday rush-hour.

'Going somewhere?'

Vi turned and found Barty standing watching her on the promenade.

'Home,' she said.

He was dressed for Zumba, splendid in turquoise. 'Ah. I rather thought that was here now.'

She half smiled, half shrugged. 'I miss my mum, thought I'd go back and see her for the weekend.'

'But you're coming back?'

That much she was certain of, even if she didn't know for how long. 'Yes. Sunday evening.'

Barty looked relieved, touching her cheek briefly before leaving her alone.

Violet watched him stroll off towards town, his back ramrod straight. He was another part of Swallow Beach she'd miss if she decided not to stay here after the summer. In the absence of Grandpa Henry, and of her mum too while she was here, Vi had unofficially allocated him as her elder, because she'd never not had someone to defer to or lean on. *Maybe that's what this is,* she thought. *Perhaps it's time I stopped looking for someone to lean on and stood on my own two feet.*

'Mum?'

Violet called out, dropping her overnight bag on the hall floor as she let herself in. She hadn't called ahead to let her parents know she was coming, partly because she wanted it to be a surprise and a little bit because she didn't want to hear anything that prevented her trip. She badly needed to get away from Swallow Beach for a few days, to clear her head of all things pier, Lido or Dearheart related. She'd taken the risk of banking on her mum being at home, and she was heartily relieved to find herself in luck.

'Violet!'

He mum came running from the kitchen, her face wreathed in delight. Vi threw herself into her mother's arms like a five year old at the end of school, breathing in her familiar scent, clinging on until she felt fortified enough to let go again.

Setting her daughter at arm's length, Della scrutinised her face. 'Is everything okay? You look peaky.' She brushed Vi's fringe aside and laid her palm flat on her forehead to check her temperature. 'You should have called ahead, I'd have made you something special.'

Vi shrugged, feeling a stone lighter already for leaving Swallow Beach. 'Just fancied a change. It was a last-minute thing.'

Della didn't look entirely convinced but didn't press for details as she sat her daughter down at the kitchen table and made them both a cup of tea. Violet drank it all in. The comfort of the home she'd grown up in, the place and the people she knew so well. That was what was missing in Swallow Beach, she realised; history. The place was steeped in it for everyone else around her there, but Vi was very much the new girl still and felt the pressure to fit in, to be accepted – a difficult enough task for anyone, and an impossible one for a blue-haired girl the Lady Mayoress had taken a dislike to. Sitting around her mother's pine dining table, Vi felt her shoulders inch down from their perpetual spot close to her ears, and her jaw ached because it was the first time in weeks she hadn't had her teeth clenched.

'So what's *really* brought you home?' her mum asked. They'd chatted about surface issues whilst her mum made the tea; how the garden was coming on, a weekend trip Della was planning to surprise Violet's father with on their wedding anniversary, how work was progressing for Vi in her new studio.

Vi cradled her hands around her cup, looking for comfort

in its warmth, even though it was a shorts and T-shirt kind of day. She thought about attempting to brush her mum's question under the carpet, but even as she tried she knew she wasn't going to be able to.

'Oh Mum,' she said, and however much she tried, she couldn't stop her bottom lip from trembling.

Della sighed and shuffled her chair close enough to pat Violet's arm. 'Come on, out with it. What's going on?'

Vi really didn't know where to start. 'Well, things are going all right at the pier, pretty much, except for the way Gladys keeps trying to interfere,' she said, looking for positives first. 'She's having a bit of a meltdown because I've agreed that the pier can be used for an awards evening. She's telling anyone who'll listen that it's going to be an orgy.'

Della's eyes opened wide. 'Why does she think that?'

'Because she's dead set on getting her hands on the pier, and she's clutching at straws,' Vi said. 'And because she doesn't like me.'

'I'm sure that's not true,' Della said. 'Why on earth would she not like you?'

Vi huffed. 'Oh, it's a long list. She thinks the Lido is a haven for hippies and weirdos, and that my use for the pier is a step away from running a brothel, and . . .'

'And what?'

Vi looked at the ceiling. 'And she disapproves of my relationship with her son. Not that I'm having one, as such, any more.'

Della looked understandably confused. Violet had told her mum about many of the comings and goings at Swallow Beach, with the notable exception of Cal.

'What I mean is, I was sort of having a bit of a relationship with him, but then his wife came back.'

'Violet!' Della said, her voice shrill. 'You were having a relationship with a married man? No wonder his mother is livid! I'm *your* mother and I'm not impressed either! And what about poor Simon in all of this?'

Vi rubbed her temples. 'Okay, so he does have a wife. But she moved to America a few years ago, just left him out of the blue, so he was doing what anyone would do and getting on with his life. It wasn't seedy, honestly. He just didn't expect her to ever come back again.'

'But she did,' Della said, dully.

Vi nodded, resigned. 'She did, and he's taken her back, and now his mother thinks I'm some kind of scarlet woman trying to ruin her son's life and bring the town into disrepute. Or I think she does, anyway. I'm paraphrasing.'

'But it's definitely over, you and this man?'

Vi sighed and looked down at her hands. 'It was over before it began, really. Ursula came back and that was that.'

Della squeezed her daughter's hand. 'And how do you feel about that?'

'Does it matter?' Violet said.

'It does to me,' her mum said. 'Because from where I'm sitting, I'd say you're the one who's lost the most here.'

Violet didn't even pretend it wasn't true; her tears would have made a liar of her if she'd tried.

'I never wanted to be the other woman,' she said, sniffing. 'And I know it was disloyal of me to fall in love with someone else so soon after Simon.'

'Oh Violet,' Della said, on her daughter's side in a heartbeat. 'It's even worse than I thought. You love him?'

Thoroughly miserable, Violet nodded. 'And he lives in the apartment opposite mine in the Lido, and no doubt she will too soon now, so if I stay there then I'm going to be living next door to them.'

'So don't. Come home,' Della said softly.

Home. It was a funny word; when she was in Swallow Beach Violet called her parents' house home, but now she was here, home conjured up the Lido, and the beach, and Cal. What a god-awful mess.

'I can't just give up,' she said, firming up her thoughts as she went along. 'And I don't want to, Mum. I've made friends there, and I'm proud of what we're doing at the pier. I've carved out the beginnings of a life for myself at the Lido.'

Vi knew her mum would like nothing more than to have her safely back under her roof again, and it *was* blissful to come back for the respite of her mother's kitchen table, but even just being here for a little while and talking about it solidified things in her mind. She'd entrenched herself in Swallow Beach over the last few months, and while she might not have belonged to one of the town's all-hallowed established families, why should that make her feel less entitled to live there? She'd allowed herself to feel sidelined by Ursula; she saw now that what she'd actually done was run from trouble instead of facing it head on. She'd been hiding herself away in the apartment when she wasn't at work, scurrying between work and home, feeling brow-beaten and small. It wasn't brave, and it was time to flick from defence mode to attack.

'The Lido,' Della said, shaking her head and laughing softly. 'Some things never change.'

'I wish you'd come,' Vi said. 'Barty said to send you his regards.'

Della frowned. 'I don't think I remember him, Violet.'

'Are you sure? He definitely remembers you.' Vi had

mentioned Barty over the phone sometimes and just assumed her mum knew who she was talking about.

'He does?' Della's mouth twisted as she thought back. 'I was so young, Vi, it was a long time ago.'

'He lives on the ground floor of the Lido, he has done for decades.'

'What did you say his name was again?'

'Barty. Barty Harwood.'

The creases lifted from Della's brow. 'Harwood? You must mean Tolly, surely?'

Vi shook her head. 'Nope, I'm pretty sure Barty's surname is Harwood.'

Della smiled, remembering back. 'No, I mean Tolly is his first name, Tolly Harwood. Or that's what my mother always called him, I'm sure of it.'

'Tolly?' Vi put her head on one side, puzzled. 'His full name is Bartholomew, so maybe?'

Della got up from the table and pulled down an old box of photos from on top of the kitchen dresser.

'I've started to sort through things since you've been gone. No sense in ignoring it all any longer,' she said, sitting back down and leafing through the pictures and old birthday and Christmas cards with sure fingers. 'I'm sure I've seen it in here somewhere . . . Ah, here you go.'

She pulled out a yellowed, flimsy newspaper cutting and smoothed it out carefully on the table between them.

'This must be from the mid-seventies at a guess,' she said. 'There's the pier of course,' she outlined it with her finger, 'and your grandmother there by the wall, and see the man standing beside her? That's Tolly.'

Vi didn't need to study the photograph; it was the exact same image the local newspaper had pulled from the archives back in Swallow Beach just a few weeks ago.

The exact same photograph Barty had studied and categorically denied any knowledge of who the man in the photograph was.

Barty Harwood.

Tolly Harwood, to Monica.

Or more simply, just T.

CHAPTER TWENTY-ONE

Oh God. She needed to go back. Barty was T; she knew it now without a shadow of a doubt. How had she missed it when it had been staring her in the face all along? Because he'd hidden it, of course. He'd been deliberately vague, deflecting her questions. She'd allowed herself to think of it as old-fashioned chivalry towards his friends, but the truth was far more basic than that. He'd lied to her repeatedly, and it cut Violet deeply. She needed to talk to him, be the brave woman he'd said she was and ask him for the truth.

But there was something she needed to do first. Climbing from her car, she walked through the park gates to the bench she'd arranged to meet Simon on and sat down. She was early, deliberately so to give herself time to gather her thoughts. It was early on Saturday morning, grey and cool despite the fact that it was the height of summer. She watched as a father shepherded his two tiny children, pushing them on the swings, lifting them onto the slide. It was all very normal, and yet Violet found it quite emotional, remembering when her own parents had brought her here for the exact same simple pleasures, Grandpa Henry too.

'Violet.'

Simon appeared beside her, dear and familiar, and she stood up and smiled, awkward.

'You came back,' he said.

She sat back down and watched as he laid down his waterproof jacket then sat beside her, prepared for all eventualities as always.

'Just for a day or so,' she said. 'I'm going back again after this.'

His face fell. 'I thought we could have dinner tonight. I've booked a table at the Taj Star.'

Violet sighed. 'I can't have dinner with you, Simon.'

'But I've asked them for that special table in the window,' he said. She could see the look in his eyes sliding from hope to disheartenment and she hated herself afresh.

'I'm sorry Simon,' she said, reaching down into her handbag on the floor. She'd thrown her bags back into the Traveller that morning ready to make tracks – she'd loosely planned to stay with her parents for the weekend, but she was itching to get back to Swallow Beach to see Barty after her mum's revelation. 'I didn't want to lead you on, or give you the impression that I'd be coming back to marry you.'

She was fairly clear in her mind that she hadn't done that, that he'd railroaded her into accepting the situation. Even still, he looked hangdog as she placed the ring box in his hand.

'You're a lovely man, Simon, and you'll make someone a brilliant husband. She'll be a lucky lady, but I'm afraid it can never be me.'

He bunched his mouth up, horribly close to crying. 'But I don't want anyone else.'

Vi leaned in and kissed his cheek, saddened beyond words. 'I never meant to hurt you.'

She got up and walked away, feeling like a cow because she was just as desolate and heartbroken, but over a different man.

Back in Swallow Beach, Lucy and Beau walked barefoot along the damp sand at the water's edge. They'd had a leisurely lunch at The Swallow, an unofficial date because Beau sensed Lucy pull back every time he moved too close. He was okay with that; he was happy to take it as slow as she needed to, because she was the most interesting woman he'd ever met and he just wanted to be close to her on whatever terms she'd let him in.

Vi made it back to Swallow Beach just after two in the afternoon, her heart both soaring and dipping at the sight of the pier jutting out over the sea. She parked by the promenade and sat for a few minutes in the Traveller, just looking.

She'd gained many things since she'd come here, but she'd lost things too, precious things, parts of herself, and every day the scales seemed to tip further against her. She'd lain awake most of the night, tossing and turning in her childhood bedroom, trying to make sense of everything, to decide what she wanted to do. Stay in Swallow Beach because she had as much right as anyone, and she'd be damned if she'd let herself feel hounded out by the likes of Gladys and Ursula Dearheart? Or sell up and find a new corner of the country that was just hers, some place without ghosts of the past and mermaids on the walls and a man she loved but couldn't have?

She knew that a wise woman would take option B. She

couldn't go back and live with her parents, but the money from the sale of the apartment would be enough to start again someplace new. Her work was portable. It was just her heart that seemed doggedly rooted here in Swallow Beach. It was wrapped around the black fretwork spindles of the pier, and painted into the intricate scales of the mermaids' tails, and caught on Cal's coat sleeves. She wouldn't run. This place was as much hers as it was anyone else's. She was going to face up to them all – Gladys, Ursula, Barty, Cal. And first thing on Monday morning she was heading back down to the undertakers armed with both her grandmother's death certificate and her own birth certificate. She was Violet Spencer, granddaughter of Monica Spencer, and she was damn well going to give her grandmother the funeral she deserved.

'Hey you.'

Vi was half in the car and half out, reaching across the seats for the handles of her overnight bag. Straightening, she slammed the door and looked at Cal, her eyes scanning the seafront for Ursula.

'It's good to see you,' he said, his dark eyes moving over her face.

'You look well,' she said. He did; the Portuguese sun had clearly agreed with him. 'Good holiday?'

'It wasn't a holiday,' he said.

Vi couldn't have this conversation. In fact, she found she couldn't talk to him at all, it was too raw.

'I need to go,' she said, locking the Traveller and avoiding his eye. 'I'll see you at work.'

'Wait, Violet,' he said as she walked away. 'Please.'

She sighed and swung back around. 'Wait for what, Cal? For you? What do you want from me?'

He looked as if she'd slapped him. 'I thought we were friends,' he said.

'Fine,' she sighed, short with him because she couldn't be anything else without making a fool of herself. 'We're friends. There. Happy now? I'll buy you a pint if I bump into you in the pub, you can help me carry my shopping upstairs. Friends.'

'That's not what I meant and you know it,' he said, stepping forward and catching hold of her hand.

She closed her eyes for a second, trying not to feel the warmth and the strength of him, then opened her eyes and looked out to sea.

'Things have changed for both of us,' she said, and he stroked his thumb over her knuckles.

'Look at me, mermaid girl,' he said, low and intimate, and her treacherous heart twisted in her chest. 'Things haven't changed for me.'

'Really? Because from where I'm standing you're fresh off a second honeymoon with your wife,' she said, pulling her hand from his, hot anger stabbing through her veins.

He stared at her. 'Is that really what you think?'

'It's what everyone in Swallow Beach thinks,' she said, shrill, half laughing so she didn't cry. 'Cal and Ursula. You're practically Romeo and fucking Juliet.'

He flinched, and she turned on her heel and left him standing there on the seafront, marching across the road to the Lido without looking back.

Lucy let herself in through the front door just after five o'clock, sand in her shoes and the taste of Beau's kiss on her lips.

'Only me,' she called upstairs, getting no answer as usual. Heading into the kitchen, she stopped dead at the unexpected sight of a huge bunch of yellow roses on the kitchen table, instantly nauseous.

And then she started to run for the stairs, yelling out for Charlie, her legs not seeming to carry her to his room fast enough. He looked up when she hurtled through his door, pulling his EarPods out and grinning at her.

'You're back then,' he said. 'How was your not-a-date date?'

Lucy stared at him, barely able to form words because of the sheer relief that he was okay.

'The yellow roses,' she said, too fast. 'Where did they come from?'

Charlie frowned. 'What roses?'

Lucy only just made it to the bathroom before she threw up.

Vi couldn't face Barty yet. She hadn't got a clue what to say to him when she saw him next, so she'd slipped through the building quietly and let herself into her apartment, closing the door and breathing a sigh of relief to finally be alone. Going through the motions, she made a sandwich and barely touched it, and the cup of coffee she made turned her stomach so she tipped it down the sink.

Crawling into bed not much after seven, she pulled Monica's diary from the bedside drawer and opened it at the last entry she'd read. She'd almost decided not to read any more of it, but knowing who T was changed everything. She needed to know what had happened, what had been so terrible that Monica's only option had been to step off the end of the pier. Her mouth dry with the knowledge that she was drawing close to the final entries, she began to read.

Oh God, oh God, oh God. My period's late. I'm forty next week, Henry and I haven't slept together for three months, and I think I might be bloody pregnant. This can't be happening, I don't know what I'm going to do. Help me. Someone please help me.

Vi closed the diary abruptly, shocked. Had Monica fallen pregnant with Barty's child? Was that what had driven her to such desperate measures? It was heartbreaking to imagine Monica's turmoil, it erupted from the stark words on the page, her handwriting less polished than previous entries, no doubt a direct result of her panicked, scattered thoughts.

Swallow Beach had killed her grandmother. Oh, she knew that Monica could have made different choices, been faithful, put the brakes on before things went too far. But Violet had learned the hard way over the last few months that it wasn't always easy to do the right thing, or to even know what the right thing was sometimes. She'd got in over her head with Cal without even seeing it coming. Who was she to judge her grandmother for doing the same thing? Monica's every diary entry showed her conflict and turmoil; she hadn't been proud of herself, and that was a difficult way to feel about yourself over a sustained amount of time without something having to give.

'Okay, Gran,' she whispered. 'I know what I need to do now.'

The mermaids around the walls gazed at her, impassive, and Violet closed her eyes and slept, exhausted. Had she been less tired, she might have taken the time to realise that Monica wasn't the only one whose period was late.

CHAPTER TWENTY-TWO

Stuart recognised her when she returned to Garland and Sons funeral directors the following morning.

'Miss Spencer,' he said.

She pulled the paperwork her mother had supplied her with from her bag.

'I'd like to collect my grandmother's ashes please,' she said. 'Monica Spencer.'

Stuart looked down at the certificates and reached for his ledger. 'I think these are all in order,' he said, reaching for his pen.

She watched as he inscribed the ledger with the details from Monica's death certificate. Back at home, her mother had pressed it into her shaking hands, tearful as she explained that, although there had been a small ceremony for her mother in the family church, Henry had chosen to leave Monica's actual ashes in Swallow Beach because it was the place she'd loved most in the world.

Vi watched Stuart scrutinise the paperwork and then complete a detailed entry in his book, pulling out a red stamp to annotate the ashes as collected. She held her breath as he pressed the stamp into the ink and then stamped it firmly in the box, feeling a sense of relief that Monica wasn't going to spend even one more night unclaimed.

'Will you require any assistance to arrange an internment ceremony, Miss Spencer?'

Vi paused, then realised he was referring to a burial of the ashes. 'Oh, no thank you. No. I've got all of that in hand already, thank you.'

Clutching the ashes to her chest like precious cargo, she turned and left the undertakers.

When Violet arrived back at the pier half an hour later, Lucy asked if everyone on site could gather in her studio as soon as possible.

'I'm leaving,' she said. 'This morning. Now. I'm sorry to drop this on you all like this, and Vi, I'll pay three months' rent or something to give you time to re-let this place, but I have to go right now.'

'What's happened?' Violet said, frightened because it was clear from Lucy's face and demeanour that something was seriously wrong. Her usually made-up face was makeup free, and her dark curls had been hurriedly dragged back into a ponytail.

Lucy looked towards the door. 'My ex-husband has found us.' She glanced around the room from face to confused face. 'For those of you who don't know, and why would you, Ian's a violent bastard of a man, and the only reason he's come for me is to cause trouble.'

'Oh shit,' Vi murmured, worried for Lucy and Charlie.

'What do you mean, he's found you?' Keris asked, urgent. 'Has he hurt you, Luce? Because the police . . .'

'No, he hasn't. I haven't seen him, but he's made sure

I know he's here.' Lucy shuddered. 'He was in my house yesterday while I was out. He left yellow roses in my kitchen as a calling card, the only flowers he ever bought me, usually to say sorry for the last beating.'

'Christ,' Keris said.

'So what, you're just going to run away?' Beau said, clearly furious. 'Wait for him to catch up with you in the next place, then run again?'

'What else do you suggest?' Lucy said, her voice rising. 'I was foolish enough to think he'd moved on with his life, but he's not that kind of man. He's vindictive. I can only think that he found that photo of me in the local paper on the internet and tracked me down. He has to win, and I'm not going to hang around and let him get to Charlie.'

'Where is Charlie?' Vi asked.

'He's in my room,' Beau said, shaking his head. Lucy leaving was obviously news to him as much as anyone else, and Vi could see him getting more and more furious.

'I can't believe the fucker was in your house,' he said. 'You should have called me.'

Lucy looked distressed. 'And put you in danger too? While I'm here, none of you are safe. He's small-minded, vengeful. I spent enough years living in fear of him to know that he'll try to get at me through anyone he thinks I'm close to.'

'This isn't the right thing to do, Lucy,' Cal said. 'If you go, you're letting him win.'

'And if I stay, he might kill me. Or worse, Charlie.'

Vi looked at Lucy. 'And if you go, he still might. You'll be forever looking over your shoulder. You can't live like that, it's intolerable.'

'Don't you think that's how I've lived since the day I

left him?' Lucy scrubbed her hands over her face, resigned. 'Charlie was in the house when he came, Vi. When I think what could have happened to my boy . . .' She trailed off, stony-faced, determined.

Vi didn't know what to say, how to help, but she couldn't let Lucy deal with this on her own.

'No,' she said, standing up. 'Come and stay with me at the Lido for a few days, just while we think what to do.'

Beau shook his head. 'You stay with me.'

Cal looked at Beau, aware that he was renting a one-room studio. 'It makes more sense if you stay at mine,' he said, glancing back at Lucy. 'I've got more room.'

'Look, all of you, stop,' Lucy said. 'I can't involve you all like this. It's my problem, and I'm dealing with it.'

'You're our friend, Lucy,' Vi said. 'And we want to help. You don't have to handle everything on your own any more.'

'Run, and he'll run too,' Keris said.

'Stay, and I'll make sure the bastard regrets rearing his ugly head within a hundred miles of you. You'll be free of him for good,' Beau said, crossing to stand beside Lucy, almost comically tall beside her five-foot-nothing frame.

Vi watched Lucy's shoulders drop, and then she crumbled, starting to cry. Keris jumped up and ushered her over to sit between them on the chaise, and Beau hunkered down on his haunches and put his hands on her knees.

'Look at me,' he said. 'I'm practically the Hulk.'

'You don't know what he's capable of.'

'And you don't know what I'm capable of,' Beau said. 'I grew up around a man like him. I know his kind, I'm not one bit scared of him. Stay and I'll protect you.'

'We all will,' Vi said, squeezing Lucy's shoulders. 'We've all got your back.'

Slowly, Lucy nodded. 'You're the best friends I've ever had,' she said.

Beau looked up at Cal. 'Looks like you've got yourself some lodgers.'

'Have my place instead,' Keris offered. 'I'll just move into Grandpa's spare room for a while.'

And so it was set. Lucy, Charlie and Beau would move into the ground floor of the Lido, and her friends would throw a ring of steel around her until her cockroach ex-husband crawled out from beneath his rock, at which point Beau would take great pleasure in crushing him beneath his boot.

They settled into a routine of sorts over the week that followed. Lucy had told Charlie just enough for him to understand the gravity of the situation but not scare him witless, and Cal and Beau worked it out between them so one of them was always visibly present on the pier during the day. It bonded them all more tightly together in a strange way, with the exception of Melvin and Linda who were away in Arizona on a couple connection retreat – whatever that was.

On Friday morning, they held a final run-through of the plans for the Good Sex awards the following evening.

'So all you really need to do is be on hand just in case there are any logistical questions from the event management team. They'll arrive here by twelve o'clock tomorrow. They're like ninjas – trust me, by four o'clock they'll have the pier Oscar ready.'

Vi nodded. The awards hadn't really inconvenienced her at all. Beau was right about the event company – they'd been on site earlier in the week measuring up, and having met them she was rather looking forward to seeing what they were going to do. There were to be a dozen round dinner tables set out along the pier and live music, professional caterers and a compere to run the evening. Fireworks had been planned as the grand finale, a spectacular sight to round off what would hopefully be a wonderful night.

The only thing Vi had taken care of herself was hiring an electrician to come and festoon the pier with fairy lights, and she'd agreed to be on site in the birdcage just in case they needed her. Beau and Cal were both attending in their professional capacities, and the plan was for Lucy to come as Beau's plus one while Charlie hung out in the birdcage with Vi. As plans went, it was pretty watertight.

The downside for Violet of Keris decamping to her grandpa's apartment was that it had made getting Barty alone nigh on impossible. He revelled in having his granddaughter as a temporary flatmate, cooking up a storm of carrot cake to send over to the pier and planning their evenings around cinema trips, dinners and theatre outings. Keris half-heartedly complained that he was monopolising all of her time, but in that affectionate way that said she was indulging him and didn't really mind.

In truth, Violet was almost relieved. She knew she had to speak to Barty, but she had no clue how to raise the fact that she knew he'd lied to her, or even what she was going to gain by doing so. She didn't need him to confirm he was T, she knew that much already. It was more visceral than that; she needed to hear that Barty had loved her gran, that she hadn't died desolate and lonely because he'd spurned her and the baby.

Vi checked her watch. It was just after lunch; Keris would be busy front of house in the birdcage for a couple of hours yet at least. Seizing the chance, she picked up her bag and headed for the Lido.

*

'Violet, my child!' Barty's face cracked into his trademark wicked smile when he opened the door and found her there a few minutes later. 'Time for a mint tea?'

She smiled, tight and fraught, nodding. 'Sounds good.'

She hadn't actually been inside Barty's apartment up to then. It was unsurprisingly different from her own, and different from Cal's too. Simple and traditional, full of photographs and mementos from a long, colourful life. While Barty busied himself in the kitchen, Vi studied the collection of framed photos on the fireplace.

Keris was easily identifiable, white-blonde and cheeky as a child clinging to a young woman's hand, her mother presumably. Barty was easy to spot too, especially now she knew him to be the man in the newspaper image. But here she saw him as a family man, and as a husband.

'Is this your wife?' she said, looking up as Barty came in carrying two china teacups, slightly rattling on their saucers.

He put the cups down carefully and came to stand beside her. 'Yes. That's my Florence.' His voice was full of tenderness as he gazed at the black and white photograph. It was a formal wedding day pose, Barty tall and proud, his wife willowy and blonde beside him in ivory parachute silk and a clutch of dark roses.

'And this is Keris of course, with her mum.' Barty touched the image of Keris as a child.

'Your daughter,' Vi said, looking for other images of the woman and not seeing any.

'Alison,' Barty said, his voice devoid of emotion.

'Is she . . .?' It was too difficult a sentence to finish.

'Dead?' Barty said, then huffed wearily. 'No, she isn't dead. She just . . . well, she wasn't a settler. Still isn't, truth told. She left Keris with us because she couldn't handle the pressure of motherhood.'

'Do you never see her?' It seemed unimaginable to Violet to lose touch with the people you love.

'Sometimes,' Barty said, his voice gruff. 'Every now and then when she needs money or she's exhausted herself and needs to clear her head.'

He didn't say it with any trace of malice or mistrust, more heartsick resignation about a situation he was powerless to change.

Inside Vi's head, the cogs whirred as she scanned the various photos, finally coming to rest on an image of Barty cradling a tiny baby beside a Christmas tree, his daughter presumably, because it was too dated to be Keris.

'That's lovely,' she asked, keeping her tone light even as her heart grew heavier in her chest. 'When would that have been?'

A thoughtful frown creased Barty's forehead as he recalled the details. 'Alison was born in a snowstorm, the worst Swallow Beach had ever seen. She was a month early and we didn't have a prayer of making it to the hospital, so she was born right here in our bedroom on Christmas Eve.'

'In 1978?' Violet said.

Barty looked at her oddly. 'Yes. How did you know that?'

Violet held his gaze, unsure what to say next, and his expression cycled from puzzled to something else. Fear, fleetingly, and then pure despair.

'It was the same year my grandmother died,' Violet said, barely more than a whisper.

'Yes.' Barty turned and walked to his armchair, suddenly looking his age as he lowered himself down and reached for his tea. Violet did the same, perching opposite him, her hands clasped in her lap.

'I know, Barty. I know about your affair with my gran.'

His face blanched, and for a moment the air crackled with tension as he made his decision: truth, or more lies.

'Monica was utterly captivating,' he said at last, with the heaviest of sighs. 'I knew it was wrong Violet, but I couldn't help myself. There isn't an excuse in the world for what I did, it was an unforgivable sin to both Florence and Henry. He was my friend, and she my wife, yet I was consumed by your grandmother. I like to imagine that she was fond of me too,' he whispered. 'Tolly, she used to call me. I've always been Barty to everyone else, but your gran always called me Tolly.'

Barty put his cup back down again untouched, because his hand was shaking so violently that tea was spilling into the saucer. Violet sat quietly, watching him, glad he hadn't made her ask him outright.

'Florence and I had been told that we couldn't conceive, and it took an inevitable toll on our marriage. Oh, it's no excuse,' he said, his mouth downturned, shaking his head slowly. 'But Monica was as blinding as a ray of sunlight, always laughing, always with that flash of devil-may-care about her that drew me in. It went from friendship to so much more with a speed that scared us both.'

Vi nodded, knowing she was listening to the other side of the story she'd already read in her grandmother's diary.

'And then Florrie found out she was expecting, a bolt out of the blue.' He covered his hand over his mouth, haunted by his memories. 'I had to end it. We'd talked about the idea of confessing, leaving Swallow Beach for some place else. But how could I do that with a baby on the way?' He stopped to gather himself together, looking at Violet with none of the usual sparkle in his blue eyes. 'I told Monica it was over, that I had to stay here because of the baby.'

'But . . .' Vi said, and then she stopped herself. Her grandmother had obviously never told Barty about their baby. What good would it serve to add to the burden of his guilt now?

'I never saw her again,' Barty whispered. 'She died three days later, and I swear to you there isn't a single day of my life when I haven't apologised to her for what I drove her to. I lived, and she didn't, and all because of what we did.'

'Barty, don't,' Violet said, rounding the table to put her arm around his shoulders, distressed by the fact that Barty had pulled his handkerchief from his pocket to wipe his eyes. 'You didn't drive her to it. It wasn't suicide, Barty. I've read her diary and I'm sure of it.'

He lifted his kind blue eyes slowly.

'Can you be certain?'

She rubbed his shaking shoulder. 'Absolutely certain, Barty. She was upset, but she was never suicidal.'

She paused to give him time to recover himself, glad that she'd come here. He'd obviously lived with the ambiguity of Monica's death for decades; Vi felt sure that her gran wouldn't have wanted him to feel responsible for what happened to her.

'I'm sorry to have brought all this back for you.'

He patted her knee as she perched on the arm of his chair. 'It never leaves me, child. I've been a blessed man, Florence and I had many happy years when Alison was a child, and Keris has been a godsend since her gran died. I've had more than I deserved, but your grandmother will forever be my biggest regret. The last thing she said to me was to rot in hell.'

Vi rubbed his shoulder, hurting for him. Her grandmother may have been captivating and charming and the life and soul, but her diary had also revealed her devil-may-care streak too, a deep seam of selfishness that Vi had tried to ignore because she wanted to adore the woman she so resembled. And she still did, because people were flawed and complicated and made mistakes.

'No one is without fault, Barty,' she said softly. 'People mess up all the time, do and say awful things, fall in love with people they shouldn't fall in love with. My grandmother was a grown woman, she was equally responsible for what happened between you, and for the choices she made afterwards too.'

'Don't blame her, Violet,' Barty said. 'If you need to blame anyone, blame me.'

'Did Florence ever know?'

Barty shook his head. 'Blessedly not.'

Vi could only hope her Grandpa Henry had been granted the same mercy, but somehow she doubted it.

Violet checked the weather report when she woke up a little after five the following morning, relieved to see that the storm everyone was starting to talk about wasn't due to blow in until the end of the weekend. The forecast for Saturday was fine and dry; maybe Beau hadn't been kidding about putting in his order for sunshine. She was due at the pier by seven to meet the electrician who was going to rig up the fairy lights, but there was something she wanted to do first. Pulling her grandmother's diary out, she steeled herself to read the final entry.

CHAPTER TWENTY-THREE

I don't believe it. She's pregnant, and suddenly I'm surplus to requirements. After all that has happened between us, she's won anyway. I haven't told him about our baby, I wish to God that there wasn't one. I've read that gin and a hot bath can help make it go away. I've bought the gin even though I never touch the stuff, but I don't know if I can bring myself to go through with it. How has it come to this? She gets to celebrate her child, and I have to wish mine dead on my birthday?

I'm going to go to the pier and drink the bottle, hopefully I'll be able to deal with it without Henry ever needing to find out what I've done. It kills me to think of the anguish it would cause him.

As final entries, it made horrific reading. Violet closed the diary and placed it back in the drawer where she'd found it, closing it and lying back against her pillows. What an awful end to such a charismatic, talented woman, wonderful in so many ways despite her faults.

She was hugely relieved not to find any mention of

suicidal thoughts, and given all that Vi had read and learned about her grandmother over the last few months, it made far more sense to think that she'd fallen to her death accidentally because of the amount of gin she'd consumed in a misguided attempt to lose the baby. Poor, poor Monica. What a dreadful state of affairs all round.

Getting out of bed with a heavy heart, Violet headed for the shower. It was the day of the awards ceremony, the day the pier would be lit up with fairy lights and fireworks. It was somehow fitting that it fell on the fortieth anniversary of Monica's death. She'd more than paid her penance – Violet intended to let her gran go in the blaze of colour and glory she deserved.

'It looks amazing,' Keris said, standing shoulder to shoulder with Violet part way through the afternoon. True to their word, the event organisers had turned up and waved their magic wand, creating a raised stage area and podium in front of the birdcage and laying out a dozen white-clothed round tables along the pier. Crystal and silver tableware glittered in the sunshine, including tall candelabras with fresh flowers wound around their arms.

'Like a wedding,' Vi said.

'There's a business idea for you,' Keris said.

'Maybe,' Vi said, although after reading her grandmother's diary the idea of people partying on the pier filled her with fresh dread. Alcohol and the sea were a lethal combination; she'd be relieved if tonight went without incident. Was it wrong to assume that the crowd were likely to be the kind of people who liked a party because of the nature of their business? It probably was; Cal and Beau were pretty regular people. Or actually, no they weren't. Vi had endless appreciation for Beau after watching how he'd stepped up to the mark this week and appointed himself as Lucy and Charlie's protector, and Cal . . . well, he wasn't like anyone else in the world.

Lucy walked the length of the pier, firing off shots of the pier from every angle.

'Spectacular,' she grinned, throwing Violet a wink as she passed on her way back inside.

'She seems better at least,' Keris smiled.

'The Beau effect,' Vi said.

Keris nodded, slanting her eyes toward Violet. 'And you? Is anyone having a romantic effect on you lately?'

Vi looked somewhere over Keris's shoulder. 'I don't have time for romance.'

'Only a little bird in a turban and silk glasses might have mentioned something about someone getting jiggy with someone else in the sea, mentioning no names, and I wondered if you might know anything about it.'

A telltale flush shot up Vi's neck. 'What the hell happened to client confidentiality?' she hissed. 'If I'd paid any money I'd have her bloody struck off.'

'Oh my God!' Keris said, her eyes dancing. 'I thought she was pissed!'

'I don't want to talk about it,' Violet said, shutting her down. 'It's irrelevant.'

'Because?'

'Because his wife is back in town,' Violet said, flat.

Keris huffed. 'For how long? She's been here a month, she'll be off again soon enough.'

Violet's eyes sparked. 'What are you saying? That I'm supposed to wait around until he hasn't got anyone better? I'm not that woman, Keris, not then and not now.' Hot tears filled her eyes.

'Hey,' Keris said, gentle as she laid her hand on Violet's shoulder. 'I know that, okay? I didn't mean to upset you.'

Vi shook her head, annoyed with herself rather than Keris. 'I don't know what's the matter with me,' she said. 'I need to get a grip.'

'You know what you need?' Keris said, giving her shoulders a squeeze.

'A slap?'

'I can do that if you like,' Keris said. 'But I was thinking more along the lines of a glass of fizzy from the eight million bottles in the birdcage. They won't miss one, surely.'

'Maybe later, okay?' Vi said, leaning against Keris. 'If I start now I might not stop, and how's that going to look?'

Keris glanced up towards the far end of the pier. 'Oh shit,' she said. 'What's she doing here?'

Vi wiped her eyes, not wanting to give Gladys or Ursula the satisfaction of seeing her crying. But it wasn't either of those people. It was Hortensia Deville.

Hortensia saw Vi coming towards her along the pier and watched as she sat down on one of the love seats set into the iron sidings, hooking her brightly decorated walking stick over the rail.

'Miss Deville,' Vi said, painting on a smile. 'I've been hoping to see you again.'

'Have you?' the older woman said, eyeing her beadily. 'Why? I told you everything I knew when you called by.'

Vi frowned and sat down beside her on the bench, choosing not to mention the fact that Hortensia had been roaring drunk when they last met and hadn't told her anything remotely meaningful.

'I wanted to ask you what you meant when you spoke to me on our open day.'

Hortensia pursed her lips into a thin line. 'I expect they've all dismissed me as a rambling old woman, told you to take everything I say with a pinch of salt.'

Violet didn't answer, because it would be impolite to agree.

'The jungle drums will have told you that I sold the pier to your grandparents,' she said.

Vi nodded, twisting her fingers in her lap.

'And no doubt they told you why, too.'

'Actually no,' Vi said. 'I don't have any idea why you sold it.'

Hortensia stared down the length of the pier towards the birdcage. 'Enchanting, isn't it?'

'Yes. I love it,' Violet said, earning herself a sharp look.

'Henry was a fool not to sell it on, or give it back to the town when it happened. I told him, even then.'

'What, Hortensia? What did you tell him?' Vi held her breath.

'There's bad luck built into the bones of this place,' she said. 'It's a poisoned chalice.'

Vi almost laughed. 'You can't really believe that, surely?'

Hortensia didn't laugh with her. 'Your gran wasn't the first to die here, you know.'

'I didn't know that, no,' Vi said. 'But it's a pier, after all. Surely there's an inherent danger to places like this? It doesn't have to mean anything as fanciful as a curse.'

The older woman raised her eyes to the skies. 'Fanciful. Far-fetched. Fairy tales. I've heard those phrases all of my life.' She sighed, resigned. 'No one listens, even when the facts are staring them in the face. Eight people have died on this pier over the last century. Seven others, beside your gran.'

Okay, so that number was higher than Violet had expected to hear. 'Eight people have drowned here?'

Hortensia shook her head. 'Not all of them. My husband didn't drown; he died fifty-six years ago defending me from flying debris in a storm. Another had a heart failure. A child choked.'

They were horribly sad stories, but in the bright wash of afternoon sunlight, perhaps not all that sinister. Violet wasn't sure what to say; she didn't want to give Hortensia the brush-off like everyone else in the town, but she wasn't going to dwell on the idea of the pier being cursed. She looked back towards the birdcage, a hive of activity as the crew of catering staff buzzed around.

'I should probably get back to work.' She gave Hortensia an apologetic smile. 'Busy one.'

Hortensia stood carefully and Vi handed her her stick.

'Don't work yourself too hard,' Hortensia said, walking slowly towards the mainland. 'Remember what Monica said about checking your diary. You need to remember to rest in your condition.'

Violet watched her go, thinking about what she'd said, and then she stopped breathing. Literally stopped breathing for a second, holding onto the railings out of necessity rather than choice. *Check your diary.* Her mind was scrambling through dates, counting backwards, forwards, losing track because she was in a hot panic.

How had she missed this? What kind of idiot was she? She knew she was needed on site to oversee things in the birdcage, but all the same she bolted for the gates, and she didn't stop until she reached the top floor of the Lido and dragged her keys out of the back pocket of her jeans. She needed five quiet minutes alone to think.

Five minutes turned into half an hour. She was late. Her period hadn't bothered turning up, and she hadn't bothered to notice because she'd been in such a state over Cal, Ursula, Gladys, Lucy, and everything else. She'd been worrying about arranging a funeral forty years too late, and not worrying at all about the possibility of a new life unfurling inside her. How had this happened? She'd always been so careful with Simon, but she'd been here just a few scant months and her life had spiralled out of any recognition.

Except she did recognise it. Her life was following a track, one laid out in looping script in the diary in her bedside table. Vi didn't need to take a pregnancy test to confirm things; the minute Hortensia had suggested it, she'd realised it was true, as if her mind had been holding back on her until it thought she could handle it. Could she?

Vi held her head in her hands. Oh God. She was pregnant with Cal's baby. Cal, someone else's husband. And then, sitting there in the silence, Vi felt something she'd never felt before. Laying her hands over her tummy, she felt protective of the tiny, fragile bloom of life in there. She felt the first stirrings of motherhood.

At half past five, Vi stood in her bedroom staring at herself in the full-length mirror. The dress code for the awards ceremony was 'red carpet ready', and even though she wasn't attending the ceremony as a guest, she'd still made an effort to brush up. She wasn't someone who'd ever really achieve much of a suntan, but all the same the sun had given her the lightest of kisses during her summer in Swallow Beach, making her appear far more rested and glowy than she felt.

Her dress was one she'd found in her grandmother's wardrobe. She'd barely touched Monica's things in the drawers and wardrobes since she'd taken over the apartment, but the midnight-blue fifties ankle-sweeping gown was perfect for the awards ceremony and too lovely to languish unloved in the back of a cupboard. Studying herself from the front and then the side, she stepped into the only pair of heels she owned. She was too edgy to ever look like a fairytale princess, but she'd managed to wrestle her blue-tipped hair into art deco waves and pinned it back on one side with the gemstone hair comb from her grandmother's bedside drawer.

Everyone would be there tonight. She hadn't enquired whether Cal was bringing Ursula as his plus one, but she presumed as much. Even Barty was coming; he'd invited himself to help out, or hang out, in the birdcage with Keris because he hated the idea of missing out on a shindig. She'd left him with a hug yesterday; no sense in adding to his guilt and it wasn't actually any of her business what he and her gran had chosen to do forty years previously.

She'd laid her hands over her tummy countless times since her realisation earlier. She didn't know what was going to happen, it was all too new, but she already knew what *wasn't* going to happen. She wasn't going to do everything in her power to make the situation go away on its own, and she wasn't going to lie or be pushed around and diminished or frightened into drastic measures. After all, she wasn't just Monica's granddaughter. She might have featured her grandmother in looks, and she loved that she'd inherited so many of her artistic traits and her spirit of adventure, but Violet was a different woman, and this was a different age. Their paths might have been eerily aligned up to now, but Vi was determined that this was the point at which they chose different roads.

Heading into the living room, she picked up the black canister containing her gran's ashes, gave herself a good-luck nod in the mirror, then picked up her purse and set out for the pier.

CHAPTER TWENTY-FOUR

'Are you sure the pier can take this many people?' Keris said, standing beside Violet in the birdcage at quarter to eight.

'Don't even say that,' Vi said. There were over a hundred people out on the pier, a hubbub of voices, the clink of crystal and cutlery, the sound of laughter as people ate their first course, all warmed by the burnished glow of the setting evening sun. Keris looked like a Greek goddess in a one-shoulder, floor-length silver-grey sheath, and somewhere out there on the pier Lucy looked every bit as glam in pillar-box red as Beau's date-not-date. It was a good look on her; for the first time since Violet met her, she looked relaxed – the Beau effect again, no doubt.

'Have you seen Cal yet?'

Violet shook her head. 'He's probably there somewhere. I haven't really looked.'

She sensed Keris's sidelong glance and chose not to look at her. The lie was so flimsy it was see-through, but indifference was all she had. She'd looked for him, she just hadn't managed to spot him yet.

'He's at the fourth table back behind the candelabra,' Keris said.

'Who with?' Vi cursed herself silently, wishing she'd had the strength not to ask.

Keris breathed out. 'He's brought Ursula.'

Vi swallowed hard, nodding. 'Okay. Thanks.'

That was pretty categorical, then. He'd brought his wife to an event on the pier. On *her* pier. It would have been less effective if he'd slapped her face. Trying not to show how much it had wounded her, she smoothed her hands down her dress and checked over her shoulder to make sure Charlie was in eyesight. He was having a whale of a time helping out the caterers who'd set up base in his mum's studio, moving the chaise to the side to turn it into a makeshift prep kitchen for the evening.

'Shall I switch the fairy lights on yet do you think?' Vi had been looking forward to the big switch-on since the electrician had strung them all up for her that morning. She'd called the enterprising guy who'd sent her his card in the mail recently, and despite the early hour she'd asked him to come to the pier. He'd been great at helping her bring her vision to life. Lighting up Swallow Beach Pier was one of the images she'd pictured in her head ever since she'd first set eyes on it.

Keris wrinkled her nose. 'Give it a little while, you want it to make everyone go *ooh*.' She craned her neck to look outside as someone tapped the microphone outside and cleared their throat to get everyone's attention. 'Looks like the show's about to start.'

A hush fell over the gathering and Barty came through with a plate of cake in one hand and a glass of champagne in the other.

'Bloody good stuff this,' he said, raising his glass, then

balancing it on the coffee machine so he could inch the door open and listen to the goings-on outside. Vi and Keris moved either side of him, and he looked from one to the other and then smiled softly to himself, the smile of a blessed man.

Charlie joined them a little later, standing alongside Violet to watch the category for 'Artisan Metal-worker of the Year', his eyes round and his fingers crossed tight. Vi swiped away a rogue tear when a delighted Beau came up to collect his award, and spotting Charlie by the door, dashed over and pulled him through the door to high-five him, laughing.

Violet made a mental note to remember that Lucy, Beau and Charlie would never have met if it wasn't for the pier; despite Hortensia's tale of doom and gloom, in her own experience it had given more than it had taken away. So far, anyway.

The awards presenter announced a half-time break after Beau's presentation and the waiters flowed through the doors with bottles to top up everyone's wine glasses and desserts to round off everyone's appetite.

Inside the birdcage, Violet drew Barty to one side.

'There's something I need to do,' she said. 'Will you trust me, Barty, and come with me?'

He raised his eyebrows. 'Anywhere, darling.'

She reached out for his hand. 'Come with me.'

Five minutes later, she'd led Barty around the balcony that edged the birdcage, a slender strip of wood just wide enough to walk on. They held onto the filigree metal railings, and came to a standstill when they were completely out of sight of the party.

'It's lovely out here, isn't it?' she said, looking at her elderly companion.

He nodded. 'I spent many an evening out here with your grandmother. Stargazing. Talking.' He shrugged.

Vi didn't want or need him to elaborate. It was one of her favourite spots too, just the vastness of the sea ahead, no anchoring glimpse of the shore behind.

'She never had a proper funeral,' Violet said. 'I looked into it after you raised it, and her ashes were left for safe-keeping with Swallow Beach funeral directors.'

'Oh my love, I'm so sorry,' Barty said, in turmoil. Vi wasn't sure if he was talking to her now or her grandmother forty years ago. He turned frightened eyes to Violet. 'Did you find out what happened to the ashes?'

She sighed. 'I went to the undertakers, Garland and Sons?'

Barty nodded, clearly familiar with them. 'I taught Maria Garland to waltz for their wedding many moons ago.'

'Well, I saw Stuart, and he found the record of my grandmother's ashes in the 1978 ledger, and then tracked them down in their unclaimed ashes collection in the cellar.'

A look of abject misery crossed Barty's face. 'She was so close all of these years and I didn't know.'

Vi shook her head, keen to assuage his guilt. 'You couldn't have done anything. It needed to be next of kin who collected the ashes, or family at least.'

'And they're still there after all this time?'

'No,' Vi said. 'I have them now.'

'Oh,' he whispered, his hands gripping the railings.

Violet reached inside her bag and eased the black canister out carefully. 'They're here,' she said. 'I'd like to scatter them tonight, Barty. Will you do it with me?'

'Child,' he breathed, staring at the ashes as if they were pure gold. 'Wouldn't your mother wish to be here?'

Vi shook her head. 'She loved her mum, but out of respect for my Grandpa Henry she just can't bring herself to come here. She doesn't think her mum would want to leave Swallow Beach.'

Henry nodded, his usually playful eyes sombre. 'May I hold her?'

Violet's heart broke a little for him as she passed him the simple canister. He clasped it to him in both hands, and then closed his eyes and pulled in a deep, shuddering breath.

'My Monica,' he said, stepping back to lean against the birdcage for support. 'My darling girl, I'm so sorry.'

Vi gave him some privacy, taking a couple of steps away along the railings, staring out over the starlit sea. It really was the most magical spot, like standing at the end of an ocean liner out on the ocean.

After a few minutes Barty moved alongside her again.

'Tell me something about her,' she said quietly.

Barty looked at her. 'I stood here with her, many times, on almost exactly this very spot.' Vi could understand why; it was like the edge of the world, away from prying eyes. 'You look so like her tonight, you took my breath away. She would have been so terribly proud of you, darling. I am, too.'

'Thank you,' Vi said.

'But you're different too, Violet,' he said. 'You're stronger, and I think that you're wiser than she was, or than I was,' he said. 'Love makes you do irrational things sometimes.'

Violet couldn't argue there.

'She was wilful, and as spirited as a child who knew no better.' He laughed softly. 'I've seen her turn cartwheels along the length of this walkway.'

Barty nodded as Vi looked along the walkway. It was barely three feet wide and about forty foot long.

'All the way from one end to the other, laughing as she went, her dark hair tumbling around her face.'

It was such a vivid picture that it brought tears to Violet's eyes.

'We weren't allowed to be in love,' he said, his eyes on the sea. 'But I loved her all the same, and I like to think she loved me too.'

Vi laid a hand over Barty's on the railings. 'I know she did,' she said. 'I've read her diary, Barty. I wanted to get to know her better, so I read it, and the one thing that I can say for certain is that she loved you.'

Barty pulled his handkerchief out and dabbed his eyes. 'Did she hate me in the end?

Oh God, this was so hideously difficult. Violet was torn between respecting her grandfather, honouring her grandmother, and not breaking Barty's already battered heart.

'No, I don't think she hated you for even a second. She . . . she was drinking before she came here alone that night.' Barty's hand stole into hers on the rails. 'I don't think she intended to take her life at all, Barty. I think it was a horrible, tragic accident.'

Barty slumped heavily, using the rails to stay on his feet.

'I always thought it was my fault,' he said. 'My punishment.'

She put her arm around him, and after a few moments, he straightened, drying his face again.

'Thank you, Violet,' he said. 'Thank you.'

She held the canister in her hands. 'Shall we?'

He took the ashes and pressed his lips to the lid. 'I love you, Monica,' he said. 'Safe travels, my darling.'

Tears slid down Vi's cheeks as he handed the ashes back with a shaky, heartbroken smile.

'Let her go, child. It's time.'

He put an arm around her shoulders as she twisted the cap off, and that was how they stood, side by side under the starlight, as Violet upended the ashes and let them scatter towards the sea below on the warm summer breeze.

'Goodbye Gran,' Violet whispered. 'Thank you for everything.'

'Goodnight my love,' Barty said. 'You're part of Swallow Beach forever now.'

Violet replaced the lid on the empty container, not even surprised that Barty had chosen the exact same phrase as Cal. Her romance with Cal had been an echo of Monica's romance with Barty all of those years ago; unexpected, life-changing, but ultimately doomed to fail.

'Come on,' she said, linking her arm through Barty's. 'People will be wondering where we've got to.'

They walked slowly back towards the party, leaving Monica Spencer's spirit free to turn cartwheels, laughing, her dark hair tumbling around her face.

At the same time as Violet and Barty were scattering Monica's ashes into the sea, the final scenes of Cal and Ursula's marriage were playing out on the promenade beside the pier gates.

'What do you mean, over?' Ursula said, her blue eyes flashing. 'You don't get to say when it's over, Cal. I say when, I say how. I came back for you.'

Cal stared at her. 'You left me a long time ago, Ursula. You left me here, and I had to find a way to make my life work without you in it.'

'And a shit job you made of that,' she said, her voice

rising. 'Carving a penny-living from making sex toys and screwing every woman in town? You've hardly been pining, have you?'

He didn't want to argue the toss. He wasn't making a penny-living. He didn't say as much though, because Ursula had been rubbing shoulders with movie-makers and millionaire businessmen for the last few years in LA, a fact she loved wheeling out to belittle his choice to stay in the small town they grew up in and run his own one-man business.

'What did you expect me to do?' he said, weary of her. 'Put my life on ice?'

'You love me,' she said.

He looked at her, and although she looked undeniably stunning, her spray-on white dress split to her thigh was too much for Swallow Beach and her red lipstick too bright against her ever-lasting tan.

'I loved you,' he said. 'I loved you on our wedding day, and I loved you for a long time afterwards. But I don't love you any more.'

'But I came back for you,' she said again, looking almost confused, as if he should be grateful for the crumbs she'd thrown him.

'Did you?' he said, loosening his tie. 'Because I don't think you did. I think you came back because your luck ran out over there, because you realised that you weren't going to find the fame and fortune you thought would fall into your lap, because waitressing for the money guys wasn't working out, and because you heard on your family grapevine that I might have finally found someone else.'

She shook her head as he spoke. 'You seriously think I'd come all the way back here because I was threatened by some blue-haired nobody?'

Cal shrugged. 'I'm glad you came back,' he said.

She flipped her eyes as if that was a no-brainer. 'You've done a bad job of showing it,' she said. 'Two weeks in Portugal and you barely laid a finger on me. I get that you want to take it slow, but Jesus Christ Cal, this is stupid.' She stepped close and tugged his tie, reeling him in. 'Take me home, Cal. Take me home and screw me. Man the fuck up, I'm sick of waiting.'

If she'd expected her speech to turn him on, she'd played it all wrong.

'I'm glad you came back, because now I know for certain that I don't love you any more,' he said. He didn't enjoy saying it, but honesty was his only weapon. 'Our marriage meant more to me than it did to you. Even when you weren't here, I wore my wedding ring for years, because I was a married man. And yes, after a while, I started to see other women; I'm a man, Ursula, not a monk. But I didn't offer them anything, because in the back of my head there was always you. You, my wife, the woman I thought I still loved. I'd sleep with other women, knowing you were somewhere else sleeping with other men, and I'd feel like a liar, an adulterous low-life cheat. I don't think you were troubled by those same worries, were you? Because you always had the upper hand with us, you always knew I loved you that little bit more than you loved me.'

She stared at him, and as he looked at her, unflinching, he watched realisation finally dawn in her perfectly made-up eyes; she didn't have any hold over him any more. Taking a few steps backwards, she half laughed, an ugly, self-defensive sound.

'You'll die here in this town,' she said. 'You'll live your days out here, watching the sea come in and out, making tat from leather, never being any more than you are today. How is that enough?'

He looked back at her steadily. 'I don't want what you want. I love this town, and I'm proud of what I do.'

'I never thought of you as dull until now,' she said, spiteful.

He shook his head. 'And I never thought of you as shallow or unkind, but you've been both of those things and worse since you came back. I've officially outgrown you, Ursula.'

He dug his wedding ring out of his pocket and dropped it in the nearest bin, watching it disappear amongst the sticky ice-lolly wrappers and empty drink bottles, then turned away and walked back through the archway onto the pier, leaving Ursula behind him on dry land.

The awards were drawing to a close in time for the firework display at ten to kick off the dancing. Violet felt euphoric even though she hadn't touched a drop of champagne all evening, taking a glass from the tray when it was offered and discreetly tipping it into one of Linda's potted plants when no one was looking.

She'd slipped away from the party for a breather, heading to one of the benches half way along the pier, kicking off her shoes and tucking her feet up under her dress to watch the fireworks. The pier had made her proud tonight, it had been an evening of true celebration on many levels. She sighed, resting her head on her hand, looking back towards the birdcage. The fanfare of awards, the promise of new love for Lucy and Beau, a fond farewell for Monica.

'Hey mermaid girl.'

She turned and found Cal sauntering towards her. He'd dispensed with his dinner jacket at some point and loosened his tie and top button, and his shirt-cuffs were folded back. Violet tried not to notice the way all of those things came together to create a devastatingly attractive man, one who looked at home in his own skin, a man rather than a boy, a man whose usually laughing eyes were serious tonight and who'd just taken a seat alongside her on the bench.

'Hi,' she said, wondering where Ursula was.

He laid his arm along the back of the bench, his fingertips close to her shoulder.

'It's gone well,' he said, nodding towards the party a little way down the pier.

Night had fallen properly now, and Vi had charged Charlie with the task of switching on the fairy lights as soon as the fireworks were done as a signal to the band to kick off the dancing. He was thrilled to be trusted with the job, and they'd gone over the simple switch ceremony a couple of times before Violet had retreated to the bench to enjoy the fireworks and the big switch-on.

She nodded. 'It has.'

What was she supposed to say? Congratulations on your nomination? She didn't know if he'd won the award he'd been up for; she'd deliberately avoided it in case she had to watch Ursula make a show of congratulating her man.

'Did you win?' she said.

He shook his head. 'Beaten to the trophy by a guy who makes sex saddles, would you believe.'

Her mouth twitched at the irony. 'Sex saddles?'

He shrugged. 'It's pretty niche.'

'You don't say.'

They fell silent again.

'Shouldn't you get back to your wife?' She couldn't keep the barbed hurt from her voice.

'Violet,' he said, low and warm. 'I'm sorry for how I've been since Ursula came back.'

She refused to look at him. 'These things happen,' she said, shrugging as if it didn't matter.

'No they don't,' he said. 'Wives don't usually disappear for years on end and then turn up again at the most inappropriate time possible.'

'And I don't usually let men lure me into the sea for sex and then go running back to their wives half an hour later, either,' Vi said, biting even when she knew she should stay aloof.

He touched her shoulder and she flinched, making him sigh. 'I can see that's how it must have looked, but that isn't how it was.'

Violet decided that she wasn't up to talking about it any more tonight. 'You know Cal, I scattered my grandmother's ashes tonight, right here off the pier.'

She finally turned to look at him when he didn't answer.

'I'm so sorry,' he said, and she couldn't tell if he was apologising about the impromptu funeral or for his own behaviour.

She nodded. 'I've decided to leave Swallow Beach,' she said. 'It's not my place after all.'

Cal moved along the bench and took her hand, warm, firm, too firm for her to quickly pull it away. 'Please don't go.'

'I have to,' she said. She wasn't saying it to score points. The moment she'd realised she was expecting a baby she knew; staying here was the wrong thing to do. She needed a fresh start, free of ghosts of the past and the complicated relationships she had with the people here.

'Violet, listen to me,' he said. 'I screwed up. I've spent years thinking I was in love with Ursula, that our marriage still meant something to me. I've avoided any relationships that came anywhere close to love, because I thought I wasn't capable because my heart was hers. But I didn't count on you.'

He bumped his thumb across her knuckles as he spoke, soothing. 'I didn't think anyone could make me feel the way you do,' he said. 'Like a man again. Being around you is like lying on a beach in summertime, Violet. You make me warm all the way down to my bones, and you make me laugh, and that night in the sea . . . God, you're so fucking beautiful Vi. I can't get the image out of my head of you, of us.'

Violet closed her eyes, because she knew what had happened as a result of that night, that they'd created a child together. Then she opened them again because there was a sudden bang, and a whoosh, and then a rainbow sky full of fireworks illuminated the whole pier, making everyone whoop and clap and stop what they were doing to watch the show.

Cal moved closer, his arm warm around Violet's shoulders, and she allowed herself that one final moment with him, because this would be her last night here as a resident of Swallow Beach. Come tomorrow, she was going to pack up the Traveller and hit the road.

As the fireworks reached their spectacular finale, she turned her head to look at him, drinking him in. She didn't stop him when he brushed the back of his hand along her jaw, or when he lowered his head and kissed her slowly, drenched in emotion.

'Please don't go,' he whispered.

Violet moved into the warmth and heat of his arms. 'I have to, Cal.'

'No one *has* to do anything,' he whispered, cradling her.

'*I* have to,' she said. She didn't believe that the pier was cursed, but she did believe that her grandmother had paid the ultimate price for loving a married man, and that it was her duty to learn from Monica's mistakes. She wouldn't stay and let the place and its people eat her alive too. She couldn't, because she had more than just herself to consider.

'Why?' he said, his dark, agonised eyes searching hers.

'Because I'm pregnant,' she whispered, and he stared at her, utterly still as the enormity of her words sank in.

'I . . .' he started, but his words were drowned out by the sudden shock of the hundreds of light bulbs strung along the pier all firing at the same time. But they didn't blaze with light.

They exploded into fireballs.

CHAPTER TWENTY-FIVE

Everyone panicked. Flames licked hot and fast down both sides of Swallow Beach Pier, confusion and screams, people in red-carpet dresses and dinner suits shouting and scrambling towards dry land.

Cal grabbed Violet, pulling her up onto her feet.

'Go!' he shouted, almost shoving her in the direction of the surge towards the gates. 'Get to safety, I'll make sure everyone gets out of the birdcage and be right behind you.'

'No,' she shouted, her heart banging, tears streaking her cheeks. 'I'm not going anywhere until I know everyone else is safe! This is my pier, my responsibility!'

He shook his head, his hands on her shoulders. 'Fucking go, Violet,' he said roughly. 'I swear, if anything happens to you, I'll never forgive myself.'

All around them people shoved and streamed, calling out the names of those they were desperate to find.

'Violet, Cal, thank God!' Keris appeared beside them, hand in hand with Barty, barefoot and her dress streaked with black soot. 'We need to get off here right now,' she said, fast and urgent, grabbing Violet by the hand. 'Come on.'

'Take her with you,' Cal said. 'Don't let her go, Keris.' He looked at Violet one last time, and then threw himself against the direction of the crowd to check the birdcage.

'It was the lights,' Barty shouted. 'Electrical fault.'

Somewhere behind them, someone screamed above the noise, high-pitched and terrified.

'Charlie! Charlie!'

Vi knew it was Lucy desperately searching for her son, and shook Keris off, shouting, 'Get Barty off here, Keris!' before she turned and fled.

'Lucy! Lucy!' she shouted, staring wildly around the orange-illuminated faces moving all around her, their expressions masks of alarm and panic. A wild-eyed man in a dinner suit scrambled over the railings, ripping his jacket, taking his chances by jumping into the sea. Another followed his lead, filling Violet's head with the haunting thought of her gran tumbling into the cold water below and washing up on the morning tide. This was unbearable. She didn't stand a chance of finding Lucy, so ducked her head down, covering her mouth as she ran for it towards the birdcage. Maybe she could find Charlie herself.

At the other end of the pier, people were reaching the gates and finding to their horror that they had been closed and padlocked. They were trapped; rats on a sinking ship, and a mad desperate struggle began of people clawing and shouting to get the attention of passersby. Keris screamed at the top of her voice, aware that Barty was probably the eldest person on the pier that evening and the most likely to suffer from smoke inhalation. A man appeared from the darkness on the other side, standing still, staring at her.

'Get help!' she yelled. 'Call the fire brigade, call the

police, there's more than a hundred people trapped on here!'

He didn't move, and then he smiled, a rictus, horror-movie grin as he held something up in front of his face. A key.

As Vi reached the birdcage, Beau came flying out the door with someone over his shoulder.

'I've got him!' he was shouting. 'Luce, I've got him!'

Violet sagged with relief, catching sight of Lucy at last, a streak of red silk as she hurled herself at Beau and Charlie sobbing, 'Thank God, thank God, thank God.'

Vi watched them start to run, hand in hand like a scene from a disaster movie, Charlie still flung over Beau's shoulder. 'Thank God,' she sobbed, echoing Lucy's words.

Everything on the pier was hot to touch: the railings, the boards underfoot, the metal of the birdcage. The flames had well and truly caught; Violet needed to get off to prioritise her baby. But she couldn't leave; not without Cal.

'Everyone's out of there,' she heard someone say as they hurtled out of the door. It wasn't Cal.

'Everyone?' she said, grabbing the man's jacket. 'Are you sure?'

'All staff accounted for,' he said, already moving away. 'Get clear love, now.'

'But Cal . . .' she said, but the guy had already moved out of earshot. She stared one way, towards the mainland, but she couldn't see through the smoke and orange glow, and she looked back towards the birdcage, agonised in case Cal was still in there.

She started to cough; her chest hurt. She had to leave. She needed to go. But when she tried to move, she stumbled, twisting her ankle as she fell down hard onto her knees, coughing. She needed to leave, but she couldn't stand up. Hot, frightened tears rained down her cheeks as pain fired through her leg. She was going to die here. The pier was going to take her, just as it had taken Monica. Hortensia had been right.

'I don't want to die,' she sobbed. 'Please don't let me die here.'

And then someone was behind her, scooping her up, cradling her like a child in his arms, telling her that he wouldn't let her die, and to hold on.

'Cal.'

'Ssh, don't try to speak,' he said. 'Just hold on tight Vi, because I'm going to run and I won't let you fall, okay? This place is going to go down, and we're not going down with it.'

She buried her face in his neck, breathing in only the scent of his skin, trusting him implicitly, thanking her lucky stars for him as he ran, the pier creaking and rocking underneath them.

'What the . . .?' he said, and she looked up and saw the crowd up ahead, people clambering over the locked gates, crushing forwards as sirens wailed in the distance.

'The gates,' he said. 'Why are they locked, Vi? Where's the key?'

She shook her head. 'I don't know,' she said, the words hardly leaving her throat.

Cal pushed through to the front, still carrying Violet, and when he reached the front he could see people dragging each other over the gates, ripped clothes, screaming fear.

'Cal!' Beau yelled, pushing through to them. 'Some fucker's locked the gates.'

Lucy was beside him, and suddenly she started to scream and punch the gates, yelling.

'Ian! You bastard, you did this!'

Vi looked on, confused, trying to work out why Lucy was shouting at the electrician who'd rigged up the lights for her that morning, and why he was just standing there staring at them instead of trying to help.

'Is that him?' Beau shouted, at the same time as a huge scream went up behind them – the central section of the pier lurched downwards into the sea, leaving everyone clinging to the land end and the birdcage an island out at sea, cut off.

Help was coming, but it wouldn't be soon enough. And then help came from the most unexpected of places: Gladys Dearheart came bombing along the promenade and launched herself onto the back of the man holding the key, her arms locked tight around his neck, clinging on as he went down under her weight, shocked. She whacked him hard over the head with her ever-present briefcase and grabbed the key from his hand, running at the gates and finding Cal on the other side with Violet in his arms.

There wasn't time for words. Gladys twisted the lock around, fumbling, and Cal reached through the gates and helped her, both of them crying as the lock sprung open.

'Stand back everyone,' Beau yelled, head and shoulders above most people. 'Gates are open, don't stampede or people are gonna die here!'

Vi's last memory before she passed out was of Beau standing with his foot pressed into Ian's back to hold him down, Charlie over his shoulder and Lucy at his side, and of Cal sitting down on the sea wall holding her safely in his lap, his other arm around his mum beside them.

CHAPTER TWENTY-SIX

Violet hadn't felt this relaxed for a long time. She was warm, and her bones were heavy. If she could just stay here then everything would be just fine.

'Nurse! I think she's waking up! Nurse!'

She really wished that people would stop shouting. Frowning, she tried to lick her lips to ask them to be quiet but her mouth was too dry to force any sound out. Oh. That wasn't right. It was no good, she needed to open her eyes and see what was going on.

Cranking one eyelid open, she swallowed painfully, blinking and then opening both eyes to bring whoever was holding her hand and saying her name into focus.

'Violet,' a nurse said, adjusting the clip on her finger and consulting a chart. 'Can you hear me, love?'

Vi nodded, and wanted to say something like *Too bloody well, thank you very much,* but then her eyes slid to the other side of the bed, to Cal. He looked awful. Dirty. Why was he so dirty?

She closed her eyes, and then it all came back in one big horrific rush. The pier. The fire. The gates. Oh God, all those people. She tried to sit up but everything ached when she jolted, especially her ankle.

'Shh, lie down for me Violet, you need to try to rest,' the nurse said, easing her back against the pillows. She looked at Cal.

'I'll leave you two to talk,' she said. 'I'll be at the desk just outside, buzz if you need me and I'll be right in.'

Cal nodded, kissing Violet's fingers once they were alone.

'All those people on the pier, Cal,' Vi said, voicing her worst fear.

Cal squeezed her fingers. 'Everyone made it,' he said. 'I promise you, everyone is okay.'

'Even those who jumped?'

He nodded. 'All accounted for.'

'Charlie?'

Cal nodded. 'He's okay. Smoke inhalation, he's in a room down the corridor. He's being kept overnight, but he's going to be fine, Violet. Everyone is – it's you everyone's been worrying about.'

Something hovered on the edge of her consciousness, then it hit her like a hammer blow and her hands flew to her stomach.

Tears filled Cal's beautiful eyes.

'My baby,' she said, her heart cracking down the middle.

'Is fine. Still there. Tiny, but still there,' he said.

For a minute, they didn't speak at all, overwhelmed by the enormity of it. Cal brushed her hair back from her forehead, held her hand. She lifted her other hand and cupped his jaw, wiping a streak of soot from his mouth.

'I thought I'd lost you. I've only just found you, and I thought I was going to lose you,' he said.

A tear slipped from the side of her eye and he wiped it away with the back of his fingers.

'Are you tired?' he said softly, and she nodded, overwhelmed.

'Close your eyes,' he whispered. 'Close your eyes, I'll stay here with you.'

She squeezed his fingers. 'Don't leave me,' she said, her eyes already drifting down.

'I won't. I promise.'

Cal watched Violet sleep. She'd been like a doll in his arms earlier, barefoot in her ballgown, too fragile, too pale. He'd gone to pieces when she'd passed out and his mum had taken charge, getting an ambulance crew to prioritise Violet, staying by his side, asking questions, taking over because he needed her to rather than because she wanted to. He had no doubt that she'd be out there in the waiting room right now, and that she'd still be there come morning if it took that long for him to emerge.

It had been a long time since he'd needed his mum, but he needed her now. He turned as the door opened and the nurse led an older couple in; Vi's parents, no doubt. They'd been called from the hospital not long after Violet was admitted a few hours back. They must have thrown themselves straight in the car and broken every speed limit to get there so soon. Their expressions reflected his own feelings; pure, naked fear.

They barely noticed him as he stood aside to let them get close to their daughter, and he backed out of the room unseen, leaving them alone.

'Mum.'

Cal spotted his mum sitting in the corner of the waiting room, alone amongst the soot-streaked walking wounded from the pier. She looked up at the sound of his voice, then stood and picked her way over to him near the doors.

'Can we go outside?' he asked, laying his hand on her shoulder. 'I could do with some air.'

'Have they checked you over properly?' Gladys fussed, feeling his brow before sitting down alongside him on a bench outside.

'I'm fine, Mum,' he said. 'Don't worry about me.'

She shook her head and huffed softly. 'I'm your mother, Calvin. I've worried about you since the day you were born.'

It was the most heartfelt thing she'd said to him in a long time.

'Why were you there tonight?' he asked.

Gladys clasped her hands in her lap. 'I only ever wanted the best for you, you know,' she said. 'Oh, I know you think I'm an interfering old prude, but I know how this world works,' she said. 'Is it so wrong to want to see your son settled and secure?'

He shook his head. 'No, of course it isn't. But you can't live my life for me either, Mum. I *am* settled and secure, just not in the way you want or expect me to be.'

He realised that she'd dodged answering his question and didn't push her for an answer; no doubt she'd been coming to try and throw a spanner in the works any way she could manage.

'I just wanted to see if you'd won your award,' she said, so quiet he almost missed it.

'Oh Mum,' he said, exasperated. She'd always been there at every prize-giving assembly, the loudest clap in the room, the mum with the biggest shouts of encouragement on sports day. He knew why, of course. Losing her husband had left Gladys devastated, and perhaps she'd tried too hard to be both father and mother to him as he'd grown up. It hadn't been too bad in his younger days, but they'd clashed badly when he'd hit his teenage years. He wasn't all that proud of some of the things he'd said and done in his youth; for all her bravado, he knew his mum had a soft streak a mile wide, even though she went to great pains to hide it from most of Swallow Beach. She was a force to be reckoned with; it must have cost her dearly to confess to wanting to come and cheer him on tonight.

'And then I hung around hoping to watch the fireworks,' she said, sounding like a little girl. 'I just wish I'd noticed that bar steward come and lock the gates earlier,' she muttered. 'I know I had those gates chained myself earlier in the summer, but to do it with people on the other side of them like that was wicked. Lambs to the slaughter.' She shook her head. 'I only shut my eyes for five minutes on that bench by the monument, knew the bangers would wake me up again.'

The idea of his mum snoozing alone on a bench with her briefcase clutched in her arms, excluded from the party, keeping an eye on him from the promenade fair broke his heart.

'You were the hero of the night,' he said, perilously close to tears. It had been the most frightening night of his life and his mum had waded in to save him.

'I know you all laugh at my briefcase,' she said. 'Never know when it's going to come in handy.'

He laughed softly and squeezed her shoulders, not letting go. 'I love you, Mum.'

She leaned against him, her shoulders heaving. 'I love you too, my stupid, wilful, wonderful boy.'

CHAPTER TWENTY-SEVEN

'Are you warm enough?'

Violet bumped shoulders with Cal sitting alongside her on the sea wall. It was a cooler day than of late, overcast and grey.

'I'm fine Cal. When are you going to stop worrying about me?'

It had been two weeks since the fire, two long, exhausting weeks. Vi had spent most of the first one in hospital being attended to by a constant carousel of visitors: Cal, her parents, Cal, Keris and Barty, Cal, Lucy and Beau, Gladys even, and Cal, always Cal. The haunted look had slowly left his eyes as she'd gathered her strength back and the doctors had confirmed no lasting damage to either Vi or their baby. Della had finally returned to Swallow Beach too; her parents were staying in the Lido apartment. Violet was staying across the landing with Cal, mostly because he couldn't settle unless she was within arm's length.

'Probably never,' he said, picking her hand up and playing with her fingers.

Violet gazed out to sea, at the blackened shell of the

birdcage strung out at sea, its windows shattered by the heat, cut off now the central section of the pier had fallen into the sea. It made for an eerie sight, iron struts standing tall of the water like the masts of a sinking ship, a terrifying reminder of the horror that had taken place there.

'It's still hard to believe it happened, isn't it?' she said, leaning into Cal. He put his arm around her, nodding.

'Let's just be relieved it wasn't worse,' he said. 'No one died. Businesses can be started again, things can be rebuilt.'

'Not that,' Vi said, nodding towards the pier.

He shook his head. 'No, not that.' He paused. 'Beau called earlier,' he said. 'They might come and see you later, if you feel like it.'

She nodded. Beau had quickly shot to the top of her all-time heroes' list after what had happened on the pier, and it was clear Lucy and Charlie felt the same way.

'I have something for you,' Cal said, digging in his pocket. 'Hold your hand out.'

She did as she was told, smiling quizzically as he laid something in her palm. She bit her lip, tearful as she looked down at the delicate shell bracelet in her hand, the slender ribbon of leather he'd made for her all those weeks ago.

'Where did you get it?' she said, touching the miraculously uncrushed shells, trying to remember.

'Lola the headless showgirl. She washed up on the beach the morning after the fire,' he said, laughing a little. 'Gave everyone a fright.'

Ah. Of course. She'd put it around Lola's wrist not long after Ursula returned to Swallow Beach. Cal's estranged wife had blown out of the bay while Vi was in the hospital, only this time she'd left without Cal's heart stowed carelessly in her hand luggage.

'I don't know if I'll ever be able to look at the beach

without feeling upset,' Vi said. She'd sat for countless hours staring out of the windows of Cal's apartment, trying to come to terms with what had happened out there.

Cal's hand slid into her hair at the back of her neck, massaging.

'You know what I see when I look at the beach?' he said, pressing a kiss against her hair. 'I see you. I see you and me together in the sea that night before everything went wrong. I'll never forget the way you looked, you took my breath away.'

He kissed her then, a slow affirmation of the love between them. Sometimes in the darkness of the middle of the night Vi questioned if it had all happened too quickly, if they'd fallen too soon, and then Cal held her and loved all of her fears and doubts away. He was a good man; strong when she wasn't, not afraid to wear his heart on his sleeve even when he'd had it broken.

What had happened on the pier that night had pressed fast-forward on their love affair; they'd both realised in the space of one fateful night that they belonged together, and that they were ready to welcome the fledgling new life they'd created into the world. Sure, it was sooner than either of them might have chosen, but in a strange way, it felt entirely as it should be, that a child should come of their unforgettable, sea-drenched union. Cal had waited in agonised fear on the night of the fire, first to know that Violet was safe, and then to hear if the child he'd learned of only hours before had survived the ordeal. His bone-deep relief had been absolute and pure; he'd known beyond doubt that he wanted this woman, and he wanted this child.

Taking the bracelet from her fingers, he slipped it over her hand, back where it belonged.

'There,' he said, holding her close. 'You're part of Swallow Beach forever now, mermaid girl.'

Vi smiled softly, her eyes on the birdcage. 'Yes,' she said. 'I am.'

Out at sea, the swallows gathered on the charred roof of the birdcage, just like always, and a pale shaft of sunlight passed through the broken windows into the shell of what would have been Vi's studio. If there truly was a curse on Swallow Beach Pier, it was lifted now. A late summer breeze blew through the birdcage, scattering ashes across the painted boards, revealing the damaged remains of the rainbow Monica had painted there all those years ago. Just one glittering, faded word remained.

Violet.

ACKNOWLEDGEMENTS

Thanks as ever to my agent Jemima Forrester and all at David Higham.

Thank you to my editor Phoebe Morgan for your kind support and encouragement, to Sabah Khan for publicity, to Rhian McKay for thoughtful copy editing, and more widely to the whole team at Avon and HarperCollins.

Continuing thanks to Emma Rogers for another gorgeous cover, I think it's possibly my favourite so far!

Heartfelt thanks to all of the bloggers, reviewers and readers.

Last but never least, thank you to my lovely family and friends.

All's fair in love and war . . . isn't it?

Fall in love with more Kat French this summer – the perfect holiday read!

You never know who you might end up with . . .

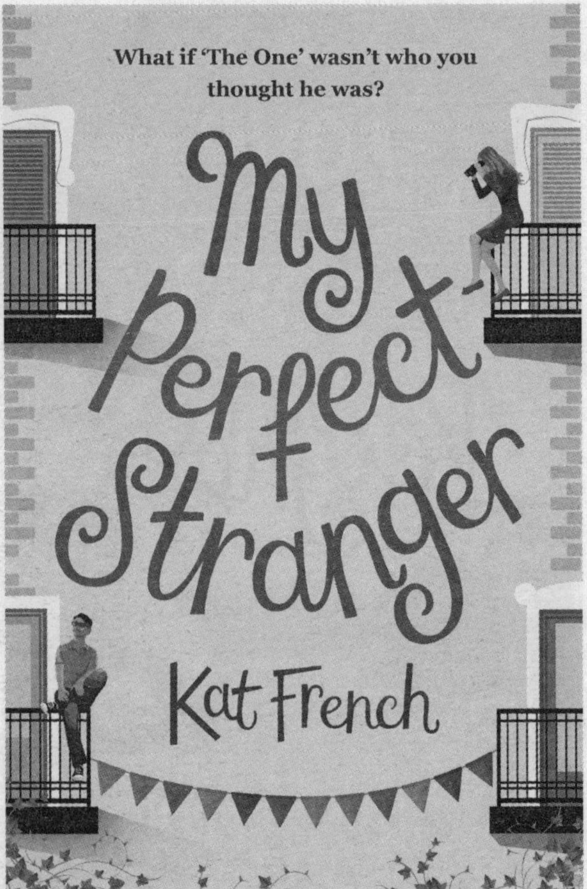

Sometimes, the boy next door might just surprise you . . .

Things are hotting up this summer . . .

Kat French is back – and there's a cowboy in town . . .

Escape to Greece with Kat French!

Three best friends – and a whole lot of trouble . . .